#stoptheglitch

CHRIS MALONE

DEDICATION

This book is dedicated to
The Hill End Centre, Oxford
hill-end.org

'A Place of Possibilities'

~ CONTENTS ~

ACKNOWLEDGMENTS

Many thanks to my publisher, Richard Mayers, for his guidance and wealth of editing experience, to my beta readers Liz van Santen and Selby Dickinson, and to my husband Ken.

Chris Malone

OXFORD

Day One

Today my phone is sitting smugly beside me, vibrating, flashing and sneering like a Cheshire Cat with a satisfied grin of control. It is the window into my life for the ephemeral conspirators who invade my room as I look out of the window on to the street below. I see too many people at all hours of day and night. Each one is glued to their device, and they are all buying stuff: drinks, clothes, sex, endless things, and food, food, food. I try to access my online sites, and the adverts just keep on flashing up. All I see is the pedalling of more and more *stuff*. We should have learnt to be more cautious after the internet collapsed catastrophically under its own weight last year. Conspiracy theories are still rampant.

The tool that gave us safety, that enabled ordinary people to find out things about other parts of the world, that helped to organise disparate lives, that joined like-minded people together across the air during the global pandemic, during floods and fires, is now my enemy.

Without asking me, *they* sent through an update that linked my phone to my computer. Now, the confidential place where I could save letters that I wanted no one to read, my overdraft statements and bad photos, is up on a public cloud, my privacy compromised. Every time I search, *they* harvest the data to sell me unsolicited goods. And meanwhile, billions of digital images pile up across the world in homage to the vanity of the human race.

They edit my preferences, telling me what *they* think I want to see. Even if they are right, I look away, because my choice has been taken away from me.

And *they* want me to eagerly scan my membership card each time I shop, building up my points for rewards in this post-pandemic world. Their reward is my data, and so I refuse to play. Each time I am offered a card, I decline, and *they* look confused.

They want me to put my small, boring personal achievements on display, so that my burgeoning number of online friends can see what a worthwhile life I lead, so employers can check that we are participating in the ways that they require, and so that the voracious advertisers can pounce.

They are turning me from a polite everyday citizen into an angry rebel, a disrupter. I am too old for this, but I can no longer ignore the nagging inside my brain, the surety that we are abusing humankind by rapidly killing our planet. Pollution is endemic, consumerism ignores the ecological impact, and there are too many people for the world we inhabit. We are all complicit in small ways, with the cumulative effect becoming potentially devastating. We are not doing enough to turn things around for the generations to come. We swing from crisis to crisis but we neglect our long-term vision.

The guilt of simply being a human being, consuming mindlessly, weighs heavily on my shoulders.

Another thing that frustrates me is the assumptions that *they* make. My anger at the systems of today do not make me a "socialist". Socialism is rapidly becoming outdated, a musty historical concept for those rooted in old ideas. I am simply frustrated, and I want things to change. "Left wing", "right wing". These labels are so archaic that they obscure the truth of today. Empty political figureheads display their ignorance of what it means to live an ordinary life. Tired and hard-working multitudes pass by unnoticed.

Where is the leadership? Certainly not on social media,

or in Westminster.

I desperately want to be able to go somewhere else, to shed the consumer babble, and to think. I desire deep thought as if it was a glass of cool water in the desert.

Looking up at my shelf, I scan with reverence the spines which declare my priorities, the jam jar full of coins for the bread, and my library card, propped up on the bookcase box. Years ago, I was given this beautiful wooden box as a present from a friend who had travelled to Sorrento. It was a tourist item, but a quality box, and I have kept it safe, despite moving house numerous times. I keep the painkillers I take for nagging fibromyalgia in it, and a couple of packets of cigarettes. It looks like a small bookcase. You can slide the lid back, and when a wooden book front drops down, a secret compartment appears, revealing a keyhole. I still have the small silver key.

Tomorrow I will place my phone in the box. I will lock it, and I will throw the little silver key out into the street for the homeless to find and puzzle over.

I will do that tomorrow. The tomorrow that, by definition, never comes.

Day Two

Decades before the lockdown, Sunday nights were always quiet, but not nowadays. It is early on Monday morning, and the street below my window is saturated from overnight rain. The sun is only just emerging over the rooftops above the shops. Light from the 24-hour pizza place opposite assaults my eyes. Sodden debris from the previous night's revellers decorates the gutters, and the street-sweeping machine drives through the dark, from left to right, from right to left, waking everyone with its irritating drone. After the restrictions of the pandemic ended, some members of society have reversed "social distancing" to the extreme.

Three residual drinkers stagger towards the station, laughing and jeering. As they pass, they kick the cardboard boxes serving as a mat for the rough sleeper, and he shifts under his dripping plastic sacks, pressing himself further into the doorway.

Glass bottles, green ones, are lined up by the bus stop, as if they are waiting for the first bus of the day. The sweeper missed them, along with the pizza boxes and plastic wrappers. One day I will move to a better place, somewhere quiet and clean, where I can think, without the pathetic clutter of mankind strewn out below me.

I might receive news today, which will push me into action, but I have been hoping in vain for the phone call, or a letter, every day for the last month. They haven't kept me very well informed. I haul on my well-worn jeans and heavy sweater, preparing for the chill of the street air, and am thinking that I should have made a trip to the laundrette, but for now I ignore the stains on my sleeves and pull on my three-day-old socks.

I leave the flat silently. The stairs are grubby and unswept. I pass the line of early light from under my neighbour's door, and exit through the back on to the passageway. I hurry with soft footsteps, passing the sleeping human bundle in the doorway opposite, and heading up the street towards my morning destination. I catch the warming aroma of fresh bread before I see the welcoming lights of the bakery, and I feel in my pocket for the two-pound coin that I placed there yesterday evening, ready for this morning's breakfast. The baker knows me well; I am generally one of his earliest customers each morning. He has already placed two hot rolls in a paper bag on the warming counter, anticipating my arrival. I place the coin on the counter, call 'Thank you', and head back with my rolls. As I turn the corner, two magpies are pecking at debris in the gutter, and I wonder if they mean "for joy."

Maybe the letter will come today.

I approach the mound, slumped in the doorway, hold my breath and bend down to give him a shake. He is already awake and I see one open eye peering blearily past the plastic sheet. He pushes his hand out from the shelter of his sleeping bag, and I see the other eye, bloodshot and sad. I press the hot roll into his hand. He sits up and says, 'Thanks,' and we smile.

'One day we will eat a breakfast banquet off golden plates in the palace of the righteous,' I say, watching him devour the roll surrounded by dirt, debris and the wet of the night.

He rewards me with a smile, and we share a moment.

I hurry across the cobbles, in the back door and back up to my safe haven. I eat the roll, wash it down with strong coffee, and prepare for the day ahead, grudgingly stuffing the phone deep into my pocket.

Rummaging in a kitchen drawer for my keys, I unearth the pieces of a photograph which I ripped up ages ago. Staring accusingly at me from the fragments are the doe-eyes on the self-satisfied face of my ex-partner. I scowl and push the pieces to the back of the drawer, behind my money-tin.

Once we used to save up for things that we wanted, I reflect. Children eagerly posted pennies in money boxes, rattling the tins to check how full they were becoming, and deciding when to tip out the clinking pile and head for the shops. We learnt to wait. Now from day one many children are showered with more than they need and social media wish lists are becoming an industry. Even parents struggling to stay on top of their lives are pressured to buy their darlings the current trend. It's not a good world to offer to new generations. I worked with children for years, watching their fresh enthusiasm become dulled by our imposed pressures, our maddened way of life. I do not want children of my own. I would always feel guilty at bringing them into a world which I despise.

One day I will opt out of all this. I will step aside, leaving the busy twenty-first century citizens to their maelstrom, and I will focus back on what really matters. But first I need my letter. Only then can I initiate my plan.

Day Three

Since the unexpected momentary failure in world systems last year, everything blinked and had to be laboriously restored. Since then, there has been a nervousness out there. Environmental campaigners have regained credibility with politicians, and it is as if the solitary preacher in the marketplace, carrying his placard declaiming "The End of the World is Nigh," is now seated around every boardroom table. The collective fear is that the "glitch" was caused by organised terrorism. In an attempt to understand it, people of different political persuasions, from world leaders to local councillors, are being brought closer together. The dread of being propelled back into a pre-digital age is promoting high level action.

Maybe some of us would prefer the pre-digital age, but no one asks.

They are frantically pumping resource into trying to find out who caused this "glitch", as it is commonly known, but I check the internet each day, as do millions of others, and there are no updates at all. They want us to think that it never happened. The financial markets are only just recovering from this second major blow; countless businesses lost many orders, and large multinationals as well as small local concerns are struggling to keep afloat. Last December, tabloid headlines declaimed that "The glitch Stole Christmas."

There has been a nervousness on the streets ever since.

Conspiracy theories continue to thrive. For my part, in 2020, after the informal parcel deliveries were finally suspended, I retreated, frightened and alone, only braving the streets muffled in scarves and outdoor clothes, which I stored in the lockup, desperately trying to keep my small flat virus free. Self-isolation for those of us who are introverts was no trouble, but the practicalities were a nightmare, and no work meant no money. We had just succeeded in regaining a modicum of normality, when we were hit again, this time by an insidious technological invader. Unlike the overwhelmingly inane public information during the virus, when the glitch hit, *they* hushed it up. We are left with a nagging suspicion, but nothing specific on which to pin our attention. *They* are relying on the post-pandemic public relief to sweep the glitch under the carpet, but I am constantly on edge as I pedal the streets of Oxford.

Day Four

My casual delivery job was meant to be a stopgap until I heard from the solicitor. I have to provide my own cycle and I only get paid for what I deliver, in cash at the end of each day. They hold no records and I don't ask. It suits me at the moment and is a stark contrast to an earlier string of social worker roles, when I ended up as fragile as my clients, the characters who I was meant to be supporting back into the multicolour fairground of modern life. All that is required of me now is to arrive on time, stack the parcels in the trailer attached to my delivery bike, and take them to their destinations by 8pm. During the day, when I run out of items to deliver, I return to the parcel office and reload. I can manage up to a hundred in a day if I really focus, and if my muscle pain is under control. The depot shuts at 8.30 each evening and so I must get there before the duty officer closes up, to collect my cash.

As well as keeping me fit, the main benefit of the delivery job has been to drag my mind away from the idiocy that is happening in Westminster, Each time my foot hits the pedal, I think of our farce of a Parliament, still tangled up with the glitch, the "emperor's new clothes", the parade of braying donkeys holding our future so clumsily in their hands. As I pedal harder and faster, I beat them into the damp dust lining the gutter.

Today begins in typical fashion. Having kitted myself out in my fluorescent garb and helmet, I haul the heavy bicycle out of the lockup in the half-light behind the shops, scramble the code, and set off for the depot. Rivulets of rainwater hiss as I pedal at speed along the cobbled street and up the gentle hill, past more homeless, huddling in shop doorways.

I collect my first consignment of parcels, pressing them on to my back carrier and tying them tight. I always select the smallest packets for the first drop, so they can be posted through letterboxes before people are awake. My knowledge of the street names has become encyclopaedic over the three years on the job, and I pride myself in not needing to look up any locations on my phone. That makes me even quicker, and they like the speed at which I work. Sometimes there is a bonus payment for exceeding my monthly target, and I cycle straight out to The Pike for supper. I know the landlord and there is generally lively political debate at the bar.

Today, I am distracted. I hope for a letter.

Maybe it is sitting on my doormat right now. I am tempted to return and to check, but fearing disappointment, I press on. The steady flow of commodities passes on and off my small trailer, items that people think they need. Single-use plastic, cheap Chinese imports and presents for friends. Things that look nice online but disappoint when they arrive, cluttering up our spaces. The parcels that I like to deliver are the books. Then, I am carrying thousands of words, often of far greater value to the human race than their price tag. I follow the postman down the street, his bag getting lighter and lighter over the months. Immediately after the glitch there was a sudden increase in actual letters, but not for long. People regained their trust in social media too easily.

By six in the late afternoon, Oxford tourists are gathering in flocks outside the eating houses, the back streets are clearing of the nose-to-tail traffic, which I sped past on my bike, and I decide to call it a day. Having collected my cash for the deliveries, I head for home with high expectations.

I heave the bike into the store, muddling up the digits on the combination lock, and climb the stairs. But it isn't here. Again.

Sitting cheekily on the worn doormat are two bright but unsolicited flyers, one advertising bargain supermarket goods, boasting beneficial price comparisons, and the other, trying feebly to persuade me to buy a stairlift. I stuff them angrily in the bin. Then I reflect, repent, and reluctantly fish the leaflets out of the bin, placing them in the recycling.

Day Seven

My routine repeats for three more days, but no letter arrives.

By Friday evening I have made myself forget about the impending communication. I return home exhausted, opening the door tentatively and glimpse the sharp corner of a crisp envelope on the mat. One large official-looking letter sits proudly, staring up at me.

It is here. At last.

I cradle the envelope in my hands, my fingerless gloves smudging the handwritten address and the solicitor's stamp. Perhaps it is simply another of those holding letters, saying that they will be in touch in due course. I sweep all the debris from the small table that is the beating heart of my one-room flat, and place the letter on it. Second class, my address. I am tempted to rip it open, but stop myself. Instead, I postpone the moment, braving my sub-standard shower, sluicing off the street-residue from my skin with the luke-warm trickle, and searching in vain for clean clothes. I throw on some of the least-dirty garments, make a coffee, and return to the table.

I want that indescribably perfect comfort of a cigarette, but when I moved here, I became nervous of my hypocrisy, and locked them in the box. I haven't touched them since, not even during "self-isolation". I dare myself, but my better, cleaner, simpler-self wins.

Unable to put the moment off any longer, I sit

ceremonially and slit the envelope open with my sharp vegetable knife, slicing harder than is necessary. I extract the one sheet of heavy paper and scan the letter for a final figure. My calculations were right.

I read and reread the formal phrases and the legal jargon. They have finally completed the probate. I am the only living beneficiary. In line with my instructions they have now also completed the sale of the properties. All expenses have been deducted, leaving just under five million, as I expected. I gasp at the immense figure that they have extracted for their services. So that is it. Done.

What happens now?

INHERITANCE

Last Year

Until last year I hadn't considered what I might do if I inherited my father's wealth. He had never forgiven me for putting two fingers up to his way of life, and we hadn't seen eye to eye for years. Last year, just before the glitch, and after the restrictions of the pandemic were lifted, I visited him in the family home, only weeks before he died.

I had risen reluctantly, but with purpose, on the winter Saturday of my visit. I dared to shovel in a double-dose of painkillers, to numb myself ready for the dreaded trip, and put my mask ready in my pocket. They were compulsory on public transport at the time. I hardly remember pedalling down to the station, or grabbing a three-pound coffee from the stand that stays open all night. It came in a single-use cup that I knew would not biodegrade, but I needed coffee, and I bought it out of protest. I really didn't want to be trekking half the way across the country to see someone who had treated me so despicably.

The journey had required careful planning as not all trains accommodate bicycles. I had checked and double-checked and I was confident that my route would be okay. Heaving a delivery bike into a train is not easy. Despite it being a weekend, there were already several eager cyclists with trendy folding bicycles waiting on the platform, executives who claim their roles are too important to work from home, and spend ten hours a day at their desks in London in the week. They never stop working at the weekend, fielding emails and preparing papers. At least my heavy bike was less likely to be stolen while I sat in the carriage, mask on.

The train drew out on time, the first of the day. My muzzy head started to clear. Only then did I think of the money, because I had begrudged spending out over thirty pounds on a return train ticket. It was an idle thought: if my investment in a train ticket resulted in an inheritance, it could offer a massive return, not that I wanted this. My father had said in his short letter, no doubt dictated to one of his helpers, that he *needed* to see me, not that he wanted to do so. There was obviously something on his mind.

I changed trains at Reading, and then Guilford, and finally disembarked, with my bike, pushing it slowly along the familiar platform of the station nearest to our family estate, stuffing my mask back in my pocket. On this platform, as a small child, I had been fussed and fondled by my adoring grandparents. In those days, a car would be sent to the station, and I sat beside our driver. Their leather cases were loaded into the boot. My Grandad smelt of tobacco. Here, years ago, I had departed for school, secretly buying sweets from the stall on platform two, and here, at the age of eighteen, I had taken the immense step of leaving for good, my mother crying on this very platform. She was frightened of being left alone with *him*.

Reaching the ticket barrier, I became stuck. My ticket was refused. Perhaps the brown strip on the back had accidentally become deactivated. I stood helpless while other passengers waved their phones at the sensor and were rewarded as the barriers clicked open for them. There was no attendant. It was difficult enough getting a heavy delivery bike through the barrier, without this. The straggle of passengers departed and I was left, marooned. I tried the ticket again, but to no avail.

Eventually a uniformed member of the station staff ambled along the platform, and without speaking, waved a disc across the sensor for the wide exit. The barrier retracted and I hurried through, cursing.

The cycle ride was only three miles, out of the village and into the hinterland of millionaires. Although I knew the route by heart, it had changed, with the sprawl of newly-built four and five-bedroom houses extending out into the countryside, obliterating the previously green serenity. Despite the gentle beauty of the outlook, as I pedalled further along the lane, the scene was tinged with dread. Had my mother still been alive, I would have had an ally, albeit an ineffective one. But I was approaching not only the firm bastion of privilege, which I so despise, but the immovable glare of my father, traditional to the roots of his thinning hair, clinging on to the past, and demanding the respect that he believed inevitably follows inherited wealth.

As I beat the pedals, my feet pounded with longstanding and deep-rooted anger, but this time I was strengthened by a confidence that had grown with age. I turned my back on my upbringing long ago, and I am quietly proud of my achievements since that day: earned rather than handed to me on a plate.

I rounded the final corner, and the small gatehouse came into view, choking me with previously forgotten memories of sitting by the glowing coals, drinking sweet tea, and listening to the down-to-earth conversations of our off-duty driver and his family. I had felt at home there, and had often escaped down the drive into the arms of his wife, our reliable housekeeper, when things were tense up at the big house. Today the gatehouse had been gentrified and sold off.

Dismounting, I pushed my bike up the lower stretch of the long drive through the stately beech trees, their boughs bare, their familiar roots lumpy underfoot. I had already decided to stow my bike behind the large turkey oak; it would be safe there for the duration of my visit. I continued on foot, smoothing my hair with my hands and preparing to be scrutinised on my arrival. The drive turned a gentle bend, and the resplendent house came suddenly into view, so familiar, so hated, and yet, reluctantly, so admired, for its history and its grandeur.

No one emerged to look out for my arrival, not even the dogs. All was still in the musty porch. I hesitated before tugging on the wrought iron bell pull. Was I expected? I had answered the letter and confirmed my arrival time. It was exactly nine thirty, in fact, the clock on the stable block had chimed as I approached the house.

I heard shuffling within, and the bellow of a familiar intonation. The door creaked open under the hand of a uniformed, masked and gloved nurse, who welcomed me curtly and ushered me into the entrance hall. The usual smell of the polished wood of ages was tinged with an indistinguishable trace of the medical. She took my waterproof and disappeared, presumably to hang it in the lobby, and I stood still, reminding myself of my beliefs, refusing to be lured back into this anachronistic and now antiseptic world of faux comfort.

Returning, she ushered me down the corridor, boasting the same wall hangings and artefacts that I had seen fifty years earlier, and we stopped outside the door to the drawing room. She knocked. How many hundreds of times had I knocked on that door, fearing reprimand, fearing punishment?

'Enter Georgiana,' he croaked, and I knew from his voice that he was defeated. I had not been called that name for many years. Still as immovable and intolerant as I remembered him, but now shrunken reluctantly into a husk, a pile of decrepitude. He glowered at the long-lost version of me appearing in his dim eyes.

He didn't even offer to shake my hand, but he did, to his credit, look into my face, seeking something, reassurance perhaps. The nurse left us alone. After he had outlined his intentions to sign over the house to me in his will, along with the other properties and his investments, I lied. When he would no longer be here, his euphemism for impending death, he wanted me to return to the family home. He droned on, in a failing voice, about the dogs, the few remaining servants, the upkeep and the investments. His final words to me were that the glory of the family should be continued through future generations. I simply said 'yes,' humouring his timeworn aspirations, but with no intention of complying. On this occasion, I could triumph over his dictatorial edict, and he would never know.

Vindicated.

Day Eight

I did not anticipate the avalanche of unsolicited messages that followed receipt of *the letter*. They flooded in, even though the glitch demolished many of the complex digital predictors in the system. Having been so careful to contain my correspondence with the firm of solicitors to paper and phone, somehow the vultures inhabiting the bastion of financial services have found me out. Now they are battling openly to share a slice of my inheritance, bombarding me with text messages and emails inviting me to invest in their illusory products, encouraging me with the promise of higher interest, flexible bonds, speculation opportunities or individually tailored savings accounts.

One of the many valuable experiences of my comfortable childhood in the mid-1970s was the opening of a post office account. I can remember holding my mother's hand, walking to the small post office in the front room of a cottage on the estate. I carried two shiny, new fifty-pence pieces in my small, sweaty hand. The postmistress used a large rubber stamp with a wooden handle, and I had to sign my name for the first time. I was handed an important-looking book with a dark blue cover, and she had written "one pound" in spidery script. When I helped out on the estate, walking the Jack Russell terriers, polishing the brasses, or ferrying sacks of dirty table linen out to the scullery, I was rewarded with payment in five- or ten-pence pieces. The five-pence coin was larger in those days, more practical than the ridiculous tiny item of today, now reduced, as was my father, to a shadow of its former self. I posted the coins into my black and red striped money tin, which I unlocked regularly, eagerly calculating the value of the coins. On achieving a pound, I would cycle to the post office, alone and adventurous, to deposit it, gaining another stamp. They later changed the familiar cardboard book into a plastic one, smelling of chemicals. It was my Post Office balance which enabled me to walk away, leaving home to nurture my late-teenage idealism.

Back home, I have selected the most promising financial advisor from a long list, thinking that she might offer me a more ethical approach, as her email had announced that my investment "would have a positive effect on society and the environment." I discarded all those with dogma about "high yield" or "easy money" and I deliberately ignored superficially enticing jargon like "inflation protection securities."

Today, my one room flat is tidy in honour of her visit. The small kitchen table has been wiped, and as I visited the laundrette after work yesterday, I look clean. From my window I can see her approaching, and my heart sinks. She picks her way along the pavement, teetering on her heels, her bright red dress clinging bravely to her contours, her eyelashes heavy with mascara. She consults her phone, and looks up at the window, noticing my eyes behind the yellowed net curtain. She frowns and makes a call. My phone rings. I hate my phone; whatever ringtone I select, it sounds invasive. In a split second I wonder whether to ignore the call, but I answer, and explain how she can reach the back door, coming down to guide her up the dirty communal stairs.

Looking scornfully at the kitchen arrangements, she declines my offer of a coffee, and launches straight into her pitch. Listening to her first few sentences, I count eleven acronyms. I pay attention, in case there is a hook upon which I want to hang my hat, but am disappointed. She allows no time for me to interject as she spouts the standard company enticements. I can choose from low risk, medium risk and high risk, tax-efficient financial products. Spouting the everyday marketing jargon with ease, she continues to blast me with intimidating vocabulary, talking about buckets, liquidity and weighted trackers. After five minutes, and after mentioning the one per-cent top-slice for her fee, she picks up on my building frustration, and asks me if her information is of assistance. I mentally calculate that her firm would pocket around £50,000, enough for a first-time buyer in London to put down a sizeable deposit on a dream home, but it would be a mere speck in their hoarded, borrowed and lent billions.

There is an awkward silence. She studies my utilitarian clothing, her eyes resting on my stumpy nails, rising to my distinctively unfeminine face. I regain my composure, and wonder whether there is a human being underneath the cosmetic doll facade.

'I am seeking an ethical holding place for this sum, for the inheritance,' I begin, adding, 'The glitch has taught us vigilance. I want a safe place ... I don't want to invest in shares, in the stock market, or in anything for that matter. I want to be able to set up a trust arrangement, and I am happy to pay for the advice that I need, but I am not interested in the options that you have outlined to me.' I glow with pride at keeping my cool, at not exploding or simply throwing her out.

Her disbelief is betrayed through cracks in her meticulously made-up face. I can see the cogs whirring in her brain. She dismisses my reference to the glitch, as they have all been trained to do, and changes tack, 'Okay, it is generally accepted that any investor will seek to grow their capital. In fact, I have been working for this firm for over five years and not a single customer has ever requested a no-return investment for such a significant sum. That tells me something. It tells me that if you want to guard your inheritance responsibly in our society in the twenty-first century, an advanced and successful jurisdiction, you will need to invest it properly. When customers lack knowledge of the markets, they pay advisors to fill that gap, and to enable them to make their own choices, but from a well-informed platform.' She raises her eyebrows in my direction, seeking my approval, searching for something familiar so that she can select another of her pre-prepared spiels. There is an awkward pause. She adds, in desperation, 'Have you considered the ethical banking sector?'

'Do you think the words ethical and banking can coexist?' I blurt out provocatively.

She smiles, 'Yes, it is a growing sector, and might meet your needs.' She rummages in her briefcase, saying, 'I was at a conference earlier this week and by chance I picked up a leaflet on ethical banking.' She hands me a folded green leaflet, smelling of perfume, and tells me that I can keep it.

I take the leaflet from her as she rises, looking longingly at the exit, aware that this appointment will not assist her performance targets. 'I will find my own way out,' she announces, leaving as rapidly as she can without seeming offensive. Clinging on to the leaflet, grateful for a piece of paper from her digital world, I watch her strut away down the street, glued to her phone. She is no doubt hoping that her next appointment will be more lucrative.

The First Weekend

The supposedly ethical bank will do for now. I have made arrangements for the portion of the inheritance for reinvestment to be safely accommodated, and the customer contact advisor explained to me how to disable the cookies so that the online bombardment of avaricious financial advisors has abated. I am taking the precaution of retaining a sizeable hoard of banknotes too, just in case.

Despite my disdain for the hollow traditions of my upbringing, continuity is important to me, and I am determined to persevere with my delivery job, to keep myself grounded and fit. I have, however, decided to devote every weekend to my future plans, and so today I explained to the chap at the depot that I will only be in on weekdays from now on. He was fine about this. They rate me highly because I am reliable and efficient, and they ask no questions.

I am planning my first weekend reconnoitre. For several months I have been keeping my eyes open for possible locations for the next phase in my life, and there is one which particularly interests me; it is called Caernef Camp. In fact, it is starting to grab my attention in the way that certain tunes get stuck in your head. I cannot think of anything else. As I pedal at speed along the streets, knocking on doors, leaving parcels in safe places, chanting the magical name, "Caernef", my mind is out on the coast. I will buy a train ticket for Saturday morning. I decide to leave the bike behind this time and rely on my feet. I will pack my rucksack ready.

I was accidentally alerted to the decaying outdoor centre, hidden in remote coastal Wales, several months ago, just before the glitch, by a friend of my ex-husband, at The Pike. Since then I have been secretly monitoring it online, fearful that another zany investor will spot the potential before I can mobilise, but having received an encouraging reply from the agent, I find that it is still available.

The first thing that attracted me to the site was the lack of any up-to-date online images. Tantalisingly, the digital mapping stopped on the access road, and the viewer could only see trees by a field gate, covered in lichen, with no signboard. It was as if the place didn't exist at all, which suits my purpose. Until relatively recently the site was used as a centre for school visits, but diminishing returns due to its remoteness, and lack of capital as the buildings have deteriorated over the years, have meant that the council is selling it off.

It may be that I will be disappointed, in which case, as I am not in any hurry, it will simply be back to the drawing board. I prepare myself for disappointment, while garnering a secret hope that this is *the place*.

Deciding not to sully the site with useless technology, I travel without my phone, in fact, before I leave, I lock the phone ceremonially in my beautiful wooden box, sliding the book panel across to hide the keyhole, and placing the key pragmatically in my shoe, ready for work on Monday. I am travelling as light as possible, with my small one-person tent, a compact sleeping bag, a single gas burner and billycan, various food items, maps and a notebook. Wearing many layers of clothing, I overheat on the first train, having to peel them off, and then pile them back on for carrying purposes as the train approaches New Street station.

It is several years since I have passed through this station, and I find that *they* have turned it into a cross between a palace for consumers and an airport. I cannot decipher the directions for platform 5b and I tour the various red, yellow and blue lounges, resisting temptations to give up and buy an over-priced coffee from one of the myriads of bustling concourse cafes. The incessantly loud, inane music blasts out of the speaker and further confuses my brain. Eventually I succeed in locating the platform in the nick of time, running from the "a" end of the platform to the "b" end, merciful that I left my bike at home. The bus-like train groans into the platform, and I spend the four hours on board preparing for my visit, studying the scant catalogue for the sale and familiarising myself with the map. By Machynlleth there are few passengers, and a flustered-looking young girl manages to load a refreshment trolley on to the train, pushing it up a rickety ramp and along the aisle. It is past lunch-time, so this is very welcome. I drink the hot, sweet tea slowly, with pleasure, and eat over-priced cheese sandwiches, which are surprisingly good.

The tiny train skirts the coast, passing through ancient tunnels which protect the track from rock falls, stopping at deserted rural stations with no more than a hut and a platform. We proceed ponderously along the single-track line. I am in no hurry to arrive, because the views out of the scratched and grimy windows are so fascinating.

We proceed slowly along the coast, and I tick off each station as we draw lazily into platforms, collect a few passengers, and continue on our way. I have alerted the train guard to my destination, since it is only a request stop. After seven-hours travelling from Oxford, the train slows and draws up at the neglected platform.

The station seems to have only one electric light, hanging precariously above the small concrete shelter daubed with old graffiti. There is certainly no digital arrivals board, and no car park. Oddly, an aluminium bin for cigarette-ends is hanging limply off the wall. Then I spot the notice, thrown, or fallen, in the hedge, decorated with brown winter debris that once grew in a tangle. I stoop and peer at the wooden board which tells me to "Alight here for Caernef Camp."

The guard gives me a cheery wave as I wait for the train to leave me behind, so that I can cross the track. There is a barrow crossing, no barriers or lights, simply a decaying sign telling me, in Welsh and in English, to "Stop, Look and Listen" and to "Beware of Trains".

Checking my watch, I see that I have over an hour before my appointment with Gareth Andrews, the estate agent from Rural Property Services. The train was actually on time. Having studied the maps carefully, I know that I can make my way on foot to the site, where I am due to meet him.

The modest station is protected by a knot of wind-blown douglas fir, and I step over a sea of fallen cones which have been rolling around on the tarmac since last autumn, and now betray the lack of traffic to this remote place. As I emerge on to the road, and walk up a rise, the vast unoccupied landscape opens up in front of me.

Turning to the left, I suddenly become aware of the coastline, and cannot stop my heart missing a beat as the distant deep blue swell catches the midday winter sunlight, black cliffs fringing the rolling heathland. Despite the track following the crest of the hill, you cannot see the site from the road, which reassures me, and I unexpectedly come upon the gateway which featured in the marketing material. The five-bar field gate is covered in moss and lichen. It has been dragged across the gateway but doesn't latch, and I slip through

CAERNEF CAMP

Saturday Afternoon

The upper part of the site houses the amenities: a makeshift car park which was once gravelled, a communal canteen and kitchens beside a locked brick toilet block, and all surprisingly unvandalized. I can also see various storage areas for fuel, bins, stacked planks of wood and concrete slabs. The wide driveway leads me downwards through an avenue of trees blasted by sea breezes, into the heart of the site, where a squirrel is digging up nuts from his store.

For the first time in recent years, I can feel the blood flowing more slowly in my veins, the muscles in my face relax, and the usual tight anxiety in my skeleton has disappeared. I nervously hope that this is *the place*. Crossing the gently sloping parade ground, overgrown with the thistles of last summer, I reach the seat where Gareth Andrews said to meet him. On the phone he said extravagantly that I couldn't miss it, as it is the best-guarded secret in the whole world, and he was right. I wonder who built the sturdy wooden seat here, on the highest point at the seaward end of the parade ground. Someone in the past treasured this view and wanted to share it with others. When the bench was made, there would have been no mobile phones, or manic online shopping, and vaccines for influenza would only have been in their infancy. The carpenter would have probably lived through the Second World War. Why does mankind repeatedly and recklessly create such folly? Had blinkered politicians through the ages sat on this bench, and paused while they feasted on the inspirational vista, our society might not have become so tortured today.

I chide myself for drifting into politics instead of deeply appreciating the scene before my eyes, and I scan the alluring horizon, the sandbanks, the swift currents, a perfect balance of serene colour, broken by a distant group of oyster catchers, their red beaks the only pinpricks of brightness. Instinctively, I freeze as I spot a solitary curlew wading peacefully in the shallow water, although I am too far away to cause alarm. The majestic bird dips its extraordinary beak, bobs its head, and then flaps gracefully off into the distance.

I leave my camping paraphernalia by the bench, take my wallet in my pocket and hang my camera round my neck as a precaution. Even here, I am alert to criminals, having spent years existing in low-cost rentals, and walking city streets at all hours. You never know who might be around the corner. I set off to explore the site, assuming that Gareth Andrews will see my kit and know that I am nearby.

Four wooden dormitories are spaced around the parade ground, but due to the slope of the land, all can face the sea. They appear sturdy and are locked and battened against the weather, with shutters over the windows preventing me from peering inside. I understand that the council withdrew its staff at the end of September and so the buildings have only been unoccupied for a few months. Debris from various activities is strewn behind one of the buildings, the items that I guess could not be reused elsewhere or sold off: holed, faded canoes, rusty barbecues, sheets of corrugated iron, rolls of fencing, a solitary parking cone and an ancient bicycle with a flat tyre.

The particulars mention a small stream running through the property, which interests me, and I can now hear running water at the back of one of the dormitories. On investigation, part of the stream has been diverted through a series of pipes and troughs, presumably to be used for outdoor washing of boots and equipment. The water is crystal clear and so cold that when I dip my hand in, my skin tingles with pain. Drying my hand on my trousers, I take photographs, and then follow a weedy gravel path downwards. Even in the depths of winter, the air smells sweet.

Further down the hill, beyond the spinney, is the warden's cottage. The agent had advertised it as a separate lot, but apparently no one was interested due to access issues. I studied the floor plan and the limited range of photographs while on the train and have already decided that it is the place for me, separate from the main residential space, sheltered by the trees, and with a sweeping view across the sea.

I approach keenly, recording the details with my camera, but am stopped in my tracks as I see washing on the line, and smoke emerging from the crooked chimney pot. Returning to the shelter of the trees, I pause for five minutes, puzzled, and angry at this pollution of the otherwise pristine vision. My supreme pleasure in being the solitary explorer discovering a derelict and needy site is shattered. The idyll is ruined. I feel heavy with disappointment, and I am all for turning back, telling Gareth Andrews that this property is not for me after all. But the fascination of the place holds me there. Who is living in the cottage? It is described in the particulars as "vacant possession".

Driven by curiosity, I compose myself and start to walk quietly towards the small, alluring house. It has no delineated garden, and there is no gate, being simply surrounded by the rough grassland and a collection of wintry bushes. At that very moment, I stop in my tracks, hidden by the wispy trees. As if scripted, the door opens, and out skips a smiling toddler, her hair braided in two short plaits. She is carrying a small basket. Completely unaware of me watching, she calls joyfully to someone in the house. The door opens again and a tall young man emerges more cautiously, looking each way, lifting the little girl up high in his arms so that she can reach the washing and placing her feet back down on the grass with extreme care. She is just about to collect the clothes pegs when he seems to feel my presence. He drops his clothes basket, grabs the girl and disappears inside closing the door quietly.

It is clear to me from their behaviour that they are occupying the cottage illegally. I reflect on the demeanour of the man, revealed in such a brief scene. He appeared genial, until he suddenly sensed my presence. His affection for the small girl was obvious, presumably she is his daughter. He didn't seem to be menacing, or aggressive. The very fact of washing clothes and hanging them out is a normal, everyday activity. I conclude that I should have nothing to fear by approaching him, but on checking the time, realise that I am due to meet the agent back at the bench.

I turn, and ascend the hill, passing confidently through the long grass, in case the residents of the cottage are watching me out of the window. I do, after all, have a right to be here. I arrive at the old wooden seat, relieved to see my belongings are still here, but see no estate agent, and so plant myself on the bench and, again, survey the scene before me, while I wait.

If I screw up my eyes, I can see faint wisps of smoke from the cottage chimney, in fact I realise that I can smell woodsmoke, gentle and comforting. The shrill call of the curlew pierces the air, accompanied by the high-pitched chattering of oyster catchers down on the shore. It is a very long time since I have been in a place where you cannot hear the human race. There are no traffic noises, no voices, and no hums or buzzes. The distant swell of the sea is calming, and I willingly lapse into a daze, transfixed by the beauty and simplicity of the scene, instinctively remaining silent and still, to blend into the tranquillity.

After half an hour I decide that Mr Andrews is not coming. This is very frustrating, given that I have travelled seven hours to meet him. I should never have left my phone at home and instantly regret making such a silly mistake. He has probably been trying to contact me. In case he has driven up, I return to the car park, and even walk out to the track, but he has clearly not arrived, so I resolve to return to the cottage to discover more about the inhabitants.

This time, no smoke lingers over the scrubby trees by the cottage, and there is no evidence of washing on the line. The previously bright afternoon is developing a wintry chill, with thick black clouds rolling in from the sea. As I walk up to the front door of the cottage, I see that it is deteriorating, with peeling paint and cracked window panes adding to the air of neglect. At once I want to fetch paint and filler, brooms and tools to rescue the needy building, but I am anxious that others have come before me. It has already been claimed. I knock, boldly, but there is only silence in reply.

I peer in through the spider's webs but in the dim light can only see heaped discarded furniture, dusty flagstones, and a pile of ash in the grate. Suddenly overcome by the solitary isolation of my position, I wonder if I was mistaken earlier. I know that this sounds fanciful, but it occurs to me that I may have stumbled upon a window into the past, perhaps seeing a glimpse of previous inhabitants of the now-deserted cottage. Brought back to my senses by a breath of cold wind, I tell myself that the two figures were real, and that they are still nearby. They are probably watching me right now.

Saturday Evening

The two enigmatic figures do not return, and as the light is fading, I choose my pitch. Despite the winter temperatures, I have planned to camp for one night, to get a feel of the remote place after hours, and also, of course, as there is no train back until Sunday morning.

I steer well clear of the cottage, giving them space, as I am convinced that they will return under the protection of the darkness, and I set up my modest camp at the sheltered end of the parade ground. The temperature is plummeting as the light dims, and I am about to snuggle into my sleeping bag for warmth before attempting to cook some supper, when nagging curiosity gets the better of me.

Greeted by a hint of woodsmoke, I emerge from my tent into the chill winter air and stumble over the tussocks using my torch to find the way. I am not disappointed. As I crest the hillside and stare down towards the luminescent sea, I spot a small flickering light shining bravely in the cottage window. I approach the dwelling and pause outside the door.

Through the cobwebs, and in the alluring glow of the light from a single candle, I can see three people warming their hands over the dancing flames of a roaring fire. The man, who I saw earlier, has a hunted look in his eyes. He holds his arm around a woman. I cannot see her clearly. The child is nestled into their feet. The woman rises and stirs something on the fire, a cooking pot, I think. The man strokes the woman's hair, and then gently massages her shoulders.

I weigh up the risks. If I return to my tent, and leave them to their solitude, they will remain undisturbed, but I look again at the fear in the man's eyes, and question myself. If I leave without any action, the family will be in danger. There will inevitably be estate agents and perhaps other prospective buyers who may be less sympathetic than me. Do I have a duty to alert them to this? On the other hand, if I knock at the door, I will startle them, again, and they may flee, leaving their supper half cooked on the fire.

My years of experience in unobtrusively assisting the homeless and the desperate serve me well. I retreat a few metres, and pick up a handful of small stones by the light of my torch. I sit on the frosted grass, feeling the damp penetrate my trousers, and I aim. The first stone falls short. The second, however, hits the exact spot on the window pane that I intended, with a clunk.

I wait. Anxious eyes appear at the window. I send a third stone with impressive accuracy, and as a result, the man opens the door. He sees me, crouching at a distance.

We face each other across the darkness, his silhouette tense. I rise slowly and cautiously, holding both of my hands open, showing him that I am unarmed, deliberately revealing my vulnerability. It is a pivotal moment. He closes the door softly behind him, and walks towards me, his hands in his pockets. I guess he has a knife.

'Friend,' I say, my breath steaming into the darkness.

'You alone?' he whispers, and when I reassure him, he responds, 'Friend.'

He holds his hand out to me, and we shake, testing each other, both offering a firm and confident grip.

'Coffee?' he asks, and I nod. He leads me into the cottage. The woman shrinks against the fireplace, her arms protectively around the child. Their belongings are sparse, lined up ready for a quick exit if needed. He fetches three mugs from the kitchen, heats water in an old pot over the fire and makes the coffee, which we drink black and strong. This cup of coffee means more to me than the endless over-priced throw-away coffees out in the everyday world. The little girl catches my eye several times, and smiles tentatively, but the parents remain tense.

I will tell them my name, Robin, which is not my original name. A week after I emerged into the world, I was named ostentatiously by my father. For reasons best known to him, he had desperately wanted a boy, who he intended to call George after a successful progenitor. To his constant frustration, through my childhood I challenged his stereotype, behaving like a boy. Thus I frustrated each parent, my father because I didn't follow the historically accepted behaviour of my gender, and my mother because I refused to dress in pink, or stay clean and ladylike.

My father bestowed the name Georgiana upon me, followed by Elizabeth, after my paternal grandmother, and then, hidden at the end of the queue, was the name Robin, chosen by my mother. She used to tell me that she wanted to call me a name that reminded her of the simplicity of nature. She once explained that during my first week on this earth, with my fuzz of red hair, a robin used to perch on the windowsill while she nursed me. Looking out into the frozen parkland, she welcomed the dash of red of her melodious companion, and she chose the name 'Robin' which was only grudgingly included by my father, who by then had lost any romantic notions about my mother and treated most of her whims with disdain.

'I am Robin,' I tell them.

Saturday Night

My unexpected companions reciprocate, telling me their names. The man refers to himself as Thomas, but has another name, which I do not recognise. He points at their daughter, saying 'This is Poppy.' On hearing her name, the child chants,

'Poppy, Poppy.'

The woman speaks for the first time, her voice tinged with an indefinable optimism. Her English is excellent, with the trace of an American accent. I don't know why I had assumed they wouldn't understand or speak English.

'We call my partner Thomas, and I am Maria. We are plant scientists. Please, tell us why you are here, and what do you know of this place?'

Something in the bare pathos of the situation persuades me to be completely open with them, and I say, 'This site is being sold. I came for a look around, with a view to purchasing it,' adding, 'It used to be a camp for schoolchildren, but it closed in September. It is a remote location out here. I am interested in reopening the camp and living here myself. I need some time out from city life.' They hang on my words, attentive and respectful, starting to lose their anxiety. 'And what brought you here?' I ask, gently probing. They are guarded in their response, telling me that they have travelled a long, long way, and that they seek somewhere safe and quiet.

We seem to have this in common and I immediately warm to these compelling individuals. They obviously lead a simple life, and sense that I seek this too. We talk of what really matters to us, of truth and honesty, of principles and kindness. We share our frustrations with the current government and our despair over the misuse of technology. They are very concerned about the possibility of future health pandemics, and further disruption caused by the glitch.

They describe the headland to me, the plants and the wildlife, fascinating even in the winter. We share a deep respect for the natural world and I tell them how I watched the curlew earlier, silently acknowledging to myself how my comfortable upbringing, my city life, and my hypocritical delivery job are so far away from the simplicity of the ideal existence that I seek. As if reading my mind, Thomas drags us back to reality, saying, 'Maria and I are very happy out here. It is peaceful, but we cannot stay. There is insufficient food, and once the camp is sold, there will no longer be shelter for us. We are talking about returning to Birmingham.'

I interrupt the devastation on their faces by asking, 'How on earth do you manage to eat, to feed Poppy?' I wonder at the bonny little person, with her plump cheeks and dimples. They laugh, and say that they have known it much harder than this, telling me how they walk four miles to the nearest supermarket and hide their shopping out in the bushes, but say that their money will not last for much longer.

'In the bushes!'

'Well, we keep milk and cheese cool in the water, and store tins of food in the bushes out on the headland.' I tell them that they are inspiring.

After a full hour of invigorating conversation, totally humbled, and not wishing to overstay my welcome, I rise, intending to return to my tent for the night.

This time it is Maria who extends an invitation to me, 'Robin, don't go yet. You can share our supper if you like?' She disappears into the kitchen and I hear chopping. 'Whoever lived here before left a lot of their things,' Thomas observes. He brings out the basket of clothes pegs and Poppy shows me how she can line them up along the hearth. Thomas hides pegs under the basket for her to find. Such a simple game gives her so much pleasure.

Maria returns carrying a stew pot and a tray of carefully prepared tiny fish, placing the pot on to a rack above the flames, while Thomas holds Poppy, nervous of the fire. We continue putting the world to rights, and I dredge my memory for finger rhymes that my mother taught me as a young child, "Two little dickie birds," "Incy, wincy spider" and "Here's a church, here's a steeple". Poppy is fascinated, and learns quickly, soon mimicking Peter and Paul sitting on their wall.

The supper begins to smell delicious, and I am very pleased to have stayed longer, as Maria places the fish over the flame. The steaming stew seems to consist of potatoes and wild herbs. Thomas explains how they catch whiting out in the estuary. 'We prefer sausages,' he jokes, adding 'but fish is good too.'

They ask me if I am serious about buying the camp, and joke that if I am, it comes with the added bonus of two willing workers. It crosses my mind that this is not a bad idea, but I need to know more about these two strangely welcoming young parents. It occurs to me that there is only one cottage, so perhaps it is not such a good plan. I certainly don't want to share my idyllic space with a toddler, however cute she seems.

'Will you tell me more about your long journey?' I ask them.

Thomas selects a handful of foraged sticks, and stokes the fire. Maria clears the supper dishes into the kitchen, and returns, glancing at him before speaking, waiting for him to nod. Then she tells me their story eloquently, while little Poppy curls up asleep in her lap, and Thomas touches her shoulder, proudly watching her lips as she speaks, but visibly distraught as the memories unfold.

ALEPPO

'Ten years ago, Thomas and I were trapped in Aleppo. We are not Syrian and we are not Muslim, although many of our friends were. My mother was originally American, but hadn't lived there for many years, and my father was a traditional Syrian Jew. Thomas comes from a large itinerant family living across the Syrian border into Lebanon. We met while studying at the University of Aleppo, just before war broke out. We are both experienced plant scientists, but were unable to graduate due to the fighting. Initially we didn't expect the conflict to go on for more than a few weeks, but we were wrong, so wrong.

'We had seen footage of the Arab Spring, and when our friends became involved in the Syrian demonstrations, we joined them. We are both fluent in English and we spoke to journalists. There was so much to fight for in Syria at that time: democracy itself, freedom of expression, justice. But we underestimated the power of the government, and when students began to be compulsorily conscripted, we knew it was time for us to leave the university behind. Looking back now, it was wise to flee as early as we did. I had been brought up to speak my mind, and that was not a safe behaviour in that place at that time, particularly not for a woman.'

I sit silently, fascinated by her words, mesmerised by the firelight, as she continues, 'Thomas had lodgings right in the centre of the city. We met there, and left together, thinking there was a break in the shelling, but we miscalculated. The barrel-bombing intensified, and the streets through which we had to pass quickly became filled with explosions and gunfire. We were forced to take shelter in a small underground room, a storage cellar with no light. I was petrified that if the only entrance became blocked, by falling masonry or by soldiers, we would be completely trapped or buried alive down there. Our companions were desperate and a couple of them seemed unscrupulous; Thomas's shoulder bag containing his passport and phone was stolen. We could not work out how they disappeared. A scuffle broke out, and while eyes were turned to the fighting men, we slipped away.

'We knew never to allow ourselves to become trapped like that again. We had to navigate the incessant shelling to work our way out of the city. It was an exercise in patience and guile amid scenes which I will not describe. The gas attacks, the random gunfire, not knowing whose side the soldiers were on, lying low, trying to be invisible. I am not sure how we reached the university, largely untouched by the shelling at that point, but we did not stop. Familiar with the area, we knew we must cross the large ring-road and head out of the sprawling city, as far away from the annihilation as possible.

'It was dusk by the time we crept through the underpass, the ring road usually so busy, only resounding with the relentless grind of military vehicles. We continued on foot as long as the moonlight lasted, picking our way further and further from the carnage.

'We travelled for many days, eventually resting at a hilltop ruin, where we could see for miles. We took turns to sleep, and made a fire, but were concerned about our dwindling supplies. Any hopes of resting there for the night were shattered as a large group of fighters selected the place for their lookout. Fortunately, we saw them running up the slopes like a herd of wild animals, and we made a hasty escape before they arrived.

'We were no longer alone as we hit the main route northwards. Hundreds of fleeing Syrians, carrying their scant rescued belongings, were also heading out towards Turkey. We joined the crowds, following blindly for days. At this point we had cash, I had my Syrian passport and my bank card. Food was becoming scarce, but we were able to buy water, and random items, as we passed through towns where unscrupulous vendors were keen to screw us for as many Syrian pounds as they could.

'We were allowed to pass into Turkey for humanitarian assistance and ended up in a camp which was relatively small when we arrived, but grew massively over the long period of time when we were stuck. At some point during our second year there, my phone was taken, which angered me, although charging it had become a challenge. I was furious with myself for falling asleep when I was on watch. It was a precarious phase in our lives, and we knew that we needed to move on, but we didn't know how.

~

'There was one notable visitor to the camp, a quiet, religious gentleman called Frere Antoine. He had come from France, and was assisting the migrants as best he could. He wasn't young. He gathered Christians for prayer, and helped small groups plan for their future, advising on the least unsafe routes through to Greece. Thomas and I befriended this well-meaning brother, and he was kind to us. He could see that we had become trapped in the camp and had no idea how to continue our journey, despite having some cash, and access to dollars in my account. We were naïve and his advice was invaluable. After several detailed conversations with him, sitting huddled together on the dusty floor, one morning we simply walked out of the camp. On foot, Thomas and I took the road to a nearby town, where we caught a bus. It took us part of the way across Turkey, towards Istanbul. Our journey to Istanbul took two days, and we had to change buses several times. People knew we were migrants; they looked at us with pity and resentment. Dishevelled and weary, we took our comfort from being together.'

As I listen to Maria telling their story, I am transported to Istanbul, which I know only from online images and news footage. I urge her to continue.

'We were elated to eventually arrive in Istanbul. Here was a large city where we could become lost in the ordinary bustle of everyday life. We checked into a hotel for one night, cleaned ourselves up, and shopped for supplies, anxious not to use up too much cash. Following Brother Antoine's advice, we went to the bus station, and managed to find out that a bus for Meric Bridge, on the border with Greece, would depart the next morning. It would be a five-hour journey, which seemed short in comparison with the buses across southern Turkey. Despite the luxury of a proper bed, for the first time since we left Aleppo, we couldn't sleep, tortured by haunting memories and anxious about the days ahead.

'We took the bus, which was hot and often filled with fumes, snatching naps in turn. As we inched our way towards Greece, we were hopeful. Brother Antoine had told us to try to cross to Greece by land, but not to declare ourselves as refugees until we reached our final destination; we wanted to reach Great Britain. The bus crawled across the countryside, eventually spluttering to a halt in a dusty lay-by a few miles short of our destination, the driver stating that it would go no further. The passengers spilled out on to the roadway, using their phones, calling for assistance and we managed to join a group of women in a taxi. Thomas helped with their luggage, and we paid cash for our ride. The taxi took us to a small sprawling rural town, and I really don't remember much more that day, except that it was a busy Saturday night and we somehow got into a rough crowd. They promised to get us across to Greece, but then kept plying us with raki. I think mine was spiked. All I can remember is Thomas keeping a clear head and desperately dragging me away when the terrible men started pawing at me. Those rogues took my bag, all my carefully protected belongings, our medications and my cash: gone.

'Thoroughly ashamed, I let Thomas support me to a safer place, and we waited for the dawn. I tried to remember exactly what Brother Antoine had told us. Through the tortured haze, I could recall something about a Bulgarian Orthodox Church. We asked several people, and were sent along busy streets to a small church. People came and went, but no one had heard of Brother Antoine, and they pointedly avoided coming over to us. We sat on some stones, bereft and alone, not sure what to do or where to go.

'One of the people who had come out of the church earlier, returned, and seeing us still hanging around, came across to us. He spoke in Greek; we didn't understand, but the tone of his voice was not aggressive, and we picked out the name Constance. After asking many unhelpful people, we ascertained from a street map that there was a second Orthodox church in the vicinity. We made our way to this second church but without much hope.

'After some time, the doors opened. A hooded priest emerged, followed by older women with their heads covered in red, white and blue cloths. They ignored us. The stream of people dwindled, and a tall man in a suit closed over the doors. Thomas left my side and approached the man, speaking in English, even trying broken Bulgarian. "We are from Syria. Brother Antoine told us to come here for help."

'The man looked at Thomas, and then at me slumped on the base of a statue. He appeared to recognise the name of Brother Antoine, and nodded, but he did not seem to speak much English, or Bulgarian. He led us to a small workshop a few streets away from the church, and handed us over to a carpenter leaving us with him. The carpenter told us in broken English to rest awhile. After some time, he came over to us with more kindness than we had experienced of late. He showed us a map on his phone, pointed to the border with Greece and indicated that he could take us right now.

'He gesticulated for us to pay him, before we left. We gave him all our remaining cash. Looking back, it was poor recompense for the risks which he took for us, but he seemed satisfied. I think he was helping people like us out of genuine compassion. He put his finger to his lips, indicating that we must be silent on the journey. He took me out to the truck first, showing me a very small compartment under the sacks. I squeezed into it and he lowered a wooden cover over me. I could hear him piling things back on top. It was pitch dark in there, very cramped and smelt sweetly of hessian and wood. I could hear him return with Thomas and tried to stop myself thinking about what was happening to him. The engine started and another man seemed to get into the cab with the carpenter.'

~

Maria pauses to drink some water, her voice becoming hoarse with pent up emotion. Thomas and I wait, in silence, for her to continue.

'The road was rough, and the truck noisy. I had never travelled in such a terrible way before, tossing and turning as the vehicle went over rocks in the road.

'Mercifully the journey was not long, maybe twenty minutes. The sweet smell of hessian had become a torment. Just as I was thinking I could not endure the suffocation any longer, feeling quite faint, the truck stopped. With the engine still running, the wooden cover was quietly lifted from my resting place, and the carpenter beckoned. I coaxed my stiff limbs into action and rose awkwardly. He shovelled me gently off the truck and on to a verge saying, "Quick."

'Sitting on the grass, breathing the welcome warm evening air, I watched him release Thomas, who had been tied under the truck. Thomas's face was a terrible white colour and he fell on to the road with a thump. Fearing the worst, I sprang forward and pulled him up. He gasped and asked for water. The carpenter fetched a bottle of water from the cab, gave it to Thomas and said, "In Greece now. You must go. Quick." It was clear that he had done this before. Just as his companion appeared from the nearby ramshackle diner, we staggered off down the road.

'We walked for days, resting by night in bus shelters, sheds and outhouses. We scavenged food and asked for tap water in roadside cafes. Eventually, having completely lost count of the days, we hit a larger town and headed for a bank.

'They enabled me to withdraw dollars, and to convert them straight into euros, charging a hefty commission. Greece was in the midst of its own financial crisis and they seemed to be pleased to lay their hands on my dollars. We were simply relieved to see the crisp euro notes in our grimy hands.

'Once outside, we split the cash in half, each taking an equal share, in case we became separated. We were no longer so naïve. We found a cheap hotel where we rested for the night, showered and set ourselves up for the journey ahead.

'In Kavala we did manage to locate someone who could help us, but we really didn't trust him. We withheld our payments until he arrived with the documents, and we insisted on checking them thoroughly before handing over the cash. This angered him and we nearly lost the deal.

'We spent time choosing new outfits, selecting touristy clothes and purchased two cheap wheelie cases, one bright pink and another a fluorescent green. Owning so few belongings, we filled the cases with odd scavenged items to add weight and in case they were opened as we passed through customs. With a long journey still ahead of us, our only goal was to step out on British soil.'

~

I envisage Thomas and Maria masquerading as tourists and I think of the swarms returning home from short breaks in Turkey and Greece, their wheelie cases filled with cheap souvenirs, and the trappings of sated holidaymakers: dirty beach wear, half-empty bottles of sun cream and a few remaining painkillers in blister packs. I visualise the pathos of their two brash wheelie cases filled with rubbish rather than being crammed with beach towels, presents for family members and cheap ouzo.

'We purchased plane tickets successfully using the fake tourist visas. Thomas's false Lebanese passport looked convincing. The day for our travel dawned, and we were at the airport very early, eager to be on our way. You wouldn't believe how smoothly everything ran. We took the short internal flight to Athens. Compared with Kavala, Athens airport was state of the art. We were petrified that we would be apprehended for false documents, but we managed to board the flight to London-Luton without incident. My heart was beating so fast that I thought I would faint. We gripped our seats as the plane took off, leaving mainland Europe way below us. This was the final life-changing leg of our long journey.

'It had taken us nearly five years to reach this moment, from that first horrifying day in Aleppo. When the plane landed at Luton Airport, despite looking like tourists, we were ready to declare ourselves as asylum seekers. We thought that would be it; we had delusions of Great Britain opening its arms to us, but I am afraid that we were overly optimistic.

'The border-force officer was highly suspicious of us and called the airport police. They marched us over to reclaim our baggage, standing close to us while we queued, waiting, waiting until the two familiar suitcases appeared. We revealed the pathetic rags filling the two brightly coloured cases. They stripped the lining, but, of course, found nothing but thin foam padding. I felt dirty and desperate at that moment. All I wanted was a cup of tea, and somewhere to sit down, but we were marched off, leaving the superfluous wheelie cases behind.

'Then, for the first time since we had left Aleppo, we were forcibly separated. They took Thomas away into a small room, and I was taken far across the tiled walkways to a police cell where I was thoroughly searched.

'As the time passed, I became more and more confused. Eventually an officer arrived and led me out of the cell to an interview room.

'I waited there for hours. It was worth waiting, because the two women who eventually appeared were of a different sort. One was carrying a cup of coffee, and the other had kind eyes. They introduced themselves as Sara and Jane, and that coffee was for me! Sara handed me the cup saying, "There's no sugar in it; is that okay?" The coffee was not too hot and I drank it as if it was nectar, thanking her profusely. Then they took me out into the fresh air, loading me into the back of a police car. My first glimpse of Great Britain was not invigorating. I was taken to a police station nearby, and into another interview room.

'Sara explained that she represented a charity for refugees. They could help me. Jane was the Immigration Officer who conducted the interview. I told her my story, as I am telling you today. She scribbled as I talked, noting down some of the details. When I finished, I turned to Sara and asked when I would see Thomas. She didn't know, but she gave me a card with her contact details on it. I was taken to another room to wait.'

~

She squeezes Thomas's hand, and continues, 'I will not bore you with the tedious details of my long-drawn-out battle with the British authorities. Suffice it to say that I was provided with basic accommodation, for which I was grateful.

'It was not until my Asylum Interview a few weeks later that I had a clue to his whereabouts. As I arrived in the reception area, I could see a list of attendees on the desk. The attendant had left for some reason, and had, unprofessionally, but fortunately for me, abandoned her list for all to see. There in black and white was Thomas's Syrian name, the name on his false passport. His interview was scheduled for 11am, after mine. I said nothing. I was learning to trust no one in the bureaucratic mess that was

Great Britain. Anyway, it might just be someone with the same name.

'All through my interview I gave concise responses, surreptitiously checking the time on my interviewer's dainty gold watch, fortunately exposed on her arm. I hurried calmly out of the interview room and back down to the waiting area.

'As I descended the stairs, I knew that it was him. The unmistakable shape of his head, his shoulders. He was sitting in a world of his own, his head resting on his hands. I walked up to him and crouched down at his feet. He looked up and he saw me.

'In that moment, we were transformed from two sad, beaten human beings into two proud survivors. At first we did not speak. We held each other tightly, embracing the comfort, the ecstasy of holding each other once again. Tears flowing freely down my cheeks. Through my tears of joy, I asked if he was okay. He kissed my tears. He kissed my wet cheeks, and I closed my eyes, drowning in my love for him.'

~

Back in the small cottage at Caernef, Thomas is stirring the embers. He places dry fir cones on the glowing ash and they spring into flame, illuminating our faces. I am so moved by Maria's story that I find it hard to speak. She looks across at me, and I reach out, stroking Poppy's sleeping head very gently.

'The day that the email finally came through, we were sitting by the fountains in Victoria Square. We had been sent to accommodation in Birmingham to sit out the virus pandemic, and as places reopened, we often spent time in the Art Gallery while Poppy slept in the papoose. On this day we heard that we had both been granted refugee status.

'By some very good luck, our papers arrived the very next day in the post. Later that day …'

'The glitch?' I interject, having worked out the chronology.

'Yes,' Thomas confirms. 'If our asylum had taken just

one day longer, we would have been right back to square one. God was looking down on us that day.'

'A job was advertised here at the camp. The details were very limited; this was straight after the glitch. All online information was suspended. We decided we had nothing to lose by coming to see the place for ourselves. We took a coach to Shrewsbury and then walked across Wales. It was while we were in Snowdonia that we were told that the job advertisement had been withdrawn. When we phoned the council, they said that the place was going to close. It all happened so quickly.

'We had never seen anywhere like Wales before, and decided to continue on our trek. We approached the camp round the coast. We slept in a ruined barn for a few weeks, creeping out here each day, watching everything being packed up. Eventually the people left. We checked every day for a week, and then took our chance. We stayed in the folly first, before we discovered this little cottage.'

'The folly?'

'I will take you out there for breakfast if you like?' Thomas offers.

THE FOLLY

Sunday Morning

After reliving their ordeal for my benefit, Maria and Thomas look emotionally exhausted. Tiredness suddenly comes upon me too, and despite their entreaties for me to sleep by their fire, I crave some solitude. We bid each other goodnight and I return to my tent, completely drained by their story. I realise that they know far more about this place than I do.

It is bitterly cold in the depths of the night, and I toss and turn, seeking pockets of warmth in my sleeping bag, but counting my blessings as I think of Thomas and Maria on their epic journey. Events from the bizarre day play through my semi-conscious mind, and I dream of gunfire on the streets of Oxford, of fleeing hoards and armed militia. Troubled, I rise before the sun, splashing water on my face from my bottle in an attempt to drag myself into the possibility of daytime. Already fully dressed in multiple layers of clothing, I open the zip of the tent door, which promotes blasts of even colder air to rush inside. I hear a polite rustle nearby. Is it an animal scurrying over dry leaves? No, it is boots on frosted grass. Thomas is waiting, staring out towards the darkness that is the sea. He hears the sound of the tent zip and turns to greet me, smiling and holding out his hand. 'Come for breakfast,' he invites. I pull on my boots.

He leads me down the slope through the darkness, past the cottage and on to a path which lay beyond my explorations yesterday afternoon. We proceed along the path for several minutes, and I can see through the gloom that we are teetering on the edge of a severe drop towards the shore. He keeps turning around to check that I am following, then he stops. The path takes us up to a grassy platform on a rocky outcrop. It occurs to me that this is madness. I am just starting to distrust his motives when I see the looming shape of a squat building, with a tower, which is obviously his destination. He flicks out a torch, shining it on a small keyhole, taking a key from his pocket and opening the door. It creaks. We enter, and I hear him strike a match, lighting two candles in jam jars. The candlelight speckles the whitewashed walls. 'Where is this?' I ask him in wonderment. He puts the match to a pre-prepared dome of dry fir-cones in a small grate. They crackle and spit, soon offering us welcome warmth.

'Maria says this is a magical place on the edge of the world,' he whispers proudly, adding, 'We came along the rocks and sheltered here for a few days before we found the cottage. It reminded us of the hilltop ruin in Syria. The key was hidden under a stone near the door.' He points through the small latticed window, saying, 'Sunrise will be over there.' He takes his phone from his pocket, taps away on it, and explains, 'You can get a signal up here on the cliffs.'

Thinking of the street sleepers at dawn, back in their Oxford doorways, I remember my phone in the box, and I marvel at my current location. If this barely-known survivor murders me here, right now, at least my ending will be in a hallowed spot. But I know that he is neither foe nor murderer. He fetches two small bread rolls from his pockets and places them on the stones by the hearth to warm. He disappears for a moment and I hear water. He returns with a metal can which he places on the fire, now energetically crackling.

'Coffee?'

'Yes. Yes please.'

'Maria found instant coffee up in the kitchen block, and

powdered milk, but that's all gone now. She is good at finding things.'

Thomas and I sit in silence drinking black coffee and eating the hot bread, while the golden disc of the sun emerges over the sea.

I find myself wondering if this remote building is included in the sale. I do remember the scribbled word "folly" just inside the red line. Please let it be true.

After our breakfast, eaten largely in silence, reluctantly, I explain to Thomas that I really must catch the first train of the day as I need to be back in Oxford for work early tomorrow morning. Once the sun has risen fully, we return along the precarious path, and I wish that I had brought my camera, for the stunning landscape in the early morning light is barely believable. Before we part, we exchange phone numbers, writing them down on a scrap of paper, and I think for a second time, that it would have been wiser to have brought my accursed phone with me on this trip. He looks bemused when I say that I left it at home. I shake his hand and wish him and his family all the best, urging him to be careful, encouraging him to guard this magical place, secretly hoping that I will return as the owner.

Before I leave, I pack up my tent and stow all that I can into my rucksack: sleeping bag, torch, several items of clothing, cooking stuff, and nearly £50 in notes and cash. I slide my maps and the paper copy of the particulars for the sale of the site down into the back of the rucksack. I creep down the slope, placing my luggage in the porch of the cottage, only taking with me my painkillers, notebook, camera, train tickets and virtually empty wallet. It is risky, but I know that they can use the items better than me.

With a light step I retrace yesterday's route to the station, anxious that the train is running, and more anxious that the guard spots me waving at the request stop. I need not have worried; the train appears, slightly late, and draws to a halt so that I can alight. It is the same guard as yesterday, and he raises his eyebrows seeing me without any luggage.

He misses nothing. I ignore his probing questions and tell him that I may be back next weekend. He retorts that I shouldn't leave it too long or they might close the station as I am the only passenger to have used it for months.

Sunday Evening

Following a seven-hour journey, I push through the early Sunday evening bustle of Oxford station, hurrying across Frideswide Square, my feet illuminated by the rainbow lights that enhance the precinct. The regular rough sleeper is already gathering his cardboard outside the business school. The skateboarding youths wheel around him in a protective arc. My street companion is not in his place yet, and I turn into the passage which leads me home.

I head straight for my work shoes, on guard by the door, and I locate the key to the box. Unlocking the box, and clutching at my phone, I am not surprised to see a host of missed calls and texts. Many are from Gareth Andrews, sent early on Saturday morning, but after I had left for the station. He apologises profusely for having to reschedule our appointment due to "family matters" and asks me to suggest an alternative time. I scroll down, and at the foot of the list is the message that I am hoping for. It is from Thomas. He asks me whether I had intended to leave my stuff in their porch; will I be coming back for it?

I compose two responses, firstly to Thomas, whose existence seems unreal now that I am back in my familiar day-to-day surroundings. I simply say, "I will be back. The stuff is yours. I don't need it. Stay Safe, Robin." Then I send a text to Gareth. It is my turn to apologise, "Sorry for late response. Rescheduling okay. Next Saturday Feb 16, same time 2.30pm? Robin."

Gareth is presumably anxious that he has not completely lost a prospective buyer, and as I expect, he responds immediately, affirming that this day and time is fine. He will confirm by email, and will resend the particulars to me. I send a second message to Thomas: "I will be back at the camp next Saturday, same time. Am seeing estate agent at 2.30. Suggest you stay away and return Sat evening. See you for supper in cottage?" I add, as an afterthought, "I will bring sausages!" I click send, but, of course, there is no instant response, as I know that he will have to go to the folly to pick up a signal.

Images of the folly play tantalisingly on my brain. I am in danger of romanticising. Just imagine living on a rocky promontory half an hour's walk from the outside world, with no power, no conveniences. If Thomas and Maria can manage, could I?

I fire up my laptop, check there is no further news on the cause of the glitch, only finding the usual enflamed social media and fake news pointing the finger at an American dissident in Russia, and I access the Caernef sale particulars for the hundredth time. Finding them unchanged, I research compost toilets.

Visibly, my life continues normally. I collect the hot rolls, share with my rough sleeper, I work, I get home late and shower, eat, and repeat the pattern. But inside my head, much is changed. The joy of parcel delivery is that it is automatic. In a relentless cycle, I clock the address, pedal hard, negotiate traffic and deliver, but there is always space in my head to dream. For the first time, my hopes for a different life seem possible. I even find myself feeling grateful to my much-maligned father for unknowingly opening this door for me. I am not proud of my actions following his death, even though they seemed so reasonable to me at the time. I can see that the solicitor achieved a decent price for the estate by dividing it up. He squeezed as much income as he could from each component, selling the then unoccupied family home to an avaricious property developer, who I notice has already applied for planning permission to convert it into ten self-contained flats. I stop myself calculating the profit that he will make.

I do not hear from Thomas.

It is midnight on Friday. I have purchased a replacement rucksack, and it is kitted out in readiness for my trip. Hoping to sleep in the folly, I pack a new sleeping bag, but no tent. I am taking my phone this time. The first challenge is that the internet has been off all evening. Is this another glitch? Every ten minutes I try rebooting, but *they* seem determined to prevent me from planning my trip. I will have to allow time to purchase the train ticket in the morning. When the internet eventually blinks into life again, my eyelids are heavy. I check the agent's site for a final fix, planning to feast on the limited collection of images of the camp before I sleep, noting again that the folly sits just inside the boundary line. As I enter the website, I cannot see the familiar picture of the gate in the trees. It has completely disappeared. I scan the pages again and again. Filled with dread, I click the "under offer" button, and there it is, staring malevolently at me, with the red triangle declaring someone else's intent to buy.

How dare someone else place an offer on it. The thought of another person taking control of the parade ground, ousting Thomas, Maria and Poppy, developing the folly as a tourist attraction, fills me with repulsion. I check my phone. There are no messages from Gareth. In fact, I heard from him earlier confirming our appointment. What is going on?

Another Weekend

My journey on the following Saturday does nothing to calm my anxieties. All the electronic departure boards have failed at Oxford, with random trains arriving at odd times and on unusual platforms. Passengers are muttering under their breath, anxious this might be another worldwide glitch. My tight connections are compounded by a large public climate demonstration in Birmingham. Although sympathetic to their cause, I resent the inconvenience, having to force my way against the tide to reach the small bus-like train, which is growling in an ominous manner. Fortunately, it does not break down, and yesterday's signal failure on the Welsh route seems to have been resolved. It was no glitch, as the systems are working fine here.

Relieved to be on the last leg of the trip, I am accosted by the same train guard as last week, who bombards me with questions each time he walks the train. 'Getting off at Caernef again?' and 'Do you know about the camp at Caernef?' then 'Have you heard of the trouble there?'

To his last question, I respond, 'No, do tell me,' and he raises his eyebrows, disappearing down the train.

On his return, he explains, 'They should never have closed it, the camp I mean. It provided employment for the locals, and the kids loved it there. Groups travelled by train, their faces pale as they arrived, but glowing with health when they left. It had a good effect on them, staying away, off the beaten track, for a few days.' Without waiting for my response, he marches off, tapping on his ticket machine.

'So what trouble is there?' I ask the next time he appears.

'Well, Glyn Vaughn, the *ex*-manager, was talking in The Prince of Wales. He is furious at the way he was treated by the council, and so sudden too. They told him that a wealthy developer is interested in the place. Might turn it into a caravan park, with amusements and night clubs. Glyn mentioned hen and stag parties, a helipad and a wedding venue. You wouldn't disturb the neighbours out there. He is getting a group together to buy the centre back for its original purpose, using his redundancy money from the council. He reckons there's loads of schools will book again, but he needs to get moving or the place will soon get run down, vandalised, even out here … What do you want with the place anyway?'

I wave my camera at him, and say that I am here to photograph the rare mosses and lichens in their winter habitat.' He shrugs and disappears down the train again.

At the station, the nameboard announcing Caernef has been dragged out of the bushes and is now propped up against the shelter, trailing wisps of dried grass and brambles. The location is no less attractive in the mist, and I pull up my collar to shield me from the gusty drizzle as I walk towards the gateway.

This time, the hidden entrance broadcasts its existence to the virtually non-existent passing traffic with a large over-painted road sign. Where letters once said "Araf", which I know from the rudimentary Welsh that I learnt at university means "Slow", it now says "Save Caernef Camp," painted roughly in black. I pause and survey this clumsy blot on the otherwise natural landscape.

The silence is broken by the noise of a distant car engine approaching; I am guessing it is Gareth, the agent. He arrives in a sleek but old Audi TT, dazzling me with his white teeth, approaching with his hand outstretched, saying, 'Robin? I thought you were a man!'

I shake his hand, greeting him amiably, 'We meet at last.'

He instantly earns my respect as he picks up the over-painted sign and throws it, upside down, into the ditch, saying, 'They shouldn't be doing this.' Turning to me, he asks, 'How serious are you, I mean, do you want a thorough tour, or are you just interested, like the others, in sight-seeing?'

He is generous with his time, once he realises that I am deadly serious, and that I am, to his surprise, a cash buyer. He takes me round the site, answers my many questions to the best of his limited knowledge of the location, and taps away on his iPad each time he says that he will find something out for me.

We approach the cottage towards the end of our tour. He marches down the slope, telling me about the old warden who lived there for twenty years, and who retired to Bangor to be near his family. Nervous, I scan the scene, but see no clues of the recent inhabitants. The empty washing line blows damply in the breeze, the front door looks as if it has lain undisturbed for months, and inside there is no ash in the grate, and no tell-tale signs of occupation. He leaves me to explore the rooms, and through glass still decorated with spiders' webs, I see him standing out on the grass, grabbing a quick cigarette while I am out of sight. He obviously has less self-control than me. It weakens his image as a suave and successful estate agent. He seems to realise this, glancing anxiously in my direction, just as I bob behind the curtains.

Two small bedrooms overlook the sea. I try, unsuccessfully, to see the distant folly on the cliff edge, and a fragment of paper catches my eye. It is stuffed into a crevice in the window frame, as if to stop a draught. I pull it out, and smile, as I read two words, "sausages tonight". So they knew I would stand here looking out to sea. I can see no more secret messages, and I roam around the downstairs rooms, inspecting the small kitchen which leads to a damp bathroom. I test the flush, and it works, the cistern refilling, so I avail myself of the facilities before braving the drizzle again.

'Thanks Gareth, and the folly?' I ask as I emerge.

'I can take you to see it if you like. It marks the easternmost end of the site. We had a break-in, perhaps kids, but no damage. It is rather exposed out there.'

I play down my interest, concealing the intense hopeful optimism that I feel even thinking of the folly. I desperately want to see it once more. I want it for my own.

While we walk along the headland path, I quiz him on Glyn Vaughn, squeezing the very last drops of information out of him. Glyn and some locals have put in a very low offer. Gareth obviously wants a proper sale, money in the bank, commission paid, rather than humouring Glyn's weak local bid to take back a financially unstable enterprise. He says that no one else is interested in buying the camp at present.

Gareth has a key. We pass through the tiny low-ceilinged rectangular room in the squat entrance to the folly, where Thomas and I sat in the candlelight, and we move into the tower. There is hardly room for us both in the small circular room at its base. Despite his business-like approach he, too, seems visibly moved by the romance of the folly. He sends me up the narrow spiral staircase, waiting at the lowest step, his booming voice echoing in the metal tube that forms the tower. 'It's not often that we get to sell a place like this.' The stairs lead straight into a look-out room clad in thick glass fronting the 180 degrees that overlook the sea. A home-made wooden bench, desk and storage drawers provide sufficient furniture for a writer or artist. The metal walls are painted white. It is a perfect retreat.

I descend and ask if he knows its history. He knows that Glyn organised its construction by a group of trainee architects who stayed in the camp for a break away from it all. They built it in a few weeks, and then it was used by small groups from visiting schools. I start to warm to this Glyn.

As we walk together back through the site towards his car, he asks me if I am still seriously interested. I play it cool. I stress that this is not a widely attractive prospect, that the buildings are already deteriorating, that the commercial potential is actually very limited. The words of the gossip in the train echo in my mind: amusements, night clubs, hen parties and a helipad. I say that I am interested, but not at the asking price, and ask how flexible he thinks the vendor will be? We haggle informally. I think he likes me, despite the fact that I do not fulfil his stereotype of a property purchaser. I tell him that I will put my interest in writing as soon as I get home tomorrow, and that my offer will be considerably higher than Glyn's.

He asks where I am staying and I have to think on my feet as I intend to sleep in the folly after supper in the cottage. I divert the conversation back to Glyn Vaughn, saying that I would like a chat with the guy, asking where I can find The Prince of Wales. Gareth tells me that he is driving back to the office and agrees to drop me at the pub, which is only a couple of miles away, and to contact Glyn. He programmes his sat nav as he drives. Apparently, there is no coverage within half a mile of Caernef, and he tells me that there is, curiously, no proper postcode as the camp doesn't actually exist in the system. Most prospective buyers might be deterred but this attracts me even more.

He speaks to his car, I hear a phone ring, and a man's easy-going voice answer, 'Hi Gareth, Glyn here. No more news for the vendor my end I'm afraid …'

'No worries, I have just shown the wealthy businessman round the site. He's called Robin FitzWilliam. I'm heading back to the office. He wants to meet you. Any chance you can be at The Prince of Wales in five?'

'Wow. Okay, I'll head round there now.'

'There you go,' he grins at me.

Saturday Afternoon

I am standing outside The Prince of Wales, beside a battered notice advertising ice creams, although it is not yet spring. This is one of the few places that was probably totally unaffected by the glitch last year. The door is open. I watch the Audi TT disappear at a speed that does not respect the sleepy village in which I find myself, and hoist my rucksack on to my back.

A spry older man is approaching the pub. His long black hair is tinged with silver streaks and he walks with loping but purposeful strides. He nods at me as he disappears inside the building. I continue standing out in the road and listen to the voices within.

'Glyn, you're early.'

'Yes, but guess what, I am here to meet the businessman. Gareth from the estate agents has just phoned me.'

'No, not the businessman with his eye on Caernef?'

'Apparently. He is called Robin FitzWilliam and I intend to give him a piece of my mind.'

'You do all you can to frighten him off. Your plan is a good one and we are behind you. We don't want some jumped up Englishman taking over the place, do we?'

'Exactly. That place is ours!'

Hearing the clink of glasses, I decide to enter the fray. The room housing the bar is cluttered with dusty village memorabilia and the flagstone floor is slimy with the damp weather. Perhaps I looked like a hiker when Glyn passed me on his way in. Drops of a black liquid fall into the drip tray of an old coffee machine, which is perched behind the draft beer. I approach the tall publican, who is guarding his bar with a grimace. I will surprise them by speaking in Welsh as I know just a few phrases.

'Paned o goffi?' I ask, loudly, so that Glyn Vaughn can hear me. The publican grunts in Welsh. It is possible that he is asking if I want milk, so I nod, paying for the coffee and carrying it over to the table where Glyn is established. I sit down opposite him, and enjoy his expression, which is defensive, simmering, and yet puzzled. I fix my eyes on his, and hold him there, luxuriating in a long pause, before I say, 'I am Robin, Robin FitzWilliam. I think you might want to talk business with me?'

His jaw hangs open in confusion while he tries to compose his sentence.

I have successfully taken the higher ground and dig in. 'Gareth Andrews said that I would find you here. I am contemplating making an offer on Caernef Camp. I understand that you are organising a local initiative but that your resource falls short of the asking price. I want to understand the economic potential of future school visits.' I emulate the assertive tone adopted by the financial advisor in the red dress, and hope that my face is appearing as steely as I intend, but he laughs, long and heartily, and I watch, suppressing a smile, not allowing him to patronise me.

'We all thought...' Glyn splutters '... we were not expecting a fiery red-headed woman.' He regains his composure, asking 'Are you the businessman?'

'Is there a businessman? Do you know of another one because I don't? I am seriously interested in purchasing

Caernef myself. I would like to work with you rather than bid against you.'

'The rumour-mill seems to have gone into overdrive,' he chuckles.

He starts to fire eager questions at me, which I evade, turning the conversation to the history of the camp. Once I get him talking, he forgets where we are, even forgets who I am, revealing his passion for the local landscape, and for the old-fashioned values which he believes the camp instils in younger generations. He gives vent to a series of cutting expletives when he moves on to describing the council.

Unwittingly, he passes my tests with flying colours. Despite looking like an old hippy, he is sharp. He displays his anger at the systems which frustrate us, yet his heart is deeply invested in Caernef. I begin to think that I can trust him, and probe further, eliciting tales of his years spent in youthwork, in education, and working in other camps like Caernef. He definitely has a wider perspective, despite liking the sound of his own voice. His Achilles heel seems to be his inability to manage money.

'So, tell me about your future bookings. You say that schools would flood back if the centre was to be reopened. How realistic is this? To be honest, I am concerned that the camp is too far off the beaten track. There is a limit to distances that customers will be prepared to travel, especially when they can book adventure holidays elsewhere, with the latest specification facilities, smart screens and streamed entertainment, and at the same price?'

He provides a compelling argument that these days, with the mounting mental health crisis and an overdependence on filling life's spaces with computer games, it is the remote and the simple which has the potential to attract new as well as existing customers, especially when forced incarceration is still fresh in memories. People, he claims, are petrified of a second glitch, and are seeking remote opportunities to escape the *real world*.

I ask him how much he has raised locally, towards the

purchase, and am not surprised to hear of hollow promises and scant savings. However, I am interested in his connections. He seems to be able to recall a skeleton staff team, which could be useful, but he says he has no caretaker.

He explains that he lives here in the village, with his family, and prefers to drive in each day. For the second time this afternoon I hear of the warden who lived rent free in the cottage for twenty years, and who has retired to Bangor. I think of the current residents, and check my watch.

'I might know a caretaker, who is available. How soon could *you* get started?' I ask.

'Immediately. Right here and now.' His total dedication to Caernef oozes out of every word.

'Who would pay you?'

'It's okay. I am living off my redundancy at the moment. I can give as much time to this project as it needs, without pay, while business builds back up.' He looks into my face, pleadingly, but still puzzled. I know that I haven't given much away. He drains his pint and saying that he will not be long, heads for the door labelled "Dynion", calling to the barman, joking, 'Don't let her leave the building!'

I decide to avail myself of the facilities too, and, leaving my raincoat on the back of the chair, head for the Ladies, labelled "Merched". I note the empty toilet roll tube as I squeeze into the cubicle, and sit on the cold ceramic, not trusting the cracked plastic seat. I can catch Glyn's voice, rising and falling through the wall. He is phoning the agent, Gareth, and talking loudly.

'Yes, it's Glyn. I know. Bloody Hell, she is something … but is she genuine … have you checked her out … Georgiana … not your usual businessman … God she's fit, and sharp. Sharp as a needle. There is something compelling about her look. She must be older than she seems.' His words drift into a burble, but then I hear him declare, 'Not sure how, but she had me on board before I knew what I was doing.'

I smile to myself at his unwitting compliments. Gareth

has obviously done his homework on me. I hear rustling, and then the unmistakable sound of a man using the toilet. Unable to locate any paper, I flush and rinse my hands under the solitary tap, shaking them rather than resorting to the limp towel. I thought they had to use paper towels or hand dryers these days for hygiene? It's actually reassuring, I want to be somewhere that still uses fabric towels in toilets. They simply need to be clean.

Glyn and I emerge from the toilets at the same time, and are forced into a narrow gap between the tables. I hold my ground, and he looks pleasantly embarrassed, perhaps realising that I might have overheard his phone call, but I give no indication of this. Returning to my seat, I quickly re-establish our previous dialogue and ask him about the railway station. 'The guard in the train said that it might be closed. We would need it to be open. A station within walking distance would be invaluable?' I ponder.

'That's nothing to worry about. As soon as the camp is reopened there will be sufficient passenger numbers. Its only during this period of closure that they are questioning its viability.' He asks nervously, 'Would you be looking to run the camp yourself?'

'I wouldn't want to be involved in the day to day running, and have no intention to interfere in the school visits, but I would live onsite, and would oversee the long-term direction. There may be more that we could be doing. The place would have to be in the black.' I get up from my chair adding, 'Your folly is genius.'

'My folly? Oh yes, the lighthouse was one of my best moments,' he comments, rising too. 'I am not good with heights, so don't go out there much. Have you seen the most recent condition survey for the camp? I can email it to you, but don't tell Gareth; I shouldn't have retained a copy when I was booted out of the council. It's a good insight into the current challenges of the place.'

Our complicit working relationship established, we exchange email addresses and mobile phone numbers, agreeing to meet up at The Prince of Wales next Saturday at 2.30. I urge him to wait for due diligence to be completed, but he is completely focused on the real possibility of resurrecting the place that was, and still is, his life. I do not stop his enthusiasm, but ask for a lift back to the station.

While he fetches his car, I quiz the barman, discovering that there are several local residents who used to be employed at Caernef: a cleaner, a cook, and a retired lecturer, who are all now out of work. I exchange contact details with him, too. He might be useful. As I leave, he asks wryly if I really speak Welsh, saying, 'We used to do B&B here, before the glitch ruined everything. If you ever need accommodation, just ask.'

I tell Glyn, untruthfully, that I am going to catch the last train of the day, which heads onwards down the line to the west. Mercifully he drops me off at the station and leaves, waving like a child who has been given a present that he thought he would never have. I wait a decent time in case he drops in at the camp on his return home. Feeling weary, right now I would rather be alone than face Thomas and Maria, despite the fascination that they hold for me. The nagging pain in my limbs is bad. I dig into my rucksack and locate the chocolate, and eat half of the bar. I then wash my painkillers down with a swig of water. Just before the train is due, I walk back up the hill to Caernef, with much to think about.

The gateway is as we left it. There is no sign of Glyn hanging around, which is a relief. Wanting to be alone with my thoughts, I settle on a low wall behind one of the dormitories, able to experience the immensity of the distant grey sea, but hopefully to remain unobtrusive.

I try to shut out the agony in my limbs, focusing on the stark reality of the prospect ahead of me. It's all very well getting a few locals onside, but the challenges of this place are considerable. I don't want to sink my inheritance into a white elephant of a money pit, or a foolish pipe dream. Caernef is not the place to be if you are old or ill. How do I know whether I am investing my aspirations in a rag bag crowd of hangers-on who cannot be trusted to throw their weight behind the project? I need to consider all the pros and cons, to force my head to overrule my heart. Once I have read Glyn's copy of the condition report, if I am still convinced that this is the right way forwards, it occurs to me to ask my Godfather, friend and mentor Reginald De Vere. He is one of the few remnants of my childhood, I even consulted him about my intentions for the inheritance, and he provided some helpful challenge, as well as gentle support. I will not go ahead unless I have his blessing.

Ambling towards the cottage, my pain under control and my mind in the right place, I see Poppy scurrying across the grass with the playful innocence of a child, carefully watched by Maria, who stands in the porch. When Poppy goes flying, the tussocks too high for her short legs, Maria scoops her up, they both laugh, and return to the cottage, closing the door.

HELICOPTERS

Autumn

It is nearly two years since we ate the sausages, fried on a small open fire, while we discussed the future. That time seems like another life, now I have exchanged the grubby city streets for the clear air of the headland. The purchase took time. Glyn defied all logic, ignored his own risk assessments, and launched into the reopening of the site with vigour on the very evening when he left me at the station. He set up a committee of local enthusiasts to support him, attracting keen volunteers who appear every weekend in their boots and waterproofs. He was determined to be ready for the beginning of the academic year. The first school parties returned at the start of September.

I didn't move out here until the folly had been refurbished, simply, and exactly as I intended. Now it is not only strengthened ready for winter weather, it is warm and watertight, with a tiny woodburning stove, retrieved from an old canal boat, double-glazed windows, rudimentary plumbing using harvested rainwater, and a small generator driven by a combination of solar and wind power. I have hidden my remaining inheritance in a metal box in the roof. It should be safe there. The trampled path used by the local builders is starting to grow over and my own path now gives away my regular route up into the camp.

At midday, when there is a school in residence, a huge and sonorous dinner bell is rung. It hangs on the front of the dining hall. Thomas transformed it from a dull and dirty thing which did not ring, to a golden symbol of our hopes. One of my greatest pleasures is to walk up the rise, watching the scurrying children all heading for lunch, and to choose my company while we share the hot, ethically sourced meal. Hearing the children tell me of their everyday lives away from the camp, seeing their faces grow ruddy from the salty air, and knowing that their mobile phones and gaming devices have all been left at home, gives me deep pleasure.

Over lunch, I am nourished by both food and conversation, then allowing myself the luxury of peaceful solitude in the folly, a calmness which I have always craved and never achieved until realising my dream of Caernef. In the few weeks that I have nestled here on the clifftop, protected by the bank of wind-blasted trees, with the sweep of the moody Irish Sea before me, I have settled into a simple routine. Rising early, before the sun, I perch in the window seat upstairs, drinking coffee and reading until there is sufficient light to walk. I have explored the vicinity on foot, accessing the small villages nearby, from the shore.

Bizarrely we have an excellent wifi signal here, following some expensive digital innovations before the reopening, because Glyn, quite rightly, insisted. Anxious parents can access our password-protected website and are reassured by the private live webcams and daily reports on activities. Even now the parents talk anxiously about the glitch all the time, fearing a reappearance of the black hole in communication systems, fearing to send their children far from home while the risk of a further glitch hangs over everyone. There is still a genuine fear that systems will fail again, or will be sabotaged.

The Government has still not told us exactly what happened that day.

The bureaucracy required to reopen the camp was daunting. Obtaining valid criminal record checks for all resident adults, including me, was a nightmare. Refugees have few documents. In the end, Thomas and Maria had to submit finger prints for checking before they could get the piece of paper declaring them fit to work with children. When eventually the paperwork arrived, having been posted in the box up at the gate, they were overjoyed, seeing their names and this address on an official document, validating their new existence. Unfortunately, there were several spelling errors in the address, but we couldn't face resubmitting the application yet another time.

I return from lunch, treading my well-worn path through the field, and nearly trip over a solitary chicken, pecking in the leaves. There is a path down the cliff below the folly which should only be taken by mountain goats. You need good footwear. I am already more adept at balancing and hanging on to the few iron posts, remnants of previous times. Late September is a perfect month to scout a new landscape, the ground is still warm, and the storms are short-lived. Maria is teaching me to recognise the plants and the berries. Some evenings I sit in front of the roaring fire in the cottage and tell Poppy stories until she sleeps in my lap, and I return by torchlight to my cosy bunk in the folly.

It is perfect in many ways, but there is much to tackle. We are far from self-sufficient, not carbon neutral, and the costs of staffing the camp way outstretch the income. Next week I have called the first meeting of my new longer-term planning group.

Well-fed after lunch, I have settled into the window seat. The rain is incessant today and I have just decided to stay in the folly for the afternoon, when my phone buzzes with a message. Ironically the signal is excellent out here. I am so far from civilisation, but digitally still completely plugged in. The message is from Reginald, my Godfather. This is unexpected and I hope that he is okay. In his characteristically curt style, he simply says, "Hope clifftop living suits. Need help. Confidential. Call me at 8pm today. Thanks, RDV."

I decide to brave the rain after all, and walk, bundled up in waterproofs, including a pair of bright yellow Gore-Tex trousers rescued from surplus supplies at the camp. Walking, the bracing air and the rhythm of feet on earth, helps me to think. Reginald has never asked me for help before. In fact, on the handful of occasions that we have interacted in recent years, it has always been me asking him for guidance. I take an inland route, fearing the slippery rocks today, and tromp along the rural roads, passed by very occasional traffic, loop round by the station, cross the track and return to the camp just in time for the supper bell.

At eight, sitting in the window and counting the flashes of the automatic buoy out in the channel, I call him. I have absolutely no idea why he wants to talk with me. He answers promptly, in his unmistakable received pronunciation. He has never quite mastered calling me Robin, and does so as if it is a word in a foreign language.

'Thank you for responding. All well with you? Good. Now, I need to ask you whether you and your trusty people at the camp can help me out with something. Something very important … to the nation?'

I remind him that he has never asked me for help before, and that, as I owe him great debts of kindness over the years, of course we will try to help out, but need to know how and what.

'Thank you. We cannot discuss this matter on the phone. Either I need to come out to you, or perhaps you would come to London. There are trains from Wales. This cannot wait.'

Intrigued, I agree to travel to him in the morning, catching the first train up the line. He thanks me again, and rings off. I select Emile Zola's *Germinal* to read on the journey, and search for my only suit from the small fitted cupboard under the stairs. Better look smart.

~

Mercifully the rain has cleared. My suit feels unfamiliar, and certainly looks incongruous as I wear it with my walking boots. In the gloom of the dawn, the four dormitories are lit up like ships on the sea, and I hear the muffled noises of children getting up for the day, soon to emerge in a chattering stream for their breakfast.

While I am changing my footwear on the wooden veranda to the boot room, up near the gate, Thomas appears. He is on his morning rounds, completing the daily safety checks for Glyn. He laughs conspiratorially.

'Look at you!'

I realise that he has only ever seen me in my old outdoor clothes, and explain that I have been called to London on business, and that it is nothing to worry about. Glyn appears across the parade ground, and, seeing Thomas and I, waves.' Despite my eagerness to leave for the train, I pause as he approaches, beaming, and asks, 'You going somewhere special, Robin?'

Thomas leaps in, pleased to be the first of the two to know my destination. 'She's off for the train, to London on business.' Glyn jokes kindly at my attire, and I leave the two of them to their morning conversation. As I turn the corner to the gate, I glance back, and they look up, both waving me on my way. Slightly embarrassed by their dedication to me, proud that they seem to wholeheartedly share my vision for Caernef; I worry whether Reginald's proposal will be in keeping with the precious life that we are creating. At the start, I was anxious that Glyn and Thomas would hit it off. They seemed to sense that I needed their relationship to work, and they quickly fell into an easy-going partnership, which I now take for granted. Two good men in such a troubled world, and Maria, the outspoken, principled and compelling Maria. What a team, I reflect.

I stand in front of the small repainted notice, subtly visible from the train for those who need to see it: "Alight here for Caernef Camp," and I flag down the approaching train. It is always an anxious moment, worrying if the driver will see me and whether the train will stop. Though highly improbable that the driver will ignore me, I am always troubled by fear that I will be missed. The train does stop. Despite the current rumbling national crisis, triggered by the glitch, outside the windows of the train, the world has barely changed. I read my old copy of *Germinal* to take my mind off Reginald's odd request, and thankfully time passes quickly as I am totally engrossed in the book.

Changing trains at Birmingham International, I am pleased that I dressed for the occasion, as I am reminded how fashion is rather more prominent here than at the camp. It is good to be prompted that rampant commercialism still rages in the outside world.

After some overpriced dry railway sandwiches, to prevent my insides from rumbling during the meeting, and several more chapters of *Germinal*, I step on to the platform at Euston, and take a cab to Reginald's office.

The golden plaque subtly announcing "De Vere Stratagems" is recently polished and stands out from the other brass name plates of private doctors and lawyers inhabiting the grand old building overlooking Regents Park. I have only visited Reginald here a couple of times, once when desperate, in my early days of independence, to ask for a reference for my first job as a social worker, and more recently after my father died, to talk through my plans for the inheritance. Today the boot is on the other foot.

Reginald epitomises all that I despise in the establishment, and yet I am extremely fond of him. I care about him because he is one of the very few people who reminds me of the better side of my childhood, the smell of brandy butter and Christmas pudding, putting the world to rights while we trod the paths of the formal garden, and for his insight. He has always been straight with me. He listens. That, I value highly, but what on earth does he want with me today?

Aware of my approach through the closed-circuit television, he opens his door wide and ushers me into his inner sanctum. He looked old to me when I was a child, and he still looks exactly the same today, his furrowed forehead and weather-worn dimples creasing up as his face opens into a broad smile.

I do not feel out of place wearing my suit.

'Robin, how delightful to see you. I am immensely grateful to you for coming all this way. How are you? And which battles are you fighting today?' We settle quickly into a comfortable and familiar conversation whereby he asks me questions, manages to illicit more about me than I have shared with anyone for years, and I learn nothing about him.

'I can offer espresso, macchiato …' he reels off a series of fancy coffees, reading the labels from the foil lids of the expensive and totally non-biodegradable pods on his polished sideboard. The machine whirrs, rather more effectively than the one behind the bar in The Prince of Wales.

'You must be wondering what this is all about?'

'Yes, indeed …' He closes the heavy door to his office and leans towards me across the desk.

'You remember the glitch I assume?' He asks rhetorically, resuming, 'I need a remote and secure venue for a day, somewhere to host a very important high-level meeting that could have long-lasting national and international implications. It would need to be totally discrete, and to remain unrevealed after the event. Complete confidentiality. A one-off.'

'The camp might be that place?'

'Possibly. We are speaking in total confidence you understand. I would need to check out a series of requirements with you, and you could then decide, "yes" or "no". If "no", we never had this conversation. If "yes", we would need to set the wheels rolling immediately.' He adds, a touch reluctantly, 'Your father hosted similar occasions a few times. Of course, I cannot ask him now …'

His clarity has always been impressive. He slides a hardback copy of *Anna Karenina*, a book which I have read several times, out from his bookcase. It is hidden between the legal volumes. He opens it and retrieves a piece of paper, which he unfolds. It seems to contain detailed plans, written in his characteristically tiny print. We discuss practicalities;

how secure *is* the site I wonder, thinking of our attempts at keeping the foxes out of the chicken run, of the miles of repaired wooden fences still covered in lichen? Glyn is on top of the security requirements for the school parties. There are endless risk assessments and daily checks. There are also cameras with the protected internet feed for parents.

He asks me, 'How easily could your closed system be compromised? We are dealing with people who employ cyber-experts. Could you disconnect all systems for the day?'

'Yes, easily. To be honest, the camp has not entered the twenty-first century yet. We use a few technologies for the school-visit business, but the place is essentially a remote headland encapsulating the things that used to matter: fresh air, silence and stunning sea views. If that's what you are looking for …?'

He nods, and calls his secretary into the room to type a high-level risk assessment while we talk. I deplore the power dynamic between the two of them, the suited senior figure, dictating, and the demure female nobody, obediently responding. I think of Reginald's wife Cynthia, who has never worked, and who seems to wait quietly at home to service his needs. I know better than to raise this right now, and stomach the blatant inequality which grates on my principles.

As he waves her out of the room, he turns to me, reading my thoughts, whispering, 'I know; I shouldn't still employ a menial secretary to type for me in this modern age, but I am not as confident as you are to abandon my entrenched beliefs.' Redeemed to a degree in my eyes by his ironic self-awareness, his sense of superiority melts for an instant into his poignant remark. He has successfully lured me back onside, and we shake over the arrangement. He emphasises that it is my responsibility to ensure that very few people know about what may be happening, and that confidentiality must be rock solid. If all runs smoothly, there will be a considerable donation to the camp. He knows that he can trust my word.

Although he offers to book me into a hotel nearby for tonight, I am determined to connect with the last train of the day back from Birmingham International. I want to head home where I will have the space and tranquillity to think.

Urgent preparations are needed.

Friday Evening

With his usual efficiency, Reginald rapidly puts arrangements in place. I deliberately wait before I take Glyn, Thomas and Maria into my confidence. I simply ask the three of them to keep Saturday and Sunday free, tell them that I will pay overtime and that no other staff will be needed. I casually imply that we will be engaging in our much-postponed long-term planning activity for the camp. The current school party leaves on Friday afternoon, which gives us Saturday to discreetly prepare. Sunday is a day off for the camp staff as, fortuitously, the next school party doesn't arrive until Tuesday morning.

Reginald is communicating with me via an encrypted messaging system which I downloaded on to my phone. I now know approximate timings and what to expect. The action begins on Saturday night when a "ghost train" has been chartered to come down the line carrying security guards, diplomats and equipment, which will be transported the short distance to the parade ground by a fleet of armoured black Land Rovers. The important visitors, I do not yet know who they will be, are scheduled to arrive before dawn. He wants to use the dormitory that has the most magnificent view across the sea. He has even checked the weather forecasts and is hopeful of a stunning sunrise. Apparently, we can expect them to be with us for no longer than an hour. They will not require refreshments or extra facilities. His cloak-and-dagger manner is both intriguing and worrying. I like to feel more in control.

Preparing the operation here is my main concern. The beds and furniture must be cleared out of the dormitory and the circular wooden table from the dining room will be set out in the bay window facing the view of the sea. There are four rather grand wooden chairs that Glyn rescued from a sale at a stately home, placing one in the entrance of each dormitory as storytellers' chairs, and we will set them out round the table. Reginald says not to use a rectangular or square table where the delegates would have to sit opposite each other. Apparently the support crews will assemble in the dining hall, with security teams on the veranda to the dormitory. We are to keep as low a profile as possible during the event. Reginald suggested just two of us, but I want the four of us on duty in case of problems.

By Friday evening, the camp is spick and span. The chickens, usually free range, are confined to their run, and the day staff have left, due back on Monday morning to prepare for next week's school visit. I walk up from the folly to see Glyn, who despite having worked since dawn, is marching with energy down to the cottage. Thomas and Maria are preparing supper and I am going to explain what will happen over the weekend.

Poppy is arranging acorns, nuts and conkers in swirly patterns on the dining table. She is not keen to tidy up and head for her bed. Glyn, with his characteristic patience, shows her that he can take a photo with his phone and will print her a copy so she can keep the picture of her amazing design. Maria deftly scoops the nuts into a basket and ushers Poppy up the stairs, promising to read to her.

Thomas is serving up a spiced vegetable stew with homemade bread. Glyn has brought a good bottle of red merlot, and we wait for Maria to reappear before drinking a toast to the camp. We don't often find time to sit together; there are always more jobs to attend to. I remind them how much I value their friendship before I launch into an explanation of the forthcoming invasion of our sacred headland.

Not unexpectedly, they ask more questions than I can answer, but they, like me, are intrigued, and mercifully they trust my judgement. Glyn raises several issues which had not occurred to me: what if the Land Rovers dig up the turf on the parade ground? We should be able to repair it using the old cricket pitch roller, which he salvaged and uses when vehicles get stuck, but how will we explain it to the staff? What if the nosey parker of a train guard gets wind of the ghost train; what will we say? How will we ensure that this visit doesn't provoke unwelcome press interest in the camp, or even some sort of retaliation?

We talk through how we can make this opportunity a success, and are generally in agreement, although I am anxious about Poppy. I didn't mention her to Reginald. Maria says she can keep her well out of sight down in the cottage.

I had not anticipated their intense interest in the glitch, not having paid much attention to the ongoing social media storm myself. Apparently the news is regularly fuelled by new speculation, with endless press interviews and ineffective politicians seemingly totally unable to get to the bottom of what happened or how to prevent it reoccurring. Glyn explains how a governmental Digital Continuity Committee has presented evidence to Parliament, but that nothing is happening, and that people are demanding reassurance. Every time the internet trips out, we fear a repeat of the split-second catastrophe when all our details were permanently deleted: family photos lost from "the cloud", bank accounts collapsed, travel bookings voided, business accounts wiped. I am ashamed of my somewhat callous attitude to date. I just thought that if you trust such systems, you are risking some sort of data compromise, but Glyn paints a convincing picture of hardworking people's lives being totally ruined by the glitch. If we can play a part, however small, in resolving this massive issue, then we agree: it will be time well invested.

A November Night

The preparations on Saturday run smoothly, and by the evening I am longing for a soak in a bath, my muscles aching from so much lifting. The four of us, along with Poppy, have shifted all the furniture from the southernmost dormitory. The circular table and chairs are set ready. We haven't been told that we can't take photographs of the preparations and so we all sit round the table as the sun sets behind the hill. The reflected pink light catches the waves and Thomas organises a selfie using the delay on his phone with a makeshift setup.

'You need a selfie stick,' jokes Glyn, and we chuckle with shared contempt at the invention of the "must have" for self-flattering tourists. The photograph shows us laughing, but looking tired and dishevelled. Poppy is sitting on Thomas's knee, grinning shyly.

We spot two silent boats on the water, their subdued lighting reflecting on the swell. Through the binoculars we spot security guards with guns masquerading as fishing equipment. The reality of the situation begins to hit us. At twenty to midnight, when the operation formally begins, we take our posts. I am in charge of receiving the ghost train at the station, while the others are ready to receive the Land Rovers at the camp. Reginald is communicating with me every fifteen minutes on the encrypted system. He will trigger army and navy backup teams if anything should go awry.

The seriousness with which he is treating this operation convinces me that the delegates must be relatively senior, but I am secretly having second thoughts. Reginald is pulling all the strings and reducing me to a mere puppet. I have always trusted Reginald, but do not trust *the establishment*, and he is very much part of that. Perhaps I should have considered this wild and ambitious plan more thoroughly before agreeing. It is too late to allow my misgivings to seep into my mind, too late to warn the others to be more vigilant. I kick the shelter in frustration at myself, immediately regretting it as the sound of my boot echoes, spoiling the silence.

On the dot of midnight, exactly as expected, I feel the reverberations of an approaching train. Despite gloves, my hands are numb with cold, as for some time I have been standing quietly in the darkness on the furthest end of the platform, with my torch turned off. The sleek silver engine, bullet nosed, and not a design that I have seen on this line before, draws into the platform. The two carriages are in complete darkness, no lights giving away their presence. The hiss as the doors open is followed by a sudden invasion of discreet black-clad people, more than the platform has probably ever seen. They are all drilled and supremely focused. I stand transfixed, while the engine continues down the line, having disgorged its secret crew.

One, two, three and more Land Rovers roar across the fir-cones. The shadowy figures pile in. I am feeling surplus to requirements, a voyeur, when a woman dressed in dark combat gear, sitting in the front passenger seat of one of the jeeps, opens the door, asking in a hushed voice, 'Robin? Climb in. Reginald said to look out for you. We will leave last, once security is through.' The vehicle waits. The other Land Rovers disappear towards the camp.

'Can I know who you are?' I ask, punch drunk from the bizarre sight of ranks of hooded security guards piling out of the ghost train.

'I'm Marcella, Deputy Director of a private cyber-security agency contracted to the British Government. The contract is managed by the senior civil servant Tustian Hayward.' She twists round to shake my hand. I am still wearing my gloves. 'We haven't worked out here before; it's the sort of place you might go on a walking holiday!'

Unsure whether this is a compliment, I comment on the weather, 'Thank goodness it is a fine night, and set fair for tomorrow. I don't think that the impact of the location on the delegates would be the same in the rain and the fog.'

'And the helicopters would have struggled to land, whereas tonight is perfect.'

I hadn't thought of the helicopters; Reginald says that they will come from Anglesey. Thomas has prepared the parade ground so that there is a clear space. I would dearly like a photo of helicopters at the camp, but this is not allowed.

'Stay here while I check the platform,' she instructs. I sit alone with the driver, who could take me anywhere against my will, watching Marcella's silhouette walk the platform, scans the bushes, and returns to the vehicle. We speed off up the road to the camp.

The events of the next few hours pass quickly as if we are in a bizarre dream. Much time is spent watching the black figures make their thorough security arrangements. The three of us are sitting in the staffroom which overlooks the parade ground. Maria has stayed down in the cottage with Poppy. Despite oceans of coffee, I am struggling to stay awake when Reginald sends me the key message: "Five minutes to arrival."

Marcella looks in again, ordering us to stay inside during the visit. I resent her tone, but bite my lip. They are punctual; it is five in the morning. We spot the first helicopter, a gnat in the distance, first two bright white eyes approaching, and then the red light flashing on the underbelly. Silence falls upon us as we each wonder who is on board, but this is soon shattered by the earth-moving sound of the twin rotor blades as it heads in from the sea, stirring up dust, setting the branches into spasms. It is enormous, dwarfing the dormitories which cling on to the hillside for dear life. Although it is so heavy, it dances daintily in mid-air adjusting for the terrain, seeking out the flattest area on the parade ground, well clear of trees. The grass is no longer lank and tussocky, but gyrates with a mystical energy. The colossal metal animal lands and we are transfixed as four figures emerge on to the parade ground, the rotor blades still turning. Security guards usher them into the dormitory that we have prepared so carefully. Once the area is clear, the helicopter rises, and with an almighty roar, sails majestically back over the sea.

I hear from Reginald, as if I hadn't seen with my own eyes: "Successful landing, now await number two." There is hardly any pause. Prepared this time, we track the second helicopter as it approaches, smaller and with a single rotor blade, again stirring up the grass and trees as if we are in a demonic whirlpool. It comes to a halt and the rotor blades slow. Eventually they stop spinning, and two men exit, hurrying into the dormitory.

'That's it, they are here now,' I say unnecessarily, breaking the silence, pulling us back to reality.

Glyn responds, 'But who are they, and what are they going to do here at Caernef?'

Thomas is alone with his memories, silent and still, retreating into himself at this moment which is weighted with expectation and mystery.

We watch the dormitory building, slouching in the darkness, not lit up as usual because they insisted on closing all the shutters, and the windows at the front are hidden from our sight. Unable to sleep due to the tension in the air, we huddle in the window, and drink more coffee, waiting for something to happen, alert for any security announcements or unexpected noises. Reginald messages, "Lie low while they talk."

I take some time out in the small staff toilet, swallow more painkillers, and splash cold water over my face in an attempt to keep myself alert. On returning to the two men, I see that they have landed in the arm chairs and their eyes are half shut. They leap up when I arrive, but I slump into a chair too, and we all doze while black figures walk up and down outside.

It is seven in the morning when we are woken abruptly by sound of the turning blades of the small helicopter, and simultaneously a message from Reginald simply says "success".

Just before it is fully light, Marcella looks in, thanks us for our hospitality, and reminds us of the importance of our complete discretion, otherwise there will be "consequences". She shakes my hand. I long for a job like hers. I wonder who she really is, whether she does ordinary things like listening to music and eating chocolate in her spare time, if she has any. She appears to play a vital part in upholding a society which I deplore, and yet she puts me to shame with my moaning and my escapism. I feel very small, and a touch hypocritical.

CHRISTMAS SHOPPING

Morning

After being passive observers of this bizarre drama, before we turn in for some much-needed sleep, we walk across the empty parade ground and down to the cottage where Maria is waiting for us with a very welcome hot breakfast. There is a strange light in her deep brown eyes. Once we are all seated around the table, tucking into our eggs, she asks us what we were able to see, and we confirm that we watched the helicopters come in, and leave, but did not see much else.

She cradles her mug of tea, warming her hands, and says softly to us, 'I saw who it was. I talked with them. This is far bigger than we imagined.' She pauses, tantalisingly. Our eyes all turn on her, eager to hear more. 'Just as the sky lit up with the pink of the dawn over the sea, Poppy woke. She was restless, so we put on her coat and wellies, and wandered out into the field. I could see the figures in the dormitory. They were shaking hands and looking out towards us. They saw me, and they saw Poppy. The security guards were alert, but two figures emerged on to the veranda, and beckoned to us. Their work seemed to be completed and they gave the impression of having sealed a good deal. As I approached, with Poppy tramping over the grass, I realised that I recognised both of them. The first man was the Secretary of State for Digital Infrastructure. I have seen him many times on the television, but never, of course, in the flesh.'

'No! Are you sure? He is at the top of the tree. He reports to the Prime Minister. It couldn't have been …?' I blurt out.

'It was. I *am* sure. The second man was that American guy who upset the American President, and who fled to Russia. What was his name? Todd something? I recognised him straight away from the news coverage before the glitch. There were suggestions in the newspapers that he was behind the threat even then. He must be behind it. That makes sense. They asked Poppy for her name, and she bravely told them. It was quite a sweet moment.'

'The man was called Humboldt, Todd Humboldt,' I say.

'That's it. Thank you. They sat on the bench while the sun rose over the sea, and they played peekaboo with Poppy. I will never forget seeing her rosy cheeks and sleepy smile while they teased her, and she cheerfully shouted "Boo!" at two such important men. Then they thanked us for providing such an unusual and inspiring venue for their meeting, and said they must leave. I heard the helicopter starting up. Security swarmed all over the place, and we walked back down here. I told Poppy, who didn't like all the noise, that she must remember that moment, and that game of peekaboo. She's asleep upstairs now. What exactly *were* they doing here? I do hope they have ended all our worries about the glitch.'

Dumbfounded for an instant by her story, we then all speak at once. We knew that the visitors were likely to be important, but … Maria modestly brushes off her encounter, and we three are in awe of her modesty. I feel no jealousy that it was Maria, and not me, who met our visitors. I do feel pride in her presence of mind, one of my close team, so bold and so calm, but I wonder that Reginald hadn't given me more responsibility, and even hinted confidentially at who was coming.

'I dearly hope that they have signed some sort of deal to prevent any more glitches,' I conclude. We agree that we will get some desperately-needed sleep and will meet again at midday to get the camp back to rights. Glyn is going to head home for a few hours, and he will drop into The Prince of Wales before he returns, to check that there are no rumours circulating locally of ghost trains or midnight patrols.

We part with a strengthened commitment to the camp, and to each other. Glyn hugs Maria, which is touching, and I stagger down to the folly, falling into my bunk in the lookout and knowing nothing more until my phone wakes me just before midday.

I feel my age, and actually regret having offered to help set the camp back to rights, but, with the resolve that I once displayed on the early mornings of my delivery rounds, I ply myself with painkillers and drag myself up the hill, half-expecting it all to have been a dream. The others look nearly as bad as I feel, but we set to the task with as much energy as we can muster. Poppy has brought her little wooden pedal car, made and painted by Thomas and Maria, and we take it in turns to supervise her circuits of the car park, which is welcome relief from the lifting. It takes a couple of hours to tidy the dining room, reassemble the dormitory furniture, to walk the parade ground and the access track, stamping out tyre marks and removing the broken branches and twigs that were sent flying when the helicopters landed.

After a final walk across the whole camp checking for evidence, satisfied that there is no trace of the strange night activities, we check the gateway. Thomas volunteers to walk to the station and back. He collects only one empty crisp packet, which is more likely to have been dropped by the school children last week. He says that a discerning detective would note how the fir-cones on the station yard are now trampled flat, but there is nothing we can do to hide that, although he did scuff them back into their usual confusion.

We are about to part, looking forward to the camp drifting back into its usual daily routine, when two things happen. The first triumph is announced by a buzzing in my pocket. A message from Reginald declares, again, a job well done, thanks me and my small team, and informs us that a faster payment of a significant sum has been made into my personal account by way of rental of the site for the weekend. How sensible of Reginald to transfer it directly to me, which will avoid any awkward questions from Glyn's Committee, or auditors. We high five, me and Maria, Thomas and Glyn, and then, of course, Poppy joins in. The donation is an extremely welcome boost to the camp coffers and we agree to decide exactly how to reinvest it when we next meet more formally. However, our greatest pleasure is from the secret knowledge that we may have contributed to the restoration of confidence in international cyberspace.

The second occurrence before we part company is a news update which Maria picks up on her phone. It says "Breaking news: British Government secures international cyber-security reassurances." We cheer for the second time, somewhat wearily, and head in our different directions.

December

Despite having largely opted out of society for the present, I still observe from afar, and am an avid follower of the news, using the accursed internet as a window back into the real world. On Monday morning our news is plastered everywhere. The tabloids declare, "No More Glitches!" with other papers confirming, "Public Reassurance: Safe at last from internet breaches," and "Britain Leads the Way: Serious international cyber criminals silenced."

I imagine the relief on the faces of all the people rebuilding their livelihoods for the second time in recent years, people whose lives were ruined, first by the pandemic, and then by the glitch. But, ever the sceptic, I know that if it has happened once, any number of signed agreements will not insure us all against future attacks on our beloved and accursed cyberspace. The identity of the dissident who talked with the Secretary of State at the camp has not been revealed. I now know that there are still people at large who undoubtably have the technology to put an end to everyday life as we know it. Their power could be far greater than that wielded through isolated acts of terrorism, or *accidental* virus pandemics.

Sitting in the window of the folly, gazing out over the grey sea of early November, a few sea birds braving the wind, I am overcome with an indefinable sadness for a life that was, before technology took over our lives, before we began to ruin our planet, before floods and fires, before the pandemic, and before the glitch. Poppy will never know the complete freedom that we experienced as children. She will always be aware of social distancing, the digital safety net, phones, cyberspace, and the omnipresent social media. She will never feel completely safe and alone in nature like we once were.

In recent years, I have grown to deplore the multiplicity of television channels with their endless game shows, the survival competitions, cheap dramas and slough of adverts for expensive protective hand gels. I have long turned my back on television, with great relief. The silence that inhabits the folly is the most precious gift given to me by Caernef, closely followed by my new friends. I resolve never to take this life for granted.

My reverie is interrupted by a flash of colour out of my landward window. Bright red, running down the hillside, is Poppy, leaving Maria behind in her eagerness to reach my folly. I have set up a small bell hanging low enough for her to reach, and she jangles it, peering inside, looking for me, with Maria puffing as she hurries to join her daughter. The cliff edge is quite close to my door.

'And who have we here?'

'It's me! it's Poppy!'

They tumble into the small room, bringing a waft of cold air with their smiles. Maria explains that Poppy is getting ready to visit the small local school, in preparation for starting in the nursery in January. She was trying on the bright red school jumper, and the sensible grey school joggers, and wanted to show me how grown-up she looked.

Unable to stand back to view her, due to the confined space, I lift her high to the ceiling and declare that she is such a grown-up young lady. We all laugh before they march back up the hill, singing "The Grand Old Duke of York".

As the winter takes hold, our school visits tail off, and there is more time for renovation of the camp. Watched by the resident robin, the bird, not me, hardy volunteers appear each day, happed up against the weather. They repair fences, build shelters and repaint the dormitories. Camaraderie is strong as the locals celebrate the resounding success of the reopened camp.

We have decided to close completely over the Christmas break. Glyn needs to spend some time with his family, Thomas and Maria are looking forward to some time by themselves, and I actually crave some solitude and autonomy. Despite the isolation of the folly, its proximity to the busy camp is not always as restful as I had intended. I play down my role here, but Glyn fuels an image of me as the saviour of Caernef, and as a result I have an unsought celebrity status. I often choose to come and go via the cliff path just to preserve my privacy.

I am planning to return to Oxford for a few days before Christmas. There are some business matters to settle with Steve, my ex-husband, and I need to collect a final bag of belongings, mainly books, which the landlord of The Pike has kindly been storing for me. I plan to spread some seasonal cheer and to drop in on old friends.

~

Sitting on the train I hear a patchwork of hopeful conversation, 'We can really enjoy this Christmas now that awful virus, and the threat of the glitch is behind us,' and 'There's no pandemic, and no glitch to spoil Christmas this year.' I had genuinely not realised how dominant the glitch had become in the public consciousness and I had under-estimated the collective sigh of relief that followed the recent announcements. Despite feeling immense pride in having played a small part in this, I still harbour nagging doubts about the future.

The train carriage is filled with people gripping their phones as if their lives depend upon them. Ironically no one is making an actual phone call; it is all internet and social media. Glancing over the legs of the passenger seated across the aisle ahead of me, I marvel at their deft fingers, swiping as if born with the skill. Our over-dependence alarms me, as do our assumptions. We take our current lifestyle for granted, and I am as guilty as these young people, blithely tapping away, filling the ether with swathes of meaningless words. I imagine the words piling up and up, eventually drowning us all in our own verbal effluent.

Saturday Lunchtime

Setting foot in Oxford again, at lunchtime on the last Saturday before Christmas, I remember why I retreated to Caernef. The annual frenzy of media-fuelled pre-Christmas celebration has engulfed the city, even more extreme after several years of low-key celebrations due to national emergencies. Kick-started by the early December student revelries, the festive period was always fraught with an explosion of shoppers, a heady blend of both locals and tourists. The pace of parcel delivery increased incrementally, just when the roads and the pavements were clogged up with eager crowds. After dark, which comes so early at this time of year, faces were bright, reflecting the fancy lights. I used to enjoy the spectacle. Oddly, I miss my delivery job. This Christmas is my first respite for many years, but I would dearly love the opportunity to leap back on the old bike, and to pedal through time into the routes that I knew so well.

A choir is singing as I saunter thoughtfully through Bonn Square. Fat, mangy pigeons peck around the expensive shoes emerging beneath the choir robes. The singers have given up their Saturday to entertain the bustling last-minute shoppers. Their well-fed mouths open in harmony, sharing with us their "tidings of comfort and joy." They are collecting for the homeless, which, initially, I applaud, but I hesitate. Locating the embarrassment of riches in my purse, I dive into the Cornmarket and notice at least a dozen rough sleepers. Some are still comatose, shoppers carefully avoiding the blanketed humps. Others sit begging. I recognise several of the faces, but there are new ones, too many new ones. Earlier in the day there were more; many have tidied up from a bitterly cold night on the streets and have left their heaped belongings, hoping that they will still be there when they return.

Overwhelmed by the pathos, the untold stories of desperation, or simply failure to play the current game of life, I return to Bonn Square and squeeze on to a bench. I deliberate that if I give money to the rough sleepers, they will probably spend it on alcohol, to warm themselves tonight, and who can blame them for that. Or drugs. I am debating miserably, irritated by the pious tones of the sanctimonious carols, echoes of past words which once held meaning, but which now draw sad attention to all that we have lost. The carols are all about men: kings, fathers, sons, merry gentlemen. Mary, over-painted through centuries, stands proud as an inspiration for women. "Let nothing you dismay," they sing. A crowd has gathered. Maybe these eager shoppers seek comfort in the familiar words. Maybe they are as desperate as I am for some sort of vision to give them hope for the future. I am spotted by one of the charity workers, called Megan, who used to occasionally join me at The Pike.

'Robin! Hi, I haven't seen you for ages. Do you have time for a coffee? And a mince pie?' I notice that the mince pies on the coffee stall have shrunk. They now come in several innovative flavours, almond, amaretto or orange, which has enabled a price hike. I shake my head, and pretend I am in a hurry. She wishes me a "Happy Christmas" and hurries off towards the market. To partially assuage my conscience, I post the cost of two over-priced mince pies into the carol singers' collecting tin and decide it is time for me to move on before I drown in my despair.

My phone buzzes in the pocket of my jeans and I guess that it is my ex-husband Steve, hassling me: "Ready and waiting." He always did hurry me along, just when I was thinking about something important. I have only seen him a few times since we parted forever, three years ago, on the day when the usual eruptions of my temper became a tsunami, and we both disgraced ourselves, descending to the level of the gutter. On that occasion, I dredged my subconscious for the most vicious words which I could call forth, my pent-up fury bursting out in an uncontrollable tirade. Since then we have avoided each other. I most certainly am not going to chew over what might have happened with him. Calming my nerves, banishing any irrational shame, I secure the feelings that I once held for him, in a locked vault.

Reginald De Vere told me that my father wholeheartedly approved of my relationship with Steve. That alone should have rung warning bells. I should have been wiser. I should have realised that the suave banker turned minor diplomat turned highly-paid advisor would see through my thin veil of social acceptability. It was inevitable that the tensions between his successful persona, and my determined dissent would come to an ugly head. He was used to getting his own way, and I had grown to oppose all that he represented. I suppose the miracle was that we lasted so long, propping up each other's insecurities.

Steve had wanted a trophy wife to parade at parties, a brood mare, a housekeeper. He was willing to shower all manner of presents and enticements. In fact I shrewdly got him to sign an agreement that following our separation our financial affairs would be our own. On reflection I think that he designed our relationship to make me feel at a disadvantage, to belittle my causes. How had I allowed myself to be ensnared by such a devious and chauvinistic partner? Embarrassed at my past foolishness, and starting to simmer with revulsion, reluctantly, I pace towards our rendezvous at The Arundel, wondering if he has summoned me because he wants to claim a right to some of my inheritance. Typical of Steve to choose one of the most expensive places in the city for our meeting. Caernef seems very far away.

Entering the vestibule, I am bowed down by the heavy portraiture and drapery. I pretend that I am an international spy attending a secret rendezvous, and saunter nonchalantly into the brocaded restaurant, scanning the pampered faces, their smiles decorated with invisible tinsel. They are taking afternoon tea with Christmas shopping companions, or are meeting colleagues for an overpriced slice of Christmas cake. Most of the customers are clutching phones. Several are taking selfies, or capturing images of the cakes before they are consumed. I cannot see Steve.

'Hi, Robin, over here!' I see that he has brought his female bodyguard and wonder if it is a girlfriend. So, he fears meeting me alone. Behaving with impeccable manners, almost as if nothing untoward had ever happened between us, he ushers me into a seat shaped like a church pew, opposite his companion. She is younger than me, more beautiful than me, and she grips the seat uncomfortably with one hand while clutching her phone with the other. 'We thought you weren't coming,' Steve announces, asking, 'Coffee or something stronger?'

I ask for coffee. While he is jostling with a group of off duty carol singers ordering at the olde-worlde bar, I ask the woman who she is. She looks young enough to be his daughter. 'Oh, I thought you knew, I am Steve's fiancé, Maria.' I think of my Maria, my fearless and courageous Maria, who had walked out of Syria, who had survived war and famine, conversed with the Secretary of State and who was, right now, probably stoking the little fire in the cottage. This slip of a girl was not a "Maria" to me.

'Oh, no, I had no idea. I am Robin.'

'I know. I have … heard loads about you. I will leave it

to Steve to explain.' She shifts awkwardly in her seat, looking nervously across the sprigs of holly, no doubt anxious for him to return. Her heavy makeup covers her facial spots with pink creamy layers and her black hair is pinned up with some frivolous Christmas clips, sparkling as she bobs her head, looking desperately for Steve, no doubt hoping he will rescue her from having to converse with me.

I decide that I despise this nervous woman, styled like a doll, and probably fulfilling all Steve's desires for a subservient and compliant lover. I refuse to speak to her anymore, but focus on staring at her, making her feel even more uncomfortable.

Steve returns with coffees. She drinks mocha. He is just about to launch into an explanation when Maria glances at her phone and gulps. Simultaneously, the jovial Christmassy mood pervading the lounge shifts. Amiable chatter is replaced by anxious looks, raised voices. 'Shit' says Steve, shaking his phone, frantically pressing buttons. The waitress on duty at the till is desperately tapping the screen, looking at the socket, checking it is still plugged in. The Christmas songs wafting out of the hidden speakers break up. Then, the word "glitch" is muttered across the room. Everyone is talking about it.

'Just give it a few minutes.' I say, adding, 'It will come back. We have had this before and it has all settled back down.'

'When it went off, there was a message,' Maria explains. 'It said something like "no more patience." Then there was a skull. This feels bad.'

'What did you want anyway?' I ask Steve, ignoring Maria's whining. He fetches two crisp old-style files from his bag. He only wants my signature, to agree our divorce. He says that he will handle everything. There is nothing that I wish for more than to divorce Steve at this point in the conversation. He is distracted by the growing uproar in the restaurant. 'Just hand it over,' I urge him impatiently. I read the terms and check the small print while the room is in chaos. Steve and this Maria flap about with their phones while I read. At the very moment that I sign both papers with my cheap biro, all the lights go out and the tables are plunged into a dim gloom. I hand the signed papers back to him, swig my coffee and leave without any customary farewell. The last that I see of him is his white face, eyes pointed at his phone. The people in The Arundel look like duplicated images from The Scream, distraught and immobile, like cartoons.

Saturday Evening

I know, deep down, that this must be another glitch, but it is unlike the previous occurrence, in that nothing seems to be coming back on. I leave The Arundel, weaving between distressed shoppers who are spilling out into the darkened streets. The Christmas lights hang, forlorn and dead, no longer lighting up dull lives with their seasonal sparkle. Very little seems to be working: no power, no tills, only feeble emergency lighting. Anyone without cash is unable to pay. The activities of human beings have been totally suspended.

It is not long before the sirens rise above the clamour of angry voices, as the emergency services launch into action. As soon as fluorescent jackets appear in numbers on the streets, panic subsides. It is replaced with a throbbing despair. Then, just like in the glitch before, electricity is restored. I am thoroughly ashamed of feeling a tinge of disappointment as the lights come back on, disowning the part of myself that wanted the drama of another full-on glitch. The neon signs, the shop windows, glow again as a wash of electric light flows over the city streets. Is it over? Is everything back to normal?

As quickly as the lights blinked back on, they now go out. The power fails, and we are in darkness again.

Looking across the city pavements, I detect a collective sigh of desperate disappointment flooding the faces of the crowds who have been ushered out on to the wintry streets.

They grab their phones and try once more to connect.

But this time the data terrorists gloat. They hold humanity on the end of a pin and they pause, revelling in their total control.

This time they have perfected their methods. I turn to my phone and see the screen light up, and slowly, ever so slowly, an image forms, a malevolent grin with broken teeth. The animated mouth, no doubt on millions of phones, opens. Suddenly a horrendous high-pitched noise fills the air. While the ancient stones of the buildings stand firm, the people crumble, falling to the pavements, clutching their ears. And the noise intensifies. Hundreds of phones all screaming with something ultrasonic, something immensely powerful like a horrendously shrill white noise.

I watch, mesmerised, as human beings are reduced to cowering animals in the darkness. I hold my own ears to fend off the excruciatingly thin, high-pitched sound. We all realise that there is only a single way to combat this, and, one by one, we switch off our phones. Naked without their digital security blanket, people stand, helpless, some talking, others crying.

The echo of the awful sound still rings in my ears. It unsettles my balance and grates on my teeth.

The streets are quickly emptying as shelter is sought in the chaotic shops, but not even cash transactions can take place because the tills are inoperable. I glance through the open doorway of a small newsagents, weakly illuminated by an emergency light. The front pages of the piles of newspapers are now totally outdated. The proprietor has closed the cover concealing tobacco products in an attempt to head off the inevitable looting.

I decide that it is wise to head for the hotel. Check-in was from 3pm, and since yesterday was the shortest day of the year, the skies are already darkening. The streets are totally clogged with immobile vehicles, their electronic devices scrambled by whatever caused this glitch. The excruciating noise hangs about like a bad smell, as people turn on their phones again and again, hoping that the attack has ended; I choose to head for the river.

I have read many books imagining post-apocalyptic societies, but these scenes are not like any of those. More insidious than an electromagnetic pulse, we seem to be individually targeted through our devices. This is pernicious cyber terrorism. It is as if *their* target is progressive society itself.

Walking through St. Ebbes, I leave the maelstrom of the shops behind me, and skirt the back doors of the shopping centre where skeins of smoke loop around anxious shop assistants taking a break from the chaos inside. I make my way through the stationary traffic and into the area of social housing where the flats look as if they were built by children trying out a new construction kit. Anxious cries pierce the air and I hasten through the alleyway. Inside the homes people are distraught. The flimsy walls vibrate with the noise of their phones. Two young children run across in front of me, looking anxiously behind, and scuttle up a fire escape, banging on a door, which is opened for them, and then slammed hard.

The playground is empty. The brightly coloured slides and swings shine out bizarrely through the growing darkness. The footbridge is silhouetted against the angry sky. I take the steps at speed and hurtle across nervously. As I reach the other bank, a group of young men all in black stride across the bridge towards the city, thankfully ignoring me. Once on the bridge I see them blocking the way for the unlucky pedestrian behind me. I hear screams but do not dare to turn back, and scurry onwards.

As I run along the towpath, I see geese paddling, blissfully unaware of the catastrophe in the world of humans.

The Abingdon Road is near. With a final spurt, I reach the pavement, speed-walk away from the city which is groaning and screaming behind me, and dive into the open doors of the hotel. I am hoping for a welcome haven, but am faced with mayhem. A group of guests turns on me, bemoaning the hotel management for failing to honour any credit card bookings. I begin to doubt my own status, and push through, announcing my name to the extremely flustered receptionist. She checks and says, 'Sorry, as you didn't pay in advance, your room is no longer available. It is policy.'

'That is totally unacceptable,' I begin, feeling the colour rushing to my cheeks. I have booked. I have a card and can pay.'

'Cash,' she demands.

'No, but ... this glitch is not *my* fault. I didn't know what would happen this afternoon. It isn't fair to ...' but she has turned away to another irate woman who seems as angry as me.

I take a deep breath, move into the far corner of the room, turn to face the wall and check my purse. I do not have enough cash on me to pay for even one night. I return to plead with the receptionist, along with hordes of other guests, but realisation emerges that there will be no comfortable bed for the night here. I cut my losses and decide reluctantly to return to the city centre, this time taking the direct route along the road, appalled by the scenes that are unfolding in the twilight. It is dawning upon me that it will not be safe out on the angry streets tonight.

I try knocking on the door of a friend I once knew, but there is no response, and I am forced to flee the gathering menace in the stairwell of the flats, which were up-market, but no longer. I hurry as inconspicuously as possible back into town, thinking of Thomas and Maria. This could be much worse. It is feeble comfort to me.

Looting begins.

Shop assistants are panicking and closing up, if they can. Electronic security grills and locks refuse to cooperate. People are yanking on them; only a few have manual override. Gangs of petty looters run past me down the Cornmarket carrying boxes and bundles, booty from small, spontaneous burglaries as shop staff struggle to gain control.

Shoppers are helping themselves to crisps, chocolate bars and bottles of soda. They exit the shop proudly, blatant criminals. The security cameras, of course, are no longer working. Shelves are quickly emptying of goods and the surge of shoppers begins to grapple with the reality that travel home is not going to be straightforward. Scuffles are developing at bus stops when people thrust themselves to the front of the growing queues, for the buses that I guess will not come.

The screeching noise of phones still haunts the city streets. Parents are sheltering in doorways, gloved hands over their children's ears. Meanwhile, the gangs are growing in size. I really don't want to hang around. I can imagine all usual street etiquette being suspended. I fear hooded figures appearing from the shadows, openly brandishing knives and batons. The police appear to have gone, and most shops are now closed up. Even the pubs and restaurants present blank faces to the street. The sound of splintering glass accompanies the high-pitched whistling of the phones, disorientating me.

What should I do, and where should I go? Despite wanting to assist people who are ending up in the path of the gangs, I know that it is not safe. Deciding that self-preservation is my priority, I head towards the station, dodging into side-streets and doorways while the gangs pass, finally standing at the foot of the building where I once rented my flat. No light shines from the windows, and I fear the raised voices inside. The wine bar opposite seems to be one of the few still open, but as I approach, I realise that this is no open bar, this is a vacant property. A gang has broken down the door and is mustering stolen alcohol. A roar of triumphant voices is accompanied by ugly words that I am not comfortable to repeat.

Instinctively I take the pathway round the back of the flats. I pass my old bike store, and wonder if it is being used by the new tenant, noticing the same combination lock, hanging in the half light, decorated with cobwebs. I flick the combination to the old code, just in case … and it clicks open. I pocket the lock and with immense relief, dart through the doorway to safety. I scan the interior, which is completely empty, and bolt the door on the inside.

THE PIKE

Saturday Night

I squat on the floor, gritty with ancient dirt. The pitch-black shrouds the interior of the lockup. Relying on the security of the rusty interior bolt, which must be a relic from days when the small room was used as a workshop, I sigh.

The distant ultrasonic wailing of phones and the sporadic screams of people in peril continue for hours. This is more serious than the glitch before. Unable to sleep, I try to rest, tense, my brain on overdrive. It is only now that I remember I had intended to meet a group of friends at The Pike this evening, before heading for the hotel. Thoughts of The Pike encourage me. Maybe there, people are buying their beer with cash, and are enjoying hot food in the bar. Should I head for The Pike in the morning?

Even in the depths of the night, the alarming noises continue. I can make out harsh voices, sirens, and always the terrible sound of the phones. I keep my device turned off. Then a different noise worries me; I am convinced that someone is trying to get into the lockup. It may be a scrabbling rat. I sit completely still until whatever it is seems to go away. I decide to walk up and down from one side of the lockup to the other, to pass the time, counting my steps, keeping active to combat the biting cold of the night.

Bound by my inbuilt moral compass, I did not join the looters, but now I find myself wishing that I had something to eat. I have half a bottle of water and painkillers, which I take despite not knowing if I am feeling any pain or am just massively unsettled. They muddle my mind and I am not sure if I am asleep or awake through the early hours. I admit to myself that I take too many of these magic little pills, but now is definitely not the time to address this.

As soon as there is a glimmer of daylight shining weakly through a crack in the old doorframe, I unbolt the door, quickly replace the padlock, muddling the code, and set off for The Pike. I do not get far without being overwhelmed with alarm and repulsion at the scene before me. It was a mistake to emerge on to Park End Street. The impromptu gangs that have taken over the disused wine bar now control the area. They are armed. I sneak back towards the lockup and try a different route.

I skirt the railway station, which is closed. I have never seen it closed up before. Massive crowds of people are huddling on the steps, in the car park. I can see wounded. There are no police. To what depths has our country sunk in the last sixteen hours? Desperate for news of elsewhere, I try speaking with a few of the people, but they don't know anything. They are so traumatised that instead of providing me with any grains of information, they hang on to my coat, pleading. I extricate myself and dodge on down the Botley Road, totally focused on staying as hidden as possible and on staying alive, thinking that the first glitch was insignificant compared with this.

The Park and Ride houses another bastion of the gangs. Cars are overturned and protective barriers have been erected. Hijacked buses are teeming with groups of young men and women. People wander aimlessly. Others crouch, inching towards their cars, trying to retrieve belongings, finding that the locks are frozen by whatever caused the glitch.

I hear distant sporadic gunfire, and still the ear-splitting shriek of phones. Why don't people just turn them off?

It takes me much longer than usual to reach The Pike. Nestled in the water meadows, for a moment the sprawling old pub seems unaffected by the chaos only a mile away, but as I approach, I see the landlord at the door gripping an air rifle. I guess he usually hunts rabbits out here. He recognises me and beckons enthusiastically. At last a coherent human being. 'Robin, how good to see you. What a terrible time. Come on in. Thank goodness for the gas ovens as we have some hot food. Please, leave your phone here.' He pushes a wooden crate gingerly towards me. It is full to the brim with mobile phones. I drop mine in, and feel unburdened.

I have never seen so many punters inside The Pike. People are sitting up the stairs, in the windows, on the floor. People are piled up like colourful presents under the cheerful Christmas tree. Their faces are rosy from the roaring fire, which is sending woodsmoke into the room. But unfamiliar characters are crowding the bar. One of these is watching my arrival and is staring pointedly at me, frowning. Every time I look at him, he pointedly looks away. I ignore any negativity and focus on the extremely welcome breakfast that magically appears: bacon and tomatoes. Apparently they have run out of bread. Someone passes me a beer, but I decline and ask for coffee. Perching by the fire, I join a group of people talking with animation. My joints thaw as I demolish the food. A luke-warm coffee is passed along the line to me, and I grip it with my hands, warming my fingers, marvelling at this pocket of good cheer only a mile or so from the total devastation that I have left behind me. People are helping out in the kitchens and the usual staff are spreading smiles with the food and drink.

But it soon becomes clear that there is no plan. More and more people, who were Christmas shopping in town, and are familiar with the pub, have arrived in the hope of something, but beyond food, warmth, company and shelter, no one knows what to do. There is no news of the effect of this glitch elsewhere. I listen to the conversation, to the frustrated tourists and furious Christmas shoppers, who were fortunate enough to know of The Pike, and who walked out here last night. I tell them about the chaos at the station this morning. A well-dressed woman says that she cannot believe there were so many bad people lurking ready for this opportunity for civil disobedience, wreaking havoc. 'The thugs are worse than the cyber-terrorists themselves,' she says. We discuss the trick enacted through our phones, and the noise, the "pulse" as they call it.

Despite the superficial good cheer here, I am frightened. For the first time in my life, I am truly and deeply frightened. This is not helped by the odd figure at the bar, who continues to stare at me.

I consider whether twenty-first-century civilisation as we know it has totally failed. The cyber-terrorists are winning. We need the Government, the councils and the emergency services to get a grip. I simply want to get back to Caernef. I want my life to return to normal.

Partially restored by the welcome, if alarmed by the lack of information and the brooding disquiet, I slip away from the crowd at the fireside, and start to plan my next move.

Sunday Morning

I realise that the temporary inhabitants of The Pike fall into two groups. The first group comprises those who have landed, and are waiting for something to happen, including the shady figures in the corners. The second type is made up of people like me, who seek to make sense of their current dilemma, and once rested, fully intend to head off home, wherever or whatever home may be in this topsy-turvy post-glitch world. I am interested in these characters. It is clear to me that, like when the previous glitch occurred, normal life will be suspended for weeks while systems are restored.

I long to be at the camp, and I need help to get there. My only option is to set off on foot, but not alone. I need a group for safety. As I scan faces and listen to snippets of conversation, I notice the loners and the thinkers, the self-sufficient survivors. They interest me. Identifying a dozen or so contenders, I try to work out who is not addicted to alcohol, drugs or the sound of their own voice. I am looking for the fittest in mind and body. I want an innovator, a problem solver, an optimist to keep us cheerful and a realist who will provide the checks and balances. I want the person who can find a meal when no meal is available.

Sadly, I come to the conclusion that actually I want Glyn, Thomas and Maria, my loyal team back at the camp, with little Poppy to keep us grounded, reminding us of the future generations, the inheritors of this increasingly blighted planet. I miss them so much, and I miss my folly, safely away from all this chaos.

The unnerving character standing at the bar, hiding his face under old scarves, is still watching me. He makes me feel uncomfortable. Not everyone in this bubble of geniality is to be trusted.

I see a quiet teenager share his food with a family that has just arrived, giving a child an apple, slicing it up patiently for him, then slipping the knife into his pocket. I single him out. There is nothing special about his appearance. He is clean shaven with short brown hair and an athletic build. After a while, he leaves the building. I follow, keeping a respectful distance. He crosses the garden and heads for the river. This route, which takes you to the path along the Thames, has been a favourite haunt of mine for several years. I pause while he settles on a bench overlooking the iridescent water.

For a moment, as the wind changes direction, the distant noises in the city cease. A grey heron is disturbed and rises from the reeds, with enormous wings spreading wide. It lands across the river and stands, stock still, like me. Hearing the engine of an approaching boat, the young man slides off the bench and stands deliberately camouflaged by a group of trees. His sixth sense serves him well as a small pleasure cruiser sputters into sight, crewed by half a dozen members of one of the gangs terrorising the neighbourhood. I watch the silhouette of a man balancing in the stern. He raises a gun, aims clumsily at the heron across the channel, and fires. His companions cheer with raucous, cruel laughter. The heron is startled and launches into the air unscathed. Standing under the trees, my young man holds his head in his hands while the motor launch disappears from view.

I give him a moment, and then saunter along the path towards him, as if on a walk on a normal Sunday afternoon. He tenses. I catch his eye and smile.

'Hi, I'm Robin.'

'Hi.'

'That heron was lucky.'

'Mmm.'

'Have you got plans? Are you heading off somewhere?'

'Not yet …'

He speaks quietly and confidently but seems to resent my interruption. He continues, calmly, 'It was too crowded in the pub. I just wanted some space to think. I am Nathan.' He holds out his hand to me and we shake. Neither of our hands is clean. 'What do you want?'

'I will be heading off soon and I don't want to travel alone.' He studies my clothes, my small rucksack, his eyes resting on my face and asks,

'Where are you heading?'

'I live in a remote part of Wales, on the coast. I have friends there, good friends. It is a camp off grid, a better place to be right now, better than here.'

He considers the scenario, asking, 'How do I know to trust you?'

I pause, and then say 'I am a tired, idealistic middle-aged woman. I have seen life; I was a social worker. I am seeking a better and simpler existence with like-minded people as far away as possible from the madness of society. Whether you trust me or not is your call.'

He asks me who I am with, and I say simply, 'Just me at the moment, but I don't want to travel alone. What about you?'

'I am a student, in my final year. I have no home to visit for Christmas and so am … was staying over. Not sure that the course will run anymore. The glitch situation seems to be long-term this time. I like the sound of going off grid in Wales, away from the trouble in the cities.'

I ask him what he is studying and he is about to tell me when we hear the sound of another boat approaching, and retreat quickly, away from the water. I note the alarm in his eyes, and test him out, asking, 'We will need supplies. Would you go back into the city if I give you a shopping list?'

'Yes. I have never stolen anything in my life before, but times are different now. I run and I am quick. People are plotting back inside the pub. There are some odd characters in there, and I really don't want to hang around longer that I have to. You give me a list.'

We return to the bar in The Pike and I look down at his feet in a pair of flimsy white trainers. 'You need strong boots, a rucksack. We need dry food like cereal bars which are light to carry, lots of them. Refillable water bottles, matches, torches, a first aid kit, sleeping bags … can you carry all that back here and stay alive?'

'Yes. When will you leave?'

I am beginning to become nervous. We are sitting ducks in The Pike, and the landlord with his small air rifle will not keep gangs at bay if they find their way out along the lane.

'Tonight at dusk, no later than four o'clock.'

'Okay. If I am not back by four, set off without me.'

That gives him several hours. I tell him the code for the lockup, explaining how to get there if he needs shelter, and watch him leave towards the river, not the road. He runs at speed without a backward glance.

I wonder if I will ever see Nathan again.

Later on Sunday

Willing my new friend to succeed, I set about recruiting a third companion. The people who I target seem hugely attracted by the thought of a remote camp in Wales, but many of them are determined to stay here near their family, near what is familiar to them. Many want to return home, but there is fear in their eyes. Few people display the spark which I seek.

As is customary in The Pike, a folk band has materialised in the main bar. The bands here are good. Ordinarily I would sink into a fireside chair and let the nostalgic fiddling transport me away from the twenty-first century, but not today. Soon the air is filled with more than woodsmoke, but the jolly refrains are incongruous. As the musicians slip into Christmas songs, their audience joins in, tense faces relaxing. I don't know what to think. The music is a welcome distraction, and is definitely raising spirits, but I am troubled by a vague memory of Nero allegedly fiddling while Rome burned.

The landlord looks in, red cheeked and beaming, no longer carrying a rifle, but brandishing a strong kit bag that looks familiar. He pushes through the crowds towards me. 'Robin, these are yours, remember!' He hands me the kit bag, heavy with books.

'Blimey! I had forgotten about these. Thank you!' He smiles jovially and shares a joke with someone across the room. They all laugh. I slip out, seeking space to examine the contents. The sturdy bag itself can be slung securely over both shoulders, and it is waterproof. The books are too heavy. I find a bookcase in the hallway, and, pushing through crowds of people, I slide the now unwanted books on to vacant shelves. I think that there was a road atlas and fumble in the depths. Yes! This will be invaluable.

Just as I am struggling to find space to breathe, I catch a familiar eye.

'Robin! Hooray! I looked out for you last night! But all that happened. It's great to see you!'

Eva was an invaluable friend to me on the day that I completely lost it with my ex-husband Steve. Not only did she turn my distraught panic into a confident triumph, but she put me up in her tiny rented attic room for a few weeks while I found a job and a flat. If there is anyone in Oxford who I would like to be with right now, it is Eva.

We reach across the people who are crammed into the hallway like sardines, and clasp hands. I tell her how overjoyed I am to see her. She sees my kit bag and observes sadly, 'You are heading off, I guess? This will not be the place to hang out in a few days when the gangs discover us. There's no hope that the Government will sort this quickly, and the police have their work cut out in Oxford. They won't have the time to get out to places like this.'

We find a vacant corner in the conservatory, which is bitterly cold, and damp, but slightly more private. We hold hands, warming our fingers, while she tells me of her ordeal last night in Oxford, her rooms being over shops, the looting, the broken windows, and then the atmosphere turning violent. I tell her all about the camp, and for the first time since I left The Arundel, I forget the current situation, as my mind is taken back to the place that I love so dearly.

'Right, so we are heading back to your camp in Wales then,' she announces decisively, adding, 'When do we leave? What do we need? I grabbed some basic kit, and cash, when I left the city last night. It is in my rucksack. My bike is out the back too. Will we take bikes or travel on foot? Public transport is gone; did you see the station and the Park and Ride last night?'

I tell her about Nathan, and she seems pleased, but says that three is not enough; we need at least one more person. A group of four can be hidden but can also split into two groups if needed. I realise that she is right and ask if there is anyone else here who she knows. There isn't.

After more discussion we agree that she will scout the building for more useful kit while I recruit the fourth member of the team. I actually intend to look out for a couple more as I am not entirely confident in Nathan's safe return.

By half past three the sky is already darkening, and with the incessant noise of sporadic fighting seemingly coming closer by the hour, accompanied by the shrill scream of phones, I am eager to be on the move. Eva and I meet in the conservatory. The bright music is still trilling in the bar, attracting the crowds, so the conservatory is fairly quiet.

After being turned down by several potential companions, I have recruited Gid, who must be in his early thirties. He declares his personality through his piercings and tattoos, and attracted me because he was energetically chopping firewood outside, his breath spurting out into the cold air. He is very keen to accompany us as he has no ties here.

Eva, Gid and I huddle close. Eva seems to approve of my new recruit. She has amassed a wealth of small useful items and has divided the stash into four pillow cases which she found in the linen cupboard. Mine smells of fabric conditioner. I peer inside and see a treasure trove of unexpected survival items: cutlery, a toilet roll, a clean and dry hand towel, a small metal saucepan and numerous tiny things rattling around. I grin; we owe the landlord. One day, when the world of humans has returned to normal, I will come back to thank him, and I will repay this small debt.

We realise that I am the only one of our group to have a watch, the others having relied on their phones. It is five to four. Having explained that we must hold off our departure for Nathan, at least until four o'clock, we all wait with baited breath. If he doesn't return in the next five minutes, we fear the worst, that he has been hunted down, or ended up in the wrong place, or has run out of time. Every cell in my body wills him to return.

The face of my watch indicates that it is four o'clock. The darkness is gathering force outside the windows. A figure enters the conservatory, coming straight up to me. It is not Nathan. It is the threatening figure who kept staring at me from the bar. My hackles rise.

THE STONES

Dusk on Sunday

'Robin, I would like to talk with you, and with you alone.'

Her voice is not at all what I was expecting. In fact, I have been caught out at my own game as I had believed her to be a man. How does she know my name? She speaks softly, peeling her scarves to reveal a face that I recognise, or I think I recognise.

'Do I know you?' is my curt reply, with two pairs of eyes on me, I remain antagonistic.

The woman is prevented from replying by Eva, who leaps into the conversation eagerly informing us, 'I recognise you - you are the politician who resigned aren't you? Your face was all over the press. You refused to stand with your party on cyber security. I remember. The big companies all targeted you. You disappeared…'

The woman in black draws her clothes back across her face, checking behind her, and remains silent.

At this point I declare that if she has anything to say to me, she can say it to the group. Starting as I mean to go on; we are a team now, and will share any key information or decisions.

She coughs. She coughs again, and finding it difficult to breathe, steadies herself by involuntarily putting her hand on my knee. We wait. There is silence in the conservatory. In the distance we can all hear gunfire. In the bar the hopeful tones of "Then let us all rejoice again" ring out. Before she can speak, the door swings dramatically open. It is Nathan struggling under a host of bundles. Blood is dripping down his forehead, but he is grinning.

'There you go Robin! I made it ... just in time ...' He tips his bundles on to the floor between us and looks desperately for my response. I can see how much he wants to please me, and I am, genuinely hugely impressed as well as relieved.

'How the hell have you managed this? And are you hurt?'

My amazed tone satisfies his need for praise, and he brushes off the injury saying, 'I hit my head in the dark in that lockup of yours. I'm okay, but boy, the streets of Oxford look more like something from the Dark Ages. We need to be off as soon as we can. Who are these people?'

I introduce Eva as my old and very special friend and Gid as a newly recruited and vital member of our party, and I turn to the mysterious black-cloaked politician, realising that we don't even know her name, saying rhetorically, and rashly,

'And this is the latest member of our band, who is coming too I think?'

Nathan has brought exactly what I asked for, and more. We quickly share out the supplies. Eva is our quartermaster. She checks that each member of the group is kitted out with warm and waterproof clothes, hats, and that distribution of equipment and food is practical and fair. Nathan distributes the remaining kit, sharing out tins of food to spread the weight. 'I remembered to get tins with ring pulls, and wind-up torches,' he says, proudly.

The politician draws me aside and whispers 'Your friend is correct; I am Meredith Brenton, the ex-MP, but I am known as Miranda. I need to be known by your friends as Miranda. I know Marcella well. You remember Marcella? She asked me to ... look out for you.'

Things begin to make more sense, and I remember Marcella, the super-fit security guard on the night of the helicopters. My initial antagonism for the strange woman softens, especially as she does not look well. 'Are you okay to travel with us?'

'Yes. I have to come with you. I will be fine.'

I refer to Miranda by name, drawing her into the group, and ask who knows the local area well. Nathan says that in his view we need to head off immediately, travelling parallel to the city, then heading north-west, leaving the trouble behind us. He says that we should strike a path cross country for the Swinford Toll, and cross the bridge on foot, adding that the path along the Thames seems safer than roads at the moment. We agree to follow the river northwards. Then we will stop to plan more thoroughly somewhere safe once we are well on our way.

Just as we are assembled, and are attempting to make a quiet exit, I notice that Eva has disappeared. Frantic not to lose her so early, I stall, but she reappears from behind the buildings with her bike.

'I don't think we will be travelling on the right paths for a bike. I'll leave it out here. Someone else might find it useful,' she whispers to me, slipping the cycle lights into her backpack.

We have agreed Nathan will lead, and the rest of us will walk in pairs in silence, one looking ahead into the darkness and the other covering our backs. Despite wanting to accompany Eva, I have paired with the enigmatic and forbidding Miranda. We cut through the garden of The Pike, and emerge on to the path. The city across the water is in darkness, and the countryside is pitch black. Weather is going to play an important part in our lives from now on, and mercifully tonight is dry, if cold and damp underfoot. No frost yet.

I take the back of the line. Nathan is at our head and sets a challenging pace. How bizarre to be in the company of these strangers, except Eva of course, on such a peculiarly alarming night. With time to think, at last, as I march along, I reflect on my choice of companions. Gid follows Nathan; he is our rottweiler, a face that I would not like to meet unexpectedly on a dark night. He is built like a wrestler. I can see his enormous shape ahead, his head ducking under overhanging boughs. Eva is ahead of Miranda. My good friend always wears bright colours and huge earrings, but tonight all I can see is a black shape tripping along. Although she is cheerfully overweight, she has dainty toes. And our uninvited guest, who obviously has much to hide, and who I do not trust, marching ahead of me, right under my eye. She is not coughing now, but is striding confidently, her black cloak swishing around her.

Despite being perilously close to the city, our route runs parallel, and we meet no one on our trek along the river bank. The leaves underfoot are beginning to crunch with frost when we reach the lock, and we emerge on to a winding lane. The pub across the water is lit up with candles, flickering in the windows like at the Pike. We give it a wide berth and take a small road, nervously. Nathan knows the route and leads the way. Miranda catches my eye and smiles but I do not smile back. After a mile, exposed on the road, I am relieved when Nathan takes us back on to paths. Helpfully, the clouds part, revealing the moon, and we can see our feet more clearly as we traverse wilder terrain. Soon in the cover of woods, we encounter fresh sounds, the nocturnal wildlife even at this time of year creating clicks and crackles which keep us alert and nervous.

I am already valuing Nathan's knowledge of the area. He leads us downhill on firm paths under the canopy of bare branches dripping with ivy. Down and down, until he gathers us in a huddle, whispering, 'Soon we will pass a cottage, and then we will hit a road. We must walk along the road past houses for a few hundred yards. The toll is closed at night. If all runs smoothly, we should be able to walk across the bridge. I will hoot like an owl if I get safely over. If not, I will return, and we will either have to steal a boat or divert for miles. I suggest we split into pairs and cross at intervals, if all is clear?' He looks to me for approval and I nod. I check my watch under the light of his torch. We have only been travelling for just over an hour, but it seems like much longer.

Nathan resumes, 'Once we are all safely across the bridge, we must clear the area. A short way beyond the Toll there is a pub, on the right. Directly opposite the pub, on our left, there is a gateway. We will meet there. Okay Robin?'

'Okay.'

Night

Four of us wait in uneasy silence as Nathan creeps on down the lane, which is still reflecting the moonlight. His rucksack is a huge hump on his back. It is not long before we hear him hooting. Eva and Gid, an unlikely pair, set off. I am left alone with Miranda, alert to her every move. She takes advantage of our moment of solitude, 'I apologise for gate crashing your party, but it is for the best, believe me. I have been working with Reginald, your Godfather. We, the British Government I mean … we knew something like this was coming. Confidentially, dialogue with the cyber-terrorists had broken down. They were threatening to attack on Christmas morning. For some reason they caught us out by striking earlier.'

I nod, and am hit by a flash of inspiration. I ask her to tell me which book might interest her from Reginald's office shelves. Looking me in the eye, and raising her eyebrows in the moonlight, her eyes sparkling, she whispers, 'Anna Karenina.' The sound of an owl hooting draws us back to the present and without talking further, we proceed towards the bridge.

We pace quietly past the sign that lists the charges for the toll. It is still only five pence for a car. We hasten across the bridge itself, the balustrades looking like rows of stone bottles in the moonlight. I see the squat toll house in darkness, no lights in the windows, and we pass, relieved. Despite having lived on the dark headland of Caernef, I am uneasy. We approach a pub where candles flicker in the windows. The car park is full with cars, unusual for this time of night. We scan the verge opposite for the gateway, and seeing it easily, dive off the tarmac under the arch of branches. Our companions are standing in front of the five-bar gate.

I take charge, whispering, 'This is not a place to rest, and we need to keep moving to stay warm. Is everyone alright?' They each nod. 'Nathan, where next?'

'We need to head north west. if I could turn my phone on, I could use the compass ...' He takes his phone out from his pocket and we all recoil.

'I remember now, I thought of that,' Nathan fumbles in the pocket of his rucksack and produces a plastic compass, looking at me to enjoy the appreciation on my face.

'Fantastic. I can lead us to a farm I know near the Rollrights, off the beaten track. I worked there in my summer break. We will take paths and minor roads, and should be there by daybreak, when we can rest. Okay Robin?'

'Okay, let's move, same pairs.'

Nathan sets a challenging pace again, but we keep up, even Eva with her somewhat rolling gait. I am determined not to appear unfit and I take pains to conceal the agony in my screaming limbs, and my nervousness, as we pass isolated cottages and skirt deserted village streets. After a while the bitter chill and the pitch darkness become a tunnel of torment, but we keep on, thankful when the moon emerges briefly and we can see more clearly where we are going.

In the countryside, humans are sleeping in their bedrooms. There is no evidence of disturbance and no noise of phones. I begin to wonder whether we are mad to even contemplate this journey, whether the gangs in Oxford were a terrible dream, or whether this second glitch is not actually as bad as I originally feared. I allow my derision for the terrorists to fuel my legs.

How dare they ruin the lives of millions of law-abiding people. How dare they provide the loop hole through which selfish and violent gangs can squeeze.

Miranda, ever astute, must have seen me grimacing. She asks tenderly 'Robin, are you okay?'

'I am furious at the audacity of these people. I was thinking about the untold damage that they have caused. It makes me ashamed to be human.' I discover that I need my mouth for breathing, and stop speaking. I know myself well, this could become a tirade of invective, and I don't want to hamper our pace.

'There are still good people,' she puffs, 'with the ingenuity to set the world back on its axis.' Half a mile or so later she resumes, 'Your Caernef sounds like a real gem. I would like to see it.'

Nathan leads us hour after hour. Every so often he pulls us into a gateway for five minutes, and we take a break. It doesn't pay to stop for too long. My limbs are screaming, tiredness causing a vicious headache, and I am short of painkillers. To compound my misery, my feet are sore from the brisk walking.

Occasionally we cross a major road but we generally travel along narrow lanes, through sleeping hamlets and past farmyards, disturbing cats. I check my watch once in a while, and see the night slowly pass, willing on the dawn and time to rest. Eva is starting to drop behind and Nathan instinctively slows our pace. We agree to go through the middle of a small town. It looks as if it has been hit by a typhoon, or a war. Even out here, shop windows are smashed, cars upturned, and along the high street the pavement is peppered with smashed mobile phones, their innards exposed, plastic and electronics spewed across our way. My feet crunch on the fallout of the glitch.

Our experience in this unassuming town convinces me that we are right to be on our secret journey. We need to leave this destruction behind us and find somewhere to think, to plan, and to rest. I now crave rest like nothing else.

How ecstatic am I to see the glow of a winter sun below the horizon, the clear crisp night beginning to give way to daylight. Nathan calls quietly backwards, 'Forty minutes by my reckoning and we can stop.' I guess that the others are as relieved as I am. Our pace quickens with the hope of respite from the incessant pressure of feet on hard ground, and the need for continuous vigilance.

It is actually an hour later when we hit a road, turn right and march to our destination. Nathan explains that he knows the farmer well and if we all wait by the stones, he will organise somewhere for us to rest.

'By the stones?'

'Yes. Here, follow me ...'

He leads us through a small gate, and there before us is a magnificent circle of ancient stones, glowing mysteriously in the sunrise, swathed in a thin mist. We all take off our loads, resting them against the gnarled rocks with relief.

'These are the King's Men, and over there are the Whispering Knights. Amazing to think that hunter gatherers would have been standing here over ten thousand years ago, just like us, but not in a world like ours ... wait here and I will be back as soon as I can.'

'Stop, you should take someone with you. I'll come too.' I say, thinking on my feet, unwilling to lose our skilful guide to the unknown. I whisper to Eva to keep her eye on Miranda, saying quietly to my dependable friend that I don't entirely trust the woman's motives for being with us. Gid is standing in the centre of the large circle of stones, keeping watch in all directions. He looks like a mythical lord, through the mist, and only needs a sword and helmet to complete the picture. Leaving our three companions, Nathan and I head back through the small iron gate.

He leads me to a nearby farm, a random collection of barns and outbuildings and a large stone farmhouse. Given the events of the past 24 hours, I would not be surprised if the occupants keep their door firmly closed to us. He presses the bell, which doesn't seem to work, and so knocks loudly on the door. We wait. After some time, we can see two shadowy figures through the frosted glass in the door.

Nathan calls out, 'It's okay, it's Nathan, Nathan Price, with friends.'

The door opens and the couple greet Nathan with open arms, ushering us into the warmth of the hallway. The man shakes Nathan's hand vigorously, beaming at him, and the woman is all smiles, running her fingers through her hair and exclaiming, 'We weren't expecting visitors after all, this morning of all mornings! I thought you might be our lost bed and breakfast guests. Nathan, how are you, so good to see you again. What terrible times.'

Nathan politely refuses when they urge us to join them in the kitchen, explaining that there are three more of us waiting hopefully out by the stones. For the first time, they turn to me, shaking my hand cautiously, telling me their names, 'Bill, pleased to meet you' and 'Eileen.' 'Robin is my new friend. When this second glitch hit, she had the presence of mind to gather a small group of trusted companions, in The Pike. We are heading for Wales, on foot, in fact we have been walking through the night and are pretty tired. No cars on the roads, no transport working. What we could do with is somewhere warm and dry to sleep for a few hours, in the daylight, before we set off at dusk. You don't want to know what it is like in the cities: gangs, looting, violence. We aim to skirt Cheltenham tonight.'

Once the couple understands our position, they offer all manner of kind hospitality, and are keen to discover more about the impact of the crisis elsewhere. I reflect to myself that Nathan has really earned his place over the first leg of our trip. What a find he was! He tells Bill and Eileen that we will go to fetch the others, and will return in five minutes. They head to the kitchen to put the kettle to boil on the wood burner, and Eileen says to Nathan, 'Meet me out by the big barn.'

We stride back towards the stones. 'I have worked on the farm for Bill and Eileen in my summer breaks for the last few years. Kind people.' Reaching the three hopeful figures, waiting in the bitter cold of the early morning, standing in the bands of winter sunlight, hoping to warm themselves, we call out, showing thumbs up. We haul our baggage back onto our backs and all walk through the gate. Nathan leads us along a new path, across the road and into a field. There, it is as if time is suspended. A solitary standing stone is silhouetted against the emerging sun, and we can see for miles across the escarpment, fields, villages and church spires. It all seems very English, and very reassuring.

'I've never heard of this place; it's magical.' Eva says.

Nathan leads us along the track to an annex, nestling in a group of farm buildings, seemingly used for self-catering guests, where Eileen is waiting with a notebook. We enter the annex, take off our heavy backpacks and head straight for the small wood burner, which seems to have been alight for some time as it is giving out a wonderful heat.

'Now, who is for coffee and who is for tea, or even hot chocolate?' Eileen asks, jotting down our eager responses, adding, 'Make yourselves at home. Like I said, Nathan, we don't have any guests today. We are thinking that they couldn't get through with all the trouble last night.'

Morning

Our faces grey with fatigue and cold, we devour the hot drinks, heartily thanking Nathan's friends, offering to pay, which they decline. Bill, the farmer, doesn't seem unduly concerned about this latest glitch. He tells us that all his digital equipment has failed, and of course the power. No television, no radio. He is relieved that he got out of dairy a few years ago, otherwise with all computerised controls seemingly scrambled, he would have been in much greater difficulty.

He leaves us, mumbling that if the guests turn up, we will have to move on. I call everyone over, 'If you are half as exhausted as me, you will be craving sleep. I suggest that we all rest until mid-afternoon. We need to reconvene before it gets dark, to plan the next stage in our journey.

How about three pm. Does that sound okay?'

No one seems to have the energy to agree or to disagree. We all have sore feet, aching muscles and weary heads. They smile and nod, and collapse on top of the various armchairs, generously leaving the double bed for me. After a few minutes, Eva creeps in and nestles up beside me, radiating welcome warmth. I sleep instantly, waking much later in the day. Eva is snoring gently. I check my watch and see that it is only two thirty. I creep past my sleeping companions and lock myself in the en-suite. Here, I sit for a while, gathering my strength, and then undress. The water is ferociously cold, but once clean and clothed, I feel ready to face the night ahead.

When I emerge, there is a polite queue outside the bathroom door, and through the next half an hour, three of my four companions take their turn to freshen up. Gid continues to sleep, dragging himself up at five to three. He takes his phone out of his pocket and we cry in unison, 'No.'

I place my book of maps on the coffee table, and Nathan sketches out a possible route. We reckon that we should reach Caernef after ten or so nights walking at the same pace as yesterday. The journey ahead of us seems interminable. We agree to travel by dark and to rest by day, but will have to review our plans regularly as we cannot be sure what we will find on the road. We will circumvent the conurbation of Cheltenham and Gloucester, cutting through the countryside, avoiding urban areas, keeping clear of the violence, the looting and the gangs.

Nathan asks, 'Robin, tell us more about the camp, to give us something to aim for while we are walking. I want to breathe the sea air, and to be somewhere which has its own story, a story of hope and simple living.'

Although I do not need much encouragement, it pains me to think of the perfect peace of Caernef. I tell them about the camp when I first found it, sad and down-at-heel, and describe the changes since it reopened, the dinner bell, and the intense pleasure of sitting beside the schoolchildren at lunchtime, the hot meals and the conversation. I talk about the isolation and the closeness to nature, about our aims for total self-sufficiency, the solar power, the rainwater harvesting and the vegetable garden. I find myself worrying about Glyn, Thomas and Maria. Are they really safe from the fallout of this second glitch? There is no way of telling at the moment. I say nothing about the folly. That is my secret for now.

Eva is beaming, having completely forgotten that we still have over a hundred miles to cover, without transport. 'And you chose us,' she muses, adding, 'You always were a good judge of character, of people's potential. I am so proud to be on this journey.'

I can tell that each of my companions, except perhaps Miranda, is really taken with the prospect of the camp. They seem to share my deep desire to be there, as far away as possible from the madness which engulfed us in Oxford.

Telling them that we have been brought together by chance, and by disturbing circumstances, I say that if our journey is to succeed, we need to believe in each other, to understand our motives and to have each other's backs. We need to move forwards as one united group. I look into the eyes of each of my four companions in turn, and say, 'No one is compelled to stick with the group to the bitter end. If you are considering leaving, and striking out alone, just talk about it with us first.'

Gid, who has championed fair play from the start, agrees, saying, 'That makes sense. You lay down the rules Boss.'

I capitalise on this comment, adding, 'Okay, and no phones, not at any time.' Eva says that the shrill whining sends her nerves jangling, and that as *they* don't seem to be intending to turn off the glitch any time soon, we must ignore the temptation to turn our phones on again, even for an instant.

Miranda interjects. 'I don't think *they* can turn it off. This whole thing has spiralled completely out of control.'

My phone is still in the crate at The Pike, but it turns out they have all retrieved theirs. I notice that Gid, Nathan and Eva persist in clinging on to their phones, perhaps hopeful that services will return to normal. I don't. I am not convinced that our "normal" is desirable any more.

Nathan is thoughtful, 'Last night, I varied my pace to that of the slowest in the group. We will all struggle at some time. I think that we should all try our best to keep up, but that whoever is leading must make sure that we travel as a group, and not strung out. We are much more vulnerable strung out …' We nod, and Eva smiles gratefully at him. We all know that she is the slowest walker, but that she makes up for it with her kind-heartedness.

Gid simply calls for honesty. He glares at Miranda while he speaks, then looking at me, he adds, 'I suggest that if any one of us is found to be untrustworthy, the others reserve the right to chuck them out of the expedition, perhaps by a majority in a vote. That seems fair to me.'

A discussion follows, with enthusiastic support for Gid's suggestion from four out of our company of five, but I notice that Miranda remains silent. Not for the first time, I wonder whether she has an ulterior motive in joining us. Gid glowers. I am not alone in mistrusting her.

Eva reminds us that we must never forget our goal to reach the safety of the camp, and to escape this mad society, to gather with like-minded friends and to somehow act against the perpetrators of the glitch. She is complimentary about my vision for Caernef, which I appreciate. Our destination is quickly becoming a symbol of our hopes, for good, honest survival in the midst of this madness. We all listen with due seriousness as Eva extols the virtues of the camp and marvels at my ingenuity in securing the place. I become embarrassed because I know that I couldn't have done this without my inheritance, but I certainly don't want to go into that here and now.

I am about to suggest that it is time to leave, when Miranda speaks, looking at Gid, 'I will be as honest as I can be, but I carry a heavy burden of classified intelligence. I respect your desire for complete openness, but must reserve my right to silence on certain matters.'

Gid explodes, 'Then leave us to our pathetic little journey and go back to where you fucking came from, back to the bureaucrats, politicians or … whatever spies who you answer to.'

We all gawp. Miranda doesn't even flinch. She turns towards him and calmly launches her steely retaliation, 'I have no choice. I must accompany you, so perhaps you might control your tongue.'

Gid turns to me and raises his eyebrows, then, gripping the sides of his chair, he says politely, 'Perhaps you could give us some insight, from your past experience; what is really happening, and what is our best chance of surviving it?'

'Look, I am genuinely sorry that I cannot be more forthcoming. We need to press on towards the camp. It sounds like an inspirational place and will give each of us the best possible chance of achieving whatever we wish in a post-glitch world. In my view, things will not return to normal this time. If we get there safely, I will share what I can with you, but not here. Please, bear with me.'

Gid shrugs, not totally satisfied. Indeed, I am uneasy too. Miranda looks around the room, cluttered with baggage and the debris of our breakfast: dirty mugs, plates, tissues and drying clothes, and says firmly, 'We must leave everywhere exactly as we find it. Your naivety in this situation is heart-warming, but I know the real dangers that we face, largely unprotected. We must move swiftly and silently and leave no trail behind us.'

The group is silent for a moment, for her words are salutary. Then Eva moves, followed by Nathan, tidying the mess, washing the cups. We all join in, gathering our belongings and packing up quickly, ready to leave. The guest apartment is restored to pristine condition just in time, as Bill, the farmer, reappears hastily and nervously.

'It's time you left.' He blurts out, casting his eye with relief over the tidy room, and grabbing the tray of clean cups. 'A man from the government came. He left a booklet of instructions. Apparently, we are in a civil emergency. He told us not to admit any strangers, particularly small groups. He showed us a sheaf of photographs of "wanted criminals opposing the state" and …' he looks at Miranda, who has hastily covered her face in her scarves again, '…and all I am saying is you must leave now. Happy to have helped you. You are not "strangers" of course as I know Nathan well, but please, just go.'

I shake his trembling hand, thanking him, and his wife, for their kindness, as the others file quietly past him, back out into the cruel winter's air.

LOCKED IN

Night and Morning

My limbs are stiff, the cold bites into my face, and my
burden is heavy. It takes me an hour or so to get back into
the groove. Then, I walk like an automaton, my feet obeying
necessity, the icy breath of the night stinging my cheeks.
Nathan sets an ambitious pace, and we fall into line, hour
after hour, hiking along lanes, through woods and past
endless fields. We avoid settlements, but are constantly
troubled by the distant moan of phones. It is never totally
silent here.

By midnight, several of us are struggling. Gid can see
that we need a break, and while we are pausing for one of
our customary short rests in a gateway, he spots a barn,
across the field. Taking Nathan, with my agreement, they
reconnoitre, returning with heartening news that in their
view, we can shelter in the barn until dawn. With relief we
cross the field in pairs. We agree that, in turn, two of us will
act as lookout, while the other three rest. The barn is being
used for the storage of farm machinery, and I unpack my
sleeping bag, settling behind a great metal monster. I curl up
on the earth floor, and braced against the cold, I give way to
sleep.

Miranda and I take the final lookout from five in the
morning. We plant ourselves in the doorway, concealed by
a farm trailer, but with a clear view outside. We don't speak
because we are fearful of disturbing our sleeping
companions, or of forgetting that we are meant to be
scanning the surroundings. I know that this is a missed

opportunity to grill Miranda.

After a couple of hours, just before dawn, Eva emerges blearily. She locates the one camping stove in our kit, a box of matches and billycan, setting a pot of bottled water on to boil. The hissing of the gas, and Eva's fumbling in the rucksacks, soon wakes the others, and we find that between us we have plenty of spoons, instant coffee and four tin mugs, all brought by Nathan from his shopping trip.

We sit in a circle, perching on our rucksacks, passing round the coffee and eating cereal bars. It is a hopeful breakfast, particularly as Nathan reports that there is a change in the weather, huge clouds having rolled in overnight. I had noticed that the air was no longer quite so cold. We walked from around five in the afternoon until midnight, protected by the darkness, and have each succeeded in sleeping for at least four hours. Unwilling to be seen marching through the lanes in broad daylight, we are unsure of the best plan for the day ahead.

Our fate is decided for us. We are packed up and ready to leave, fearing the arrival of farm workers, and aware that we are not far from roads, when we are held in our tracks by a long, loud whistle. This is followed by a massive hiss.

'What the hell is that?' Gid exclaims. We listen, fascinated, finally concluding that it is the unlikely sound of a steam train. We cross the field and follow the noise. Walking into a village, we are soon aware that a few people are emerging from their homes, and are wearing colourful scarves with woolly hats, carrying bags with flasks and packets of crisps. We feel conspicuous with our baggage, but no one questions us.

Following the stream of people who are heading towards the whistling, we join the long queue that is already across the forecourt of the small brick-built heritage railway station. Thinking on our feet, and keen to put some miles under our belts on a faster mode of transport, we send Nathan as our scout. He discovers that the heritage steam train is leaving for Cheltenham. 'I had forgotten that it's

Christmas Eve,' he says, adding, 'This is the local enthusiasts club refusing to give up their Christmas Eve Special!'

We send Eva to ask them if we can join in. She persuades them with her charm and smiles, and they tell us to grab tickets.

The queue moves through quickly, a jovial guard takes our cash and hands out old-fashioned buff tickets stamped with the words "One return" with today's date. We are soon on the platform. It is populated with die-hard steam-railway enthusiasts, refusing to be beaten by glitches or anything else, which is both bizarre and reassuring in the circumstances. Hand-made signs have been strung along the hoardings announcing "Christmas Eve Special WILL run. 9.30am. Return tickets £15 cash only."

Our train is ready and waiting, whistling and sending forth huge bursts of steam, drowning the distant moaning squeal of phones.

Miranda and I enter a carriage and choose a seat. This is a bizarre experience. I cannot decide whether it is exciting and heart-warming or whether it is ridiculous. These cheery people genuinely think that they are going for a nostalgic pleasure-trip to Cheltenham. I wonder what we will find there.

Determined to take advantage of this time with Miranda, I quiz her further. The carriage is packed, and we are pressed together on a double seat. I am sure that human beings were smaller when these beautiful old carriages were made. The last fifty years has seen untold gluttony, the junk-food revolution, as well as an explosion in comfort eating and sedentary lifestyles. This glitch will see to our excess; no one will be ordering food to eat on their sofas in half-time at the moment.

'So, what do you think will happen now? You must have inside information,' I ask Miranda casually and quietly, my words cocooned in the babble of the steam enthusiasts.

She seems relieved to talk to me, unburdening herself, her words gently escaping from beneath the scarves which cover her real identity. 'The original intention was to hit the banks hard, very hard, and to redistribute wealth by the back door.' This is an unexpected response and I push her further,

'Whose intention?'

'Under the cover of far-right extremism, you know the sort, racists and bullies who make a load of noise, there is a cell of far-left extremists. I despise them now, but at the time I was carried along in a fervour of toppling the twenty-first century order. They are fiercely anti-establishment but have lost sight of their original aims, prepared to make millions of law-abiding people pay the price for their misguided solution to the inequity of wealth in the world.'

'But millions of hard-working people would lose everything that they had striven for, over years, over their lifetimes. This action wouldn't only hit the super-rich?'

'Exactly.'

A small dog dressed in a Father Christmas coat, trots up the aisle between the seats, wagging its tail, and the revellers coo over it.

'They were using current news headlines as cover: the threat of new viruses, climate change, the interminable fallout from Brexit, rumbling impeachment stories. When another headline was brewing, they would plot their action. Hidden in plain sight, they tested out their cyber-terrorism, they kidnapped and bribed key journalists, and they lobbied politicians, which is how I was drawn into this sorry and misguided episode. This is a massive conspiracy, and those who were lured into it, like me, are not only frightened to speak out, but must hide from the eyes of the terrorists. They tracked our location using our phones, checking all that we did online. I, like you, abandoned mine at The Pike. It's ironic that we are only a few miles from GCHQ here, where the best brains in the land will be desperately trying to solve the glitch, isn't it?'

A jovial ticket collector appears, sporting flashing Christmas badges which light up his smart uniform. Along with the multitudes around us, we show our tickets.

'I believed in their cause until …'

Her words are lost as a raucous rendition of "We Wish You a Merry Christmas" sings out, the revellers singing with gusto.

'I believed in their cause until my eyes were opened. Then they tortured me, because I refused to cooperate with their requests to put them in touch with our friend, who visited your camp. I had been party to confidential information on the identity of those responsible for the original minor attacks on parliaments; you may not remember. It was before the first glitch.'

'Tortured?'

Unobtrusively, she slides her sleeves up her arm, revealing extensive scarring on the soft, white underside. I recoil, empathising with the pain which she must have experienced. I place my hand on hers, trying to convey an indefinable emotion: admiration, pity and respect.

'So, what do you think will happen next?' I ask again, in a whisper.

The train is slowing, people are rising from their seats, putting on their winter coats, which they had placed in the overhead racks.

'They intend to topple the banks, to topple wealth as we have ever known it. They are hoping to establish a new Year Zero and to level the playing field of life. Investments will have gone up in a puff of smoke. Bank accounts will have already been totally voided, debts written off and overdrafts forgotten. This is not about technology, or mobile phones at all. That is a distraction. It is about enforced redistribution of wealth. *'Blessed are the meek, for they shall inherit the earth.'*

We step down on to the platform, hidden in the scrummage. I would rather be strong and courageous than "meek". The pine trees wave in the gentle breeze, and a murder of crows rises suddenly into the air, alarmed by the cacophony of steam and voices.

Christmas

The blinkered steam enthusiasts emerge from the train towards the exit, and then stand in puzzled huddles, as military jeeps appear, soldiers leaping out, shaking their heads and pointing back down the line. We do not wait to see what transpires. I am nervous, as for a few minutes I lose sight of Miranda, but she reappears, her face showing her age, her mouth tight. We want to appear as inconspicuous as possible, and we now need to leave the odd scene well behind us. We have no desire to travel back down the line.

While attention is focused on the confusion, we take the bit between our teeth and march purposefully in the opposite direction to the throngs of people, through the exit and on to a main road. We take a road bridge across the railway track and dive through a gap in the hedge into the shelter of hedgerows which run around fields of stumpy green winter wheat. Nathan uses the compass and we lose no time, establishing a brisk pace. The cheery whistle of the steam train becomes more and more distant.

Nervous to be travelling in broad daylight, we avoid roads wherever possible and we do not take a break for at least two hours. By midday our track takes us out to the banks of a river. Nathan leads us along a reasonable path on the river bank. The limpid water reflects the heavy clouds, and the tranquillity of the scene raises my spirits, but we feel exposed on the bank, and soon head for a spinney of gnarled trees, where we stop. Eva looks exhausted.

We agree that we could do with a place to rest until we are protected by the darkness, and we nervously approach some isolated buildings nearby. The grand old black and white house is silent, with no cars outside and no lights on. It is protected by burglar alarms, which we guess have not been working since the glitch, but we decide to steer well clear. Disappointed, and about to head on along the track, we pass a small stone building, its iron gate swinging in the wind. I peer inside. The dim light glancing through the high windows reveals a small, simple stone chapel, with two empty rooms separated by a Saxon archway, unadorned and unoccupied.

Consensus is to rest here, and, quietly latching the iron entrance gate behind us, we troop into the inner ancient stone chamber, pulling out our sleeping bags for warmth. The stones underneath us are cold from centuries of damp air. Although out of the wind, it is not the most welcoming of resting places, but seems private and sheltered.

We discuss the distance that we have covered, Gid bemoaning our lack of a vehicle. We agree that, on foot, not only does our progress seems painfully slow, but we are exposed and vulnerable to whoever happens to be out and about. Although the train did help us on our way, we admit that it only benefitted us by a few miles, as we had to double back on foot, away from Cheltenham. The roads are still largely empty, with no domestic vehicles running at all, making the train journey seem even more unreal. Eva asks, 'When will They get cars up and running again, like last time?' We don't know. Nothing is clear to us at all. There are no phones, there is no internet and where we once had access to information and current news, there is a vast black hole.

Nathan and Gid have been talking earnestly in the corner. Gid approaches us to share their thinking, saying, 'We need a vehicle. Eva is right. Walking the whole distance to the camp through the midwinter weather is possible, but not desirable. Now, I know some guys at a place ten miles or so from here as the crow flies, just off the M50. They store old vans and trucks for spares, some of them pre-dating digital systems; there are vehicles from over twenty years ago. If we could pick up one of these, Nathan here thinks that he could get it going. He says that he's good with car engines, and old ones at that. We'd need fuel. I think we should give him a chance at it?'

Nathan nods enthusiastically, explaining, 'We would

travel at night, burn the rubber before everyone else gets their cars fixed.'

So, it is agreed that we will head for Gid's mates under the cover of darkness. Buoyed with a glimmer of hope from this plan, we settle to rest, four of us burying our heads in our sleeping bags, and two of us alert in case of any eventuality, although that seems unlikely out here in such a quiet, dead-end location on Christmas Eve.

I am only half sleeping, resting my aching legs, thinking of Thomas and Maria, and longing to be in my folly. I fix my eyes on the hunched figures of Eva and Gid, huddled together for warmth, taking their turn on lookout, when I see their shapes twitch. I hear something too. Footsteps?

We sit as still and as silent as the ancient stones around us. Then we hear a sharp 'click' followed by the sound of shuffling feet, fading into the distance. I slide out of my sleeping bag, and leap up, following Gid into the outer of the two stone chambers, dreading the worst. My fears are realised as Gid fingers the padlock which now secures the metal grill firmly across the doorway. He calls out, but no one comes.

We frantically scan every wall but find no more possible exits, only ancient arched windows filled with thick old glass, not designed to open, and too high to reach anyway. There is definitely only one door, and we are locked in.

'We are such fucking stupid idiots,' Gid remonstrates.

'Shit,' I add, in the knowledge that we are not only totally incarcerated, but that tomorrow is Christmas Day and we may be stuck in here for some time.

Once we have checked all possible methods of escape to no avail, presuming ourselves safe from predators, we give up on vigilance and we all sleep.

I am troubled by disturbing dreams of Caernef. I arrive back and find the camp in ruins, a malevolent figure similar to Miranda has taken up residence in the cottage and there is no sign of my friends. The shrill calls of seabirds get louder and louder until my head feels as if it will burst. I drag myself back into consciousness and face the reality that I am trapped in a silent stone dungeon with no key to the lock, over a hundred miles from my folly. I sigh. Eva, who isn't asleep either, reaches across to me and strokes my arm. 'Try not to worry,' she whispers. I wriggle nearer to her and we lie silently together, waiting for the dawn.

We spend Christmas morning in surprisingly good spirits, lighting a fire for warmth, and setting up a makeshift dining room on the wooden benches which line the walls. We feast on hot tinned meatballs with spaghetti in tomato sauce, from the random tins of food which Nathan had scavenged only just over a day ago. Miranda announces that she is a vegetarian, and only eats the spaghetti. 'It's not the time for namby-pamby middle-class habits,' mumbles Gid, I think ungraciously.

Eva serves up steaming tinned rice pudding, and we pass round the two bottles of beer which Nathan had stashed in his rucksack. While we are sharing stories to pass the time, Miranda visits the toilet area which we have set up in the far corner of the other room. She returns, looking restless, then wanders back over to the doorway again and again. She asks for Nathan's strong torch and calls me over.

'We need to get moving. I think I can pick this. You hold the torch steady. That's it.' She fiddles and pokes with a piece of wire, starting again on several occasions. Her patience is formidable. She doesn't give up, grimacing as she concentrates. Eventually there is a satisfying "click", and the padlock drops off the catch. The iron door swings open and we cheer with immense relief.

Gid is the first to come across to shake Miranda's hand. She has earned her place in the company tonight. With relief, we tidy the rooms which have been our makeshift home, removing any evidence of our presence, bundling up rubbish for disposal en-route and loading our rucksacks ready to leave. Eva grits her teeth and takes the containers that have been used for toileting outside. Coming back empty-handed, she asks if anyone has wipes so that she can clean her hands.

We escape the ancient ecclesiastical prison at dusk on Christmas Day and head hopefully for Gid's friends.

Christmas Night

We appreciate our freedom all the more for having been inadvertently imprisoned, and we stride with renewed energy under the weak moonlight, making quick progress. There are very few habitations out here by the river, but after half an hour of trekking along the dark river bank, we approach a riverside pub, with static caravans and boats moored rather too close to our route for comfort. On hearing voices, we cut quickly inland and loop round the sprawling habitation. Nathan makes his way back through the group to speak with me while we continue moving forwards along the river bank.

'Robin, we are going to have to cross this river at some point. I know one way, a road bridge alongside another pub. In about twenty minutes, we need to climb the bank in pairs and cross quietly, like we did back near the toll, but this time it is much earlier in the evening. We will have to be vigilant.'

'Come on. It's a pub. Let's go in and rest,' urges Gid. Eva looks hopefully at me as she is clearly struggling with the pace.

'But …' I am reluctant to delay.

'It is tempting, but we must press on. We really don't want to lose time, and heaven knows who might be holed up inside,' Nathan urges.

Gid reluctantly agrees. Relieved, as we really are too tired for disagreements, I am decisive, 'Okay, same pairs. Hoot again once the way is clear.'

'Yes, that worked well before.' Gid mumbles, his head down.

We press on to the bridge and cross successfully. We want to reach Gid's friends before they turn in for the night, and so do not stop even to rest. The thought of a vehicle is attractive and I am really hoping that this plan works out.

After another couple of hours walking as fast as our legs allow, we find ourselves stumbling down to the side of the silent motorway. So many times, over the years, I have longed for the incessant noise of traffic to cease, but not like this, not as a result of mankind being emasculated by extremists. Despite my weary limbs, anger simmers in my veins. Distracted by the journey, and by my new companions, I have forgotten how desperately I want to beat the terrorists. I want to beat them at their own game.

Several hundred metres along the hard shoulder, Gid spots the motorway exit which he says he recognises, but before we can climb the bank up to the road, we are startled by a distant sound of engines, a low growl heading rapidly towards us, grinding on the tarmac of the motorway. We step back from the barrier, under the mass of bare branches silhouetted against the dark clouds. A huge swarm of powerful motorbikes surges into view with a deafening roar. For a moment I think that they are slowing for us, but their black helmets point forwards, and with a squeal of brakes, they swerve as a pack, racing up the slip road. Four bikers remain on the motorway. They rev their engines, performing loops and arcs, their headlights sending swirling beams of light across our faces. We are frozen. They play some more, and then, with a squeal, disappear far into the distance, leaving the air ringing, exhaust fumes filtering through the trees.

'What a terrible din, and how frightening,' Eva whispers, but Miranda, Nathan and Gid disagree. Their eyes are like saucers, as they crave control of such powerful machines, in their eyes magnificent. We pace up the bank in a reflective mood. It is as if the enforced curfew shrouding us since this latest glitch, has been lifted.

'Time to accelerate our progress, I reckon. Heaven knows who will be out on the roads once vehicles are back up and running,' I observe, encouraging Gid to hurry and to report back to us as soon as possible. We shelter out of the wind in the trees, not wishing to reveal ourselves up on the road, where a silent depot, Gid says for road grit, sits on the bank.

Gid lopes off into the distance with Nathan, and we settle down to wait. The blisters on both of my feet scream when we stop, and despite the cold, I loosen my boots. The pine needles are soft and fragrant, reminding me of the railway station at Caernef. Eva huddles up with the child-like enthusiasm of a little girl, asking me to tell her a story while we wait, like I used to when we were trying to sleep in her small attic in Oxford. Miranda shuffles into the huddle. We are an odd collection of human beings in a strange situation. Miranda wants to hear more about the camp, but I resist the temptation to tell them about the night of the helicopters, being careful to keep that to myself. Instead I recount a tale of two brave refugees making their way across Europe to the little cottage which I had hoped to have for my own. I don't tell the story as well as Maria; my voice is not as soft and passionate as hers, but they aren't to know, and it passes the time while we wait.

Just as my narrative transports us to the estuary off Caernef, to catch fish, we hear the crackling of twigs, and tense our muscles, relaxing when Nathan comes into view, alone.

'They are tricky customers,' he tells us, 'but they could come up with the goods. Gid is trying to get a Honda Acty pickup started. Arriving on Christmas Day without any alcohol to give them, perhaps wasn't the best of timing. They want cash, which we haven't got, so I have come to see what we can put together for them. Any ideas?'

We root through our rucksacks, but only come up with a ridiculously small amount of cash and a pathetic collection of items without much value at all. I am stumped.

'Tell me about these people,' Miranda asks, speaking softly from the shade under the pine branches.

'There are several families together for Christmas around a big wood burner. They have loads of food, and booze, but are not going to share that. Someone is playing a piano. Two guys came out with us; one seems to be in charge. The other is his son, I think. They have been drinking. I didn't see much else.'

Miranda rises, taking her shoulder bag from her rucksack and tightening her cloak around her. 'Take me to them; it's worth a try,' she says, winking at me.

I go to stop her, not fully understanding her motives, but Eva puts her hand on my arm, saying 'Let her go Robin, there's no harm.'

Nathan and Miranda disappear into the distance.

'No harm? Are you mad?' But my friend calms me down, saying that Miranda has volunteered to go and to try, whatever trickery she chooses.

'But …'

'But nothing. Are you honestly saying that you trust that woman?'

Eva is uncharacteristically critical, 'Robin, she is devious. Don't you let her take you in. I wouldn't be at all surprised if she has been planted in our company by someone wishing to cause you harm.'

I sit moodily and reflect. What have Eva and Gid noticed about Miranda that I have overlooked in my desire to court her approval? I think back to the nightmare which troubled me when we were locked in the chapel. Maybe my subconscious was telling me to be wary of the inscrutable woman who appeared in my dream as the devil incarnate.

Our wait under the pine trees seems interminable. I cannot help feeling anxious for Miranda, fearing that she is risking some act of foolish bravado just to get us on our way. I divert my attention by gently rifling through her rucksack, but find nothing to incriminate her. We hear a distant engine sputtering, stopping, and starting up again.

Eventually Nathan trots back down the small escarpment, through the bare trees. We peer into the darkness, desperately trying to read his face before he reaches us.

'We're in business. Miranda has swung a deal. The old Honda pickup was used for local deliveries until a year or so ago. It still runs,' he calls out, beckoning. We heave our rucksacks on to our backs. I lug Miranda's, and we climb up the bank on to the road bridge above the motorway. The high-pitched sputtering of an engine fills the air, alarmingly loud on such a lonely night. Nathan leads us to the pickup, rattling and shaking on the forecourt of a large scruffy house. The back of the pickup is open with low sides and is covered by an old-style oil-cloth tarpaulin, seemingly inhabited by all the spiders and creepy crawlies from miles around. We load the baggage on to the back and work out that three of us can fit into the cab, and two of us can squash together under the tarpaulin.

We stand on the forecourt, anxiously waiting for Miranda to reappear, while the engine turns over. Nathan checks the bodywork with his torch. He pulls at the rubber seals, hanging off like strings, and inspects each tyre. 'Tyres okay,' he says. He gets Eva to flick the lights on and off, checking each one. Although the headlights produce a steady beam, the back lights are clearly broken. 'Come on Miranda, I don't dare turn her off.' He sounds as anxious as I feel.

Eventually, in the murky shade at the side of the building, I spot Miranda with the outline of a man, exiting the house by a back door. They stand closely together, staying in the shadows. I see him roughly bob forwards towards her. He tries to pull her back, but she slithers from his grasp and runs towards the sound of the engine.

'Don't ask, let's go. Quick,' she says to the assembled audience, with a strange glint in her eye. She climbs on to the back of the truck and settles down in the far corner along with Nathan, while Gid revs the engine. Eva and I climb with relief into the cab.

OCCUPATION

Later Christmas Night

Gid has decided to take the A-roads for speed, under the cover of darkness, and has my map book perched on top of the grimy dashboard. Nathan will knock on the back window of the cab if the passengers in the back of the pickup need to stop. We plan to swap over halfway. It is cold and damp in the cab, but must be unbearable in the back of the truck. Despite the engine running well, we are all anxious. The wipers don't work at all, so if it rains, we will be in difficulty. We eat up the miles, sitting in silence. I doze, hardly daring to believe that by morning, we could reach the camp. It is barely five days since I left the folly, in such good spirits, with no inkling of the chaos which lay ahead.

Losing myself in my thoughts, diverting my brain away from my aching limbs, I run through the challenges which are facing us. From Miranda's accounts, I deduce that an international far-left cell of cyber terrorists exists, and that certain unknown individuals are determined to be the authors of a new human era. They seem to have attacked the cyberspace which we take for granted, knocking out all digital capacity and sending some sort of pulse or signal through the mobile phone networks. This, I deduce from Miranda's hints, is only a smokescreen, setting the millions of everyday citizens into uproar. What we are not seeing due to the lack of any news coverage, is the repeat of the untold damage and disruption which was experienced after the first glitch. While we are bumping along in this old pickup, medical services will be immobilised, the most vulnerable in our society will be in dire straits, certainly suffering the most. Especially since the pandemic, I am not confident in the effectiveness of the business continuity plans in the Health Service, or in councils for that matter. I certainly spent two weeks, coughing and self-isolating in my tiny flat and no one counted me in the statistics or offered any assistance. The first glitch, which came hot on the heels of the demise of the pandemic, was generally seen as a one-off, and what with the turbulence in the Government, even I can see that systems are not at all robust. We were not ready for the scale of attack which we are now experiencing, and the power grids have not held up at all this time. I could have foreseen this failure of supply, as I kept saying that there are far too many contracts, sub-contracts and "switches" for our own good.

We can see that most means of transport are temporarily inoperable. Hopefully people are working on restoring essential services. I think back to our experience on the steam train. Perhaps it is laudable to provide Christmas cheer for the traumatised, but I can't help wondering why there hasn't been a coordinated effort to get things back up and running this time. The image of hopeful but baffled revellers disembarking to find the military turning them back, resurfaces in my mind.

Maybe there is even more disruption which we are not seeing? Without any social media, and with no broadcasting, we are completely in the dark. We simply don't know. Sadly, the immediate chaos has prompted greed and violence rather than a concerted and united effort to combat the cyber bullies and to get things back up and running. I am ashamed rather than frightened, and I want to act, but am not sure how. I cannot help thinking that heading for the camp is the coward's way. I crave its security, safety and the solitude which the peaceful headland offers. I just want some quiet normality, but without supplies of food, life at the camp will be tough. Very tough.

I hold my head in my hands, trying to make sense of it all. Eva, who has been lost in her own thoughts as we hurtle along the empty roads, takes my hand and asks if I have a headache. I tell her that everything aches, and most of all my brain. I am trying to make sense of everything, but failing miserably. Ever practical, she offers me some paracetamol, which she has squirrelled away, handing me a half-empty bottle of water. It is a kind gesture, and I accept gratefully, swallowing the two white tablets as if they will solve all my problems. Gradually the sharp aching in my limbs softens, and I close my eyes.

They wake me at the halfway stop. We are well-into Wales, where an intermittent drizzle is soaking everything, including the windscreen. I stagger out of the cab and dive straight under the tarpaulin, while Miranda, who seems to be avoiding me, climbs into the cab, and Nathan takes his turn at the wheel, operating one wiper manually before starting up. Gid, a mountain of muscle, squeezes reluctantly beside Miranda in the cab, his turn at the wheel complete. Eva is, at least, well cushioned. She disappears into her sleeping bag under the tarpaulin. We set off. I settle in a lying position, grabbing the side of the pickup to steady myself. Peering out, I see that the drizzle has stopped. Nathan is a surprisingly fast and smooth driver, which goes some way to offset the damp chill. The pounding of the boards in my back, the incessant roar of wheels on road and the acrid smell of the exhaust combine to disgust me. I think that I could manage this for a short distance, but the thought of hours in this hell freaks me out. I suppose it is better than walking, and think again of Thomas and Maria crossing the border in the carpenter's truck. I watch the shiny black road disappear behind us, as we pass the occasional glow of candles in windows in remote villages and farms, on this bizarre Christmas night.

It is a thoroughly unpleasant few hours tempered only by the satisfaction of seeing the miles stretch out behind us. I have directed Nathan to The Prince of Wales. I want to approach the camp alone in the morning, to prepare Glyn, Thomas and Maria for the arrival of this motley but brave group of strangers.

After several more hours on the road, as agreed, Nathan pulls to a stop just up the road from the pub. The noise of our engine blasts through the tiny village and we see curtains twitching and anxious faces peering out at us. We sit silently, our engine and our lights off, until we are confident that the inhabitants have gone back to their beds.

Eva looks all in. She is either sleeping or feigning sleep, her eyes screwed up tightly. Using my small torch to guide me, I climb over the side of the back of the truck. I rap on the glass of the cab and as Nathan is sitting nearest the door, we agree that he will accompany me to The Prince of Wales.

'Do you know the publican well?' he asks me.

I whisper that I have met him a few times, but cannot remember his name, and we approach the pub, which is in darkness except for one emergency exit sign shining green through the night. The incongruous board advertising ice creams is still standing on the forecourt. We hammer on the front door. The hollow booming of our knocking echoes, and the lights in the windows of a handful of buildings in the street below us flick on. We knock again, and this time hear sounds inside.

To his credit, the publican, having grabbed his dressing gown and stuffed his feet into slippers, does not complain. He stands half asleep and bewildered on the step.

'Hi, it's Robin, Robin from the camp at Caernef …'

'Robin, bloody hell, what are you doing up here; is there a problem at the camp?'

'No, at least, I don't think so. We haven't come from the camp. We have travelled from Oxford. I was stranded there. I want to go to the camp in the morning. We need shelter for the rest of tonight. Please.'

'Shelter, of course. Come on in. There's no electric. It's another glitch I'm afraid. Was it the same in Oxford?'

'Yes. Chaos. There are three more of us. We travelled

together. This is Nathan Price.'

'Three more,' he mutters, shaking Nathan's hand, saying, 'Price is a good Welsh name. I am Rhys,' He ushers Nathan indoors while I fetch the others. I realize that I had not known his name before; he had simply been "the publican at The Prince of Wales." Glyn called him "barman". He says that he hasn't seen Glyn, or his family, since the glitch a few days ago, and is assuming that they are staying at the camp over Christmas, like the old days.

Soon we are all lined up along the bar, which carries the debris of a Christmas gathering earlier in the day. Miranda has come to life; she collects clean glasses and organises a strong drink for each of us. The Publican, Rhys, locks the front door and leads us to two small upstairs rooms, which were once used for bed and breakfast, but have long been mothballed. There are two king-size beds between the five of us, and a small bathroom down the corridor. Warmed by the alcohol, and immensely relieved to be so close to our destination, we grab what bedding we can find, and crash out.

I wake with a very thick head, the daylight hurting my eyes, and realising where I am, stagger to the bathroom, where I attempt to wake myself with cold water. It is late and has been light for a couple of hours. Rhys is tidying the bar, and as I appear, he provides me with a steaming black coffee, apologising that there is no milk. We compare our experiences of this glitch. He has had no contact with anyone from the camp, but comments that it is the place to be after a glitch as it is pretty well self-sufficient. I had genuinely forgotten how much we have achieved there, and as the coffee penetrates, I start to feel more human. Over the next half hour my weary companions emerge, and Rhys calmly produces more coffee along with seemingly endless anecdotes. There is a geniality in the bar, a normality, which seems to relax my companions, and we entertain Rhys with accounts of our journey. I am so eager to see the camp again that I forget my aches and pains. I had hoped to be on my way much earlier.

Gid scans the room, peering over his coffee cup, 'Has anyone seen that snake Miranda?' We check upstairs. We check the bathroom, the bedrooms, even the pickup out in the street. Mercifully she hasn't taken that, but we have no doubt that Miranda has disappeared.

Boxing Day

I decide to take Gid with me to Caernef this first time. We plan to find Thomas and Maria, to check that all is okay, and to arrange where Gid, Eva and Nathan can stay. At the camp, there are backup supplies of power and water, with a small generator and the stream, which flows through the pipes at the back of one of the dormitories. There will be ample stores of vegetables, and of course eggs from the chickens, although they may not be laying at this time of year.

While Gid and I go to Caernef, Eva and Nathan offer to help Rhys get the bar scrubbed and shipshape. It seems that most of the village spent Christmas Day here in candlelight. Miranda has indeed disappeared. Unsettled, we agree to be vigilant. What is she up to?

It takes a great deal of persuasion to get the trusty Honda pickup to start, and we are low on fuel. In the light of day, we can see that it is a rusted wreck. Heaven knows how we managed to travel all the way across Wales in it. We attract much unwanted attention, as villagers come out to see what the commotion is. Eva tries to put their minds at rest by beaming and waving us off. Eventually, and with the help of a bump start, we head off down the familiar road to the camp. I glance back and see Eva chatting with the people in the street. Our spirits are high as we are now so close to our ultimate destination.

I direct Gid, and he drives the rusty old truck up the road which is so familiar to me, turning into the wooded area, and up to the gateway to the camp. The wheels grind on the muddy gravel, and the engine sputters as we enter the car park. I want to show the camp off to Gid, but I fear that something is not right. The camp feels odd. As I peer out through the windscreen, I can see the woodpile is soaked, the tarpaulin having blown loose. Thomas would never have let that happen. Perhaps they have gone somewhere else because of the glitch.

'Gid, what is that over there? Behind the dining hall, I can see black shapes in the shadows. Gid takes it all in, choosing not to get out of the truck until I lead the way. He turns to me with a quizzical look on his face.

'Robin, do Thomas and Maria have motorbikes?' he asks, as our engine idles.

There is just time for me to shout 'Watch out ...' before they are upon us. The noise of our vehicle could not have announced our arrival more emphatically, and we have been seen. Four or five armed and helmeted troops run up the rise and surround the truck, pointing their guns at us.

Instead of surrendering, or entering into conversation with them, Gid shoves me down into the footwell, slams his boot on the accelerator and skids into a complete turn. His actions catch them by surprise and for some reason they hesitate before shooting, allowing us to clear the trees on the rise. We hear a weak spatter of gunfire once we are through the gate and out on to the open lane.

'Well Robin, this is turning out to be quite a trip!' His measured voice helps me to gather my senses, my heart pounding in panic and my whole body shaking in fear, which I attempt unsuccessfully to conceal. 'For some reason they want us alive,' Gid comments with ridiculous calmness, as I sit up and direct him along the lanes to a quiet spot where I used to walk, from which you can access the camp along the coast.

'Not much diesel left. We need to stop.'

I direct him to the right into a farm gateway. There is no way to conceal the truck, if they are following us, so we bale out and run. Gid prompts me, 'Speed and stay focused;

you know this place. Where do we go?'

Realising that he is now totally dependent upon my navigation, and with my feet back on the familiar terrain surrounding the camp, something clicks in my brain, and I take the lead with confidence, providing clear directions as we run. I strike out along a narrow path which I have used on many occasions. We emerge on to the headland which runs parallel to the cliffs of Caernef. We dive down the rough path. Our pace slows due to loose boulders and the steep gradient. Instinctively, we stop briefly and listen, but can only hear the roar of the breakers below us. There is no sound of pursuers.

I am nimble on these small paths, and it is Gid who is finding his feet. I set an ambitious pace, eager to impress the courageous giant stumbling in my wake. I reflect that, only four days ago, I made an excellent choice. I knew, when I saw him wielding the axe, creating his huge mountain of firewood, that he would be an asset.

Unwilling to descend to the level of the waves, realising that the tide is high, I take us along a precarious path that leads to the folly. The very thought of the folly sends my heart into spasms. We release a shower of scree, which tumbles down the rock face and we freeze, fearing that we have given away our location, but all is quiet.

If there was a boat out on the water, which there isn't, we would appear as two tiny figures scurrying for our lives across the rock face. I know that we are only a hundred metres from the folly now. We are slightly below the promontory upon which it proudly stands, and we cling to rocky handholds as we hoist ourselves up on to a short platform of rock with an overhang protecting us from above. I used to sit here watching the estuary birds through my binoculars.

Gid smiles and gives me a thumbs up. He doesn't seem to be at all worried by the turn of events, saying, 'I wish I had a phone; I would have filmed this ...,' he whispers. We squat on the rocks and listen, but can hear no sound of humans. I finger the key to the door of the folly which has been safe in the pocket of my jeans throughout this whole escapade. Touching Gid's knee, I point, as the curlew peacefully dabs its long beak into the surf. 'What is it?' he whispers, and as if on cue, the serene bird produces its unmistakable warbling call, the evocative signature of the headland.

'The world of humans may fall apart, but the curlew still fishes at Caernef.'

Surely nothing can stop us now. 'Gid, I am going to crawl up on to the cliff alone. I want to see if they, whoever they are, have occupied the folly or not. With any luck they will only be in the camp, and we can …'

I never cry. It was instilled into me as a very young child, and I am proud of my dry eyes, even if I can't on occasions control my temper, but now, at the thought of unlocking the door of the folly, I feel tears welling, and I blink them away. 'If the folly is undisturbed, I will come back for you. If I don't return after twenty minutes, go and get help.' I can see that the prospect of clambering all the way back to the road, remembering the route alone, causes him slight anxiety, but he nods, still grinning. He seems to feed off the excitement. With his help, I hoist myself up, over the lip of the hollow and on to the mat of sea thrift. I can see the folly now, and crawl slowly towards it. Sheltered by a clump of gorse, I scrutinise the view, my whole being alert for noises, for clues.

I can tell that the folly is untouched. I tiptoe unobtrusively up to the door and turn the key. I quickly check that each room is exactly as I left it before I departed for Oxford, and allow myself a few minutes. It is my first solitude since the night in the lockup, and my march out to The Pike. At last, time to think. But I must be quick!

As the breakers roar at the foot of the cliff, and the wind buffets my proud little tower, I run through all that has happened. I knew all along that Miranda was not to be trusted. She wanted something from me, and still does. I wouldn't be surprised if we discover that the band of vigilantes who jumped us just now is connected with her. It has something to do with the Minister's secret visit to the camp. She said that she knew Marcella, the cyber-security expert. Maybe she simply knew of Marcella. Miranda also knew about the volume of *Anna Karenina* on Reginald's bookshelf; perhaps she wasn't trusted by Reginald after all, perhaps she spied on him, or worked with someone who did?

I remember Gid, and hasten back down the stairs, sidling out of the door, latching it as quietly as I can, turning the key, just in case. Running to the cliff edge, I keep low, now lying on my stomach, peering down. Gid is smoking a cigarette, his gold earring is glinting in the weak sunlight. He is watching the curlew, and on hearing me, looks up. 'All clear,' I whisper. He offers me his cigarette, and I hold the glowing stub, battling with desire to take one long, slow drag, wanting to appear tough in his eyes, but knowing that I have conquered that challenge once already. I close my eyes and inhale the smoke without putting the cigarette end to my lips, and hand it back to Gid once he has launched himself up on to the thrift. He takes a final draw, scuffs the end under his boot, and follows me to the folly, where I unlock the door, and we disappear inside.

Later Boxing Day

Gid seems enormous in the folly. In the emotion of the moment, he wraps his arms around me in an exuberant and spontaneous hug. I smell the smoke on his coat, and he pats me on the back. Two survivors.

'Letting go of me, he asks, 'Robin, who are those soldiers and why are they there?'

'Do you think that Miranda …?'

'Yes, I do. We need to find out how many of them there are here. They seem heavily armed, and look dangerous,' he says, unnecessarily.

'Did you notice that they deliberately didn't shoot us. They want us alive. Why?'

'I have no idea, Gid, no idea, but I am nervous ...' Ecstatic to have my familiar belongings around me again, despite the tenuous circumstances, I make coffee, and produce a tin of biscuits, the ones I usually offer little Poppy. 'God, what about Poppy, Thomas and Maria, and Glyn. Where are they? Are they taken prisoner or in hiding? What has happened here Gid?'

Gid doesn't know. He swigs his coffee and devours several biscuits. I slide an old wine cork on to the tip of a small, sharp vegetable knife, and place it carefully into my boot, handing him a broader knife, which I use for bread. He slides it into the long leg pocket of his trousers. I hope that we do not need to use them. I have always been proud of my mettle, but have never physically harmed anyone, not even when Steve drove me to the depths of anger.

We load up with supplies. 'Robin, you know this headland like the back of your hand. Would you be comfortable heading off alone now, checking out the cottage and the camp, while I wait here? You will be able to blend into the landscape better than me. Don't take long, and don't get involved. Just check things out and get back to me as quickly as you can. Then we can plan. I think we will need to return to The Prince of Wales somehow for re-enforcements.'

My fury at Miranda is welling up, but I must remain calm. 'Yes, good plan.' Even I find myself hankering after a phone. Mine will be out of battery in a crate at The Pike. Instead, from my desk drawer, I take the small binoculars which I use for birdwatching and my camera. I leave Gid to discover the pleasures of the folly, and I head off, cautiously.

Treading softly, I skirt the wood, staying under the cover of the trees. I can see the cottage through the branches. Two armed soldiers are guarding the door. I continue silently up the rise until I have a good view of the parade ground. Initially all seems quiet, but then I spot three people sitting inside one of the dormitories. They are not looking towards the wood, and are completely unaware of me. I peer through the binoculars.

There is Miranda, arguing with two men, shaking her head. I recognise her instantly, raise my camera, and as if photographing birds, zoom as far in as I can, focus, and click the camera shutter. Time to return to Gid.

I admit to a pang of jealousy when I see Gid's face at the upper window. That window seat is mine, and mine only, but I forgive him as he descends the stairs ready to leave, asking, 'Well?'

'I saw Miranda; look.' I show him the photograph. 'That bitch is in one of the dormitories with two men. I couldn't see any more there. Two soldiers are guarding the door of the cottage. There cannot be more than five of them in total, though I might be wrong.'

'Time we went for re-enforcements then.'

I grab a box of painkillers, and some chocolate, shoving them into my pocket, lock the door of the folly and this time lead the way down towards the shore, intending to take the most direct route possible to reach The Prince of Wales on foot. It will be quicker than using the truck, which is running on fumes. I know that we will be walking for an hour or more, but that is easy compared with our recent route marches. Once in the height of summer, and in high spirits due to the resurrection of the camp, Glyn, Thomas, Maria and I, and of course Poppy, took this route, stopping to eat a picnic in the glorious sunshine. On that day, we were totally oblivious of the impending challenges, and certainly never imagined that our beloved camp would be ambushed, that the streets of Oxford, indeed the streets of all the towns in the land, would have succumbed to a simmering public anger resulting in nights of fear, riots of daily violence, and a complete lack of law and order.

'We are in a hell of a mess,' I observe.

We break into a jog, keen to cover the two miles as quickly as possible, but I develop a stitch, so we slow a little.

I ask Gid what he thinks Miranda is up to, and he provides a staccato commentary as we pass bare orchards, heaps of unwanted rotting apples, skirting hedgerows, watched by the odd group of scavenging seagulls.

'That woman is dishonest.'

'I realise that now.'

'She is obviously in with a crowd of fucking bastards who think they can change the world by evil means.'

'Mmm.'

'Eva says that she was a politician and that she resigned.'

'But at that time loads of them were resigning. Looking back, I'm not sure that she did anything courageous or principled.'

'She is hard bitten that one, brazen, tough, but dishonest.'

'She said that she was involved with a far-left group masquerading as far right, and that the glitch was all about redistribution of wealth.'

'Do you believe that?'

'I'm not sure. I'm not sure of much just now.'

Gid stops to catch his breath, and we stand by a slimy green stile. Before we climb over, he says to me,

'Robin, I knew about you before you saw me there at The Pike,'

'Oh?'

'You used to come to The Pike on and off, didn't you? A guy I knew pointed you out. He called you "The Lady of the Lamp" because he saw you, after dark, alone and muffled up and giving out stuff to the street people. Never frightened. Always generous. He thought a lot of you.'

'Blimey, that was a while ago now.'

'People don't forget these things.'

INQUISITION

Afternoon

With immense relief, Gid and I reach The Prince of Wales in time for a late lunch of hot leftovers, concocted by Eva. We take Rhys, the barman, into our confidence, and of course Eva and Nathan, describing what we found at the camp. Rhys is devastated. He cannot believe that such things are happening out here in this quiet wilderness. Had I not appeared with the estate agent that afternoon, Caernef would probably still be a forgotten backwater... a forgotten backwater with a derelict camp decaying on the clifftop. I am painfully aware that I have brought trouble to the place which I hold in such high esteem, the place which I now call home.

We are all seriously concerned about Thomas, Maria and Poppy. They were spending Christmas together at the camp and must have become engulfed by the dangerous idiocy of Miranda's armed renegades. And Glyn, where is he and is he okay? Swept along by our enthusiasm to rebuild the camp through the last year, I haven't paused to consider my feelings for Glyn, but right now, with his life possibly in danger because of my actions, I am confronted by a complex mix of intense friendship and the sort of deep love that you might feel for a close brother. At the start, and very briefly, he was my enemy, but he quickly became my fellow conspirator.

The urgency of the situation hits us. Rhys can access diesel for the pickup as he knows a farmer, on the edge of the village, whose old Massey Ferguson is up and running.

He will walk down there with Nathan and Gid, and they will hitch a ride on the tractor. They will get our old truck running and then will return to the pub by a circuitous route, avoiding the camp.

While they are gone, bowed with anxiety, Eva and I clear up the debris of lunch, and then occupy the snug, off the bar, with a large pot of tea, and loads of sugar. We sit close to the radiator, hungry for warmth after several chill days on the road.

'I was thinking about my flat,' Eva laments. 'It was totally wrecked. Thank goodness I was renting. But all my stuff. It's heart breaking.'

'Once things have settled down, we will go back. What will you miss most?'

'My photos, my pieces of art, and my personal things, silly small things like jewellery, clothes, books. The things that made me who I am. I'm sort of lost without them.'

'I know that feeling of being lost. It's as if the usual world has been flipped upside down and everything is scattered around. Let's focus on what really matters. What really makes you "you": your generosity, your good cheer, your knack of turning a disappointment into a hope. That's what matters, especially at the moment.'

Eva smiles, and pours more tea. We settle into one of our comfortable philosophical debates. She, as always, champions human kindness, and I gently remind her of the evils of the world. I remember the chocolate that I grabbed from the folly, and produce it with a flourish. Eva loves chocolate and it cheers her up. It feels good to give *her* something nice for a change.

'Robin, what do you think will happen now?'

'We will finish the chocolate, Gid and Nathan will get the pickup running, and we will all return to the camp, overcome the soldiers with our makeshift weapons, bury their bodies on the clifftop and live happily ever after.'

She laughs nervously, not sure whether to take me seriously, 'There's no way we can overcome armed men …'

'No, but we will have to trick them somehow. Maybe Miranda will help us?'

'Dream on!'

At this moment we hear an engine, not the pickup, but a tractor. It draws up outside and Rhys hops out, lifting several large sacks of vegetables, stacking them on the road, then dragging them to the door of the pub. We help Rhys carry the booty into the large larder while the old tractor disappears down the road.

'These are for the villagers. I will put up a sign, and we will cook a vat of fresh soup. Your friends will be back soon; all went to plan.'

With the pickup refuelled, and now outside the front door of the pub, the four of us, Eva, Gid, Nathan and I, plan our next move. We are realistic enough to know that we cannot overpower the soldiers, or easily outwit Miranda, and we decide to take a more conciliatory approach, that is if the soldiers do not seek us out first. This feels shrewd to me and stands a better chance of success. We nervously fill a generous hamper, containing spirits, wine, and a selection of food items which Rhys can spare: packets of crisps, nuts, jars of olives and gherkins, and the piece de resistance, an enormous tub of home-made gingerbread, which a villager had donated on Christmas Day and which had become hidden at the back of the kitchen. I have a quiet word with Rhys, writing him an IOU. I can pay him cash once I am back in residence at the folly, where I have secretly hoarded my savings, in the box in the roof. Thank goodness I didn't rely upon the fancy investment accounts pedalled by the financial advisor.

Although our gut feeling tells us to stick together as a group, we agree that one of us must stay at The Prince of Wales, as backup, in case a rescue operation is needed. Nathan volunteers, saying that he is quick on his feet and can run the couple of miles between the pub and the camp if needed. We long for working phones, or at least some means of communication. How did human beings manage in years gone by? Messengers on horseback and Morse code come to mind. I think ahead; if this situation lasts for a long time, we must get horses at the camp.

Gid tries turning his phone on, for the hundredth time, but the excruciating noise starts up and he has to switch it off immediately.

We agree that we will drive up into the car park at the camp, and offer an olive branch to the gang there, share the booze and the food and find out more about them. After all, they did seem to be firing to scare rather than to actually hit us. Nathan will make his way down in the morning to check the state of affairs.

It is mid-afternoon by the time we set off, hopeful, but more nervous than we are admitting, with the full bottles of booze clinking in the back of the pickup.

Late Afternoon

There are two armed guards waiting at the gateway to the camp. This time we do not overreact. They bar our way. I hop down from the truck and walk up to them with a swagger, confident but not cocky.

'Hi, I'm Robin. These are my friends Gid and Eva. We know Miranda. We have brought you supplies: spirits, wine, food.' I gesture towards the back of the truck, adding, 'We have no guns, and come in peace.'

The damp winter air hangs in the trees and the cawing of rooks echoes in the bare branches. The two men, for I can now see they are not proper soldiers, whisper together. The taller one bends down to his bag, taking out two plastic cable ties. He checks me for weapons, but is not thorough and the small vegetable knife remains hidden in my boot. His voice is kinder than I am expecting. He tells me that he is called Anton and apologises for tying my hands. He snaps the cable ties into place, tight enough to prevent me from slipping my wrists out, and leads me up the drive.

The shorter man waves the truck through the gate, while

I seethe inside, incensed that these imposters have the audacity to control access to my property. I work hard at remaining calm. We reassemble near the parade ground. Anton holds me at a distance. The other guy uses his gun to control Eva and Gid's movements. They unload the boxes from the truck and carry them across the parade ground into the dormitory where I saw Miranda through my binoculars. The shorter man manhandles Gid out of the cab, removes the bread knife from his trouser pocket, uttering an expletive, turns off the engine of the pickup, pockets the key and checks our cargo. He then ties Eva and Gid's hands behind their backs. Eva looks distraught. Gid takes it all in his stride, joking with them, no doubt trying to put Eva at ease.

They lead the three of us into the dormitory, which feels cold and damp. They shout through the open door for Miranda. She arrives with a third man. He has a cruel look about him. On seeing us, he scowls, but once he sees the gifts which we have brought, he rifles through the boxes avariciously. So, there are three men and Miranda, and presumably at least one more man down at the cottage.

They play their game well, ignoring us and talking in a huddle, making us sweat. Gid smiles at Eva and I, making faces, raising his eyebrows. I frown at him. No point in taking risks or antagonising them. I can feel the vegetable knife pressing against my ankle. Miranda is avoiding making any eye contact with us.

They have pushed back the furniture in the dormitory and are using the large wooden table, which is strewn with papers and phones. Phones? The surly man looks again into the crates of food and drink which we have brought and gestures for Anton to unload. They seem hungry and attack the odd selection of items, devouring the strange collection of offerings and pouring one of the stronger spirits into the plastic cups which the children use for squash. Miranda doesn't drink. I know her by now; she prefers to keep her head completely clear and to rely on her natural bravado.

I am desperate to know whether Thomas, Maria and Poppy are in the cottage, and Glyn, where is he? For a while, Miranda's gang ignores us completely, and we sit obediently, our hands bound. This provides an opportunity to study our captors. They are dressed for the circumstances, in strong protective clothing and black boots. The men are unshaven. Miranda looks different now. She has shed her cloaks and scarves and just wears black jeans with a thick black jumper. They all wear fingerless gloves, reminding me of my delivery days. They actually seem less organised than I expected.

When they have eaten their fill, with the debris still littering the table, and the smell of crisps and pickles in the air, the sour-faced man addresses us. He assumes the role of leader, 'We work for a movement called "Redistribution". This is not about us as individuals, but it is about ensuring a fair and equitable future for the human race. We will not harm you if you cooperate. There is one piece of information which we need from you, Robin.'

Anton drags me towards a chair placed directly across the table from the leader. I sit, and look into his face, feigning patience, awaiting instructions. I am not one to jabber on, and usually find that silence can be more powerful than chatter, but the tension in the air between us is palpable.

All eyes are on me. I wait, weighing up our captors, deciding whether I will cooperate. At this instant, a phone lying on the table buzzes. The leader glances at it, picks it up and taps on the keys. There is no shrill blast. Gid cannot resist saying, 'Good God, that phone is okay. How do you do that?' They totally ignore him, instead focusing on me. The third man now draws up his chair. They have been calling him Mandeep.

In soft and enticing tones, the sour-faced man reminds me of the night of the helicopters, 'Robin, take your mind back to the weekend of November the twenty-third, the night when the helicopters landed here at the camp. You were here that night, we know. You communicated with

Reginald De Vere, you enabled access, and you watched the delegates arrive. You will have seen the MOD helicopter arrive. It is the second helicopter which interests us. We need to know who met with the Secretary of State here that night. Can you tell us that? If so, we will untie you and your friends, and will leave you to the rustic joy of your camp, because we have work to do elsewhere.'

I desperately want them to be gone, but I know that I must not tell them who visited that night, even if I do not know why. Without hesitating, I speak in a low deliberate voice, as if taking them into my confidence,

'If I had seen, I could tell you who it was, but we were kept well clear. I saw the helicopters land, but I did not see who was involved. Truthfully, Marcella and her troops were very careful to keep us separate from the action.'

The leader bangs the Gin bottle down on the table, muttering to Miranda, 'So what are you going to do now; that's exactly what the others told us. *They don't know.*'

This at least confirms that they have others, I assume in the cottage. Is it Thomas and Maria? And Glyn? I sit silently, remembering Miranda's account of their organisation, far left hiding in the far right, intent on total reboot of the economic system. I decide to make a move, 'Talk to us about your cause. I may not have the very information that you need, but am prepared to engage in dialogue.' I stand up and stare furiously at him, manage to retain my control, and hope to intimidate their offensive leader.

He glares at me, launching a tirade which takes me aback, 'You fucking privileged madam, as if you could help us! It is people like you who turn our stomachs. Do you realise, this glitch is all about people like you, it is all about overturning the centuries of inherited wealth, and it is about starting again, from zero with everyone equal. It is about putting the banks where they belong, in the gutter, and about showing people like you the consequences of your hoarded wealth, your fancy ways.'

A stupefied silence hangs in the dormitory. Eva looks

as if she will burst with indignation. I signal to her to remain quiet. Surprised at the calmness in my voice, I respond by asking, 'So, for you, the glitch is an attack on the banks in order to upend society, to force people like me to face up to the realities of poverty and destitution?'

'Yes, for us, the glitch is an attack on the banks, and on people like you.'

'But you don't control the glitch.' Gid's voice booms from the corner of the dormitory. This time they do not ignore him, and Miranda mutters with the leader, then approaching Gid. She stands full height, her athletic build now visible without her disguise. Gid is being held down on the chair, his hands tied behind his back. She looks down on him, and sneers, 'If we controlled the glitch, we wouldn't be here today, trying to find out who does, would we?'

We seem to be talking at cross purposes, and I can feel the tension escalating. I am sorely tempted to give them the name that they seek, to be rid of them. I have not spoken untruthfully, because I did not see who the second man was that night, but of course Maria saw, and she told me. It seems that whoever they have in the cottage is keeping shtum too.

'Hold on there, let's rewind a bit; I think you may find that we are on your side here,' I observe, but their leader is on a roll,

'That's rich coming from you!'

'Robin, do you realise what we are saying?' Miranda interjects.

'No?'

Miranda spells it out for me, 'Look, this time the glitch is pretty permanent. Systems are wiped. The only money now is cash. Anything that people have stored up in their accounts, it is all gone. Mortgages are cleared, anarchy rules. We know all about your inheritance. You are one of *them*, but all your millions from dear daddy, they are gone. Gone up in a puff of smoke. Now you are just like the rest of us. You'd better face up to it.'

I consider Miranda's comments, and my determination not to reveal the name that they seek is strengthened a hundredfold.

Dusk

The pale winter sun has just disappeared over the horizon, the sky is darkening and the air temperature is dropping rapidly. At least we are indoors, but the cavernous space is becoming bitterly cold.

Miranda tidies the mess on the table, talking with her friends in low tones, and exchanging words with Eva. Gid, his hands still tied, bristles in the background. I slide unobtrusively beside him on the bench. Neither of us has use of our hands, but he whispers, 'when they laid into you, how did you keep your cool? Well done!'

'Patience needed now,' I urge him, in a low voice.

'They seem to be holding your friends in the Cottage.'

'Yes.'

'They are not as strong as they make out. What's your plan?'

'Let's get them talking and get them onside.' Gid's disgruntled face tells me all. There is no way that he sees talking as the solution here, but he says, grudgingly, 'You give it a try.'

The wine and the food seem to sooth their ungracious leader, who they call Karl. He yanks Gid and I towards the table, and we all sit round. I begin to remonstrate, but Karl's hand clamps over my mouth. The door opens, and another of their company leads two cowed figured in through the door, bringing a blast of cold air with them. My heart races. They shake off their hoods and I see the weary faces of Thomas and Glyn, lined and anxious. For a moment their eyes adjust to the bright light in the dormitory. Then they turn, and see me. Glyn's face melts into a great, but troubled, grin, and Thomas winks at me. They say nothing.

Where is Maria, I wonder, and little Poppy? Seeing my

two dear and trusted friends fills me with confidence and I cannot resist the temptation to take charge any longer. I feel compelled to speak out. I surprise Karl, the leader, as I stand up and launch straight into a desperate attempt to get things back on track.

'Okay, I think that we have more in common than we realise. You have nothing to lose by listening to me. Firstly, welcome to Caernef Camp.' I pause, and smile, but am unable to open my arms to them due to the cable ties, which are starting to irritate my wrists. 'Here we are creating a haven, an escape from the materialistic world. Not only do we offer educational breaks for school children, who arrive here leaving the trappings of our digital society behind, and who learn to survive for a week with very little, but we have also created a sanctuary for those who seek to escape the pressures of an affluent society, which is obsessed with money and with technology. In this camp, we are all equal, and we are all valued. It might sound naïve, but it is an ideal to which we all sign up. It matters to us.

I pause, staring into his eyes, emboldened and resolute.

My audience is reluctantly attentive, and encouraged, I continue, 'For whatever reason, in the topsy turvy mess that has followed the latest glitch, you have arrived here uninvited. You have imposed your values upon our community, bringing weapons, tying our hands. You tell us that you seek to revolutionise the world order, to put an end to inequality, and you think that you are within touching distance of controlling cyberspace, and therefore controlling systems, such as the banks, but you need the digital tools which one human being seems to have mastered, a human being who came here, here to Caernef. Who is this ingenious character? If you could work with him, or her, then you think that you could perfect your plan, and take the world of humans back to the start again, to a new Year Zero.

'In a small way, that's what we have attempted to achieve here. We have tried to get back to the basics which matter. So, I suggest that we start our relationship over again. You untie us, treat us with some respect, and let's see whether we can put our heads together to move forwards. What do you say?'

Before our captors can reply, Glyn stands up. 'She's right. These are wise words,' he says. Miranda smirks to herself, in a manner which suggests a grudging admiration, and she looks at Karl, expecting him to respond. He shrugs his shoulders. His cheeks are flushed and his head is not as clear as it was before he unpacked the alcohol. He defers to Miranda. She, I am reluctant to admit, is magnificent. Having lost her cloaks and intrigue, she speaks clearly and directly,

'We apologise for treating you with disrespect. It was remiss of us. This latest glitch has fostered mistrust. Anton, untie them.'

Once released, Glyn, Thomas and I embrace each other warmly. I introduce them to Eva and Gid, and hands are shaken. I am simply so relieved to see Glyn and Thomas again. We do not mention Maria, not with our former captors on the alert, But Miranda is astute. She turns to me, demanding, 'So, which one of these two is the Syrian, and where is his partner? They refused to talk to us.'

Thomas comes forward, 'I am Thomas, and my partner Maria is not here. She travelled to meet friends on the day of the second glitch and has not returned. I am hoping she is still with our friends.'

Miranda brushes this off as merely inconvenient, and turns to Karl, 'Tell them about our cause. Perhaps we can recruit them.'

Karl clears his throat and speaks in a strong voice, tinged with anger, 'There is only one planet Earth. We are simply its custodians. Over the centuries, as the human race has multiplied, the rich resources of the planet have become overexploited. We have disregarded the warnings, and are now facing the very real scenario that our demands on this planet are outstripping what it can offer us. The planet is fighting back, throwing fires, floods and viruses at us.'

Despite his appalling behaviour towards us, since our arrival in the camp, we all listen with curiosity, as he continues, 'Over the centuries, the human race established systems for bartering, for trading, for buying and selling. By the twenty-first century, the dynamic between those who have the wealth and those who earn their living has become both corrupted and blurred. Huge financial reward for virtually no effort is now entrenched. People with capital invest and reap the profits. Celebrities like footballers and superstars attract completely disproportionate rewards. Meanwhile hard-pressed workers flog their guts out for scant recompense: nurses, teachers, street-cleaners, and small businesses struggle to balance the books. Significant debts are commonplace. Many of us are existing on a raft of credit. Inane celebrity is worshipped and, especially of late, principles are swept aside.

He continues, 'The time has come to call a halt to this madness. There is an appetite out there. People want to take back control, but just serving them with an indiscriminate glitch is not going to achieve anything more than stirring up fear, prejudice and violence. We need to make contact with whoever is behind this act of cyber-terrorism, and to turn it to the advantage of the human race.'

For a moment we all let his words sink in. He looks embarrassed and sits down, still glowering. Miranda hands me one of the phones lying on the table. She shows me how the encryption works and sets the entry as my fingerprint. It is similar to the system used by Reginald. Then she says, 'Hang on to this. Keep it switched on and fully charged. We will use it to contact you. No news is good news. It is there for occasional and important messages. If you get any clues to the identity of the person who visited Caernef, the person behind the glitch, get straight in touch. Send a bland message like "need to talk" and then call us, using this.'

They start packing up their kit, preparing to leave, collecting any food and drink left on the table and stashing it away. Apparently, they came on motorbikes, once Miranda had contacted them from The Prince of Wales. Desperate to see the back of these intriguing but troubling characters, I remain quiet.

Before they leave, Miranda comes up to me, 'I am truly sorry Robin, I was led to believe that you knew who it was. I was under instructions …' She looks at Gid and glares.

Before he leaves. Anton hands the key to the old pickup back to Gid, and then they all depart, disappearing into the darkness, leaving me holding their phone.

Evening

As the roar of their motorbikes recedes into the distance, we are about to celebrate. I have never felt so elated, but Gid calls us together abruptly, ushering us out into the cold. 'They're canny; who knows what listening devices they may have planted in there. Is there somewhere else we can go?'

Thomas invites us to walk down to the cottage, saying to me, 'We must get to Maria and Poppy. We must find them, urgently.'

'Aren't they with your friends?'

'No, I made that up to protect them. As soon as we saw those thugs with their guns marching down to the cottage, pushing Glyn, his hands tied, Maria took Poppy out the back door and they hid in the coal shed. That was over a day ago. There were guards on the cottage doors. I haven't seen them since.'

I know that old coal shed well, having helped Maria to clear it out in the summer. There is, at least, no coal in it anymore, but it is draughty and packed with sacks of potatoes from the vegetable patch, wooden boxes of apples and carrots, and all manner of other gardening junk. Not the place to shelter a four-year-old on a bitter winter's night unless you are absolutely desperate.

While Gid and Glyn bond, checking that our guests have indeed left the area, we run down to the cottage, and search frantically for Maria and Poppy, our cries echoing eerily over the headland. The coal shed is empty. Before we can settle down to talk over the events of this extraordinary day, we know we must find them. Breaking into pairs, we take strong torches, scanning hedgerows and outbuildings. We check all the buildings in the camp with no success, and I chide myself for not thinking of the folly earlier. They could conceivably have run down there unnoticed in the dark. I am paired with Thomas. He is distraught with worry and I feel responsible.

How many times have Thomas and I walked down to the folly together since that magical first breakfast at dawn? We have never carried so much anxiety on our shoulders. As soon as we rise over the hump of the field, we see a low light in the window. They must be there.

Thomas sprints down to the folly, faster than me. He pounds on the door, and I see Maria's worried face peer out. He disappears inside. I give them a few minutes before sauntering back home.

'Robin,' Poppy cries, rushing to hug my knees, closely followed by her mother.

Maria greets me like a long-lost and beloved sister, saying, 'What a horrendous experience. Have they gone? I could see that you had been here recently; I didn't understand. I had to break your bathroom window to get in. I have stuck a piece of board across it for now. We can mend it.'

'Forget the window. Thank goodness you are both here.'

'They wanted to know the name of the visitor that night: Todd Humboldt.' Thomas tells her while I am listening to Poppy tell me all about the adventure in her piping voice.

'We obviously weren't intended to have a quiet life,' she mutters, wryly, as we lock the folly and return to the cottage, where our troops have assembled, and are overjoyed to see us all piling in from the cold night.

We crowd round the fire, which is crackling

enthusiastically, and chew over the extraordinary events of the day. 'Thank goodness you didn't even know the name of that person that they wanted so much. And I'm so sorry you lost your savings Robin,' Eva observes kindly, remembering the comments made earlier by our then-captors.

'Oh, it's fine. Don't worry. I don't believe in banks. The money is safe, and will be just what we need while we build this place back up. What a good job I opted for wads of cash rather than stocks and shares,' I respond, smugly.

Gid overhears this and cannot help exclaiming, I assume with conspiratorial surprise, or maybe with admiration, 'Shit.'

We eat, we settle, and we sleep. In the morning, Nathan appears. More introductions are made, accommodation and duties are organised, and an emergency survival plan is devised for the camp, its longer-standing, and its new residents.

And so it was that our proud and diverse company assembled at Caernef Camp: Glyn the intrepid educator, Thomas and Maria, the brave survivors, the cheerful little Poppy, Gid, the ferocious, Eva, the peace-maker, Nathan, with youth and ingenuity on his side, and me. Who am I? I have still completely failed to jettison the services of a mobile phone, having been handed one by my co-conspirator, or my enemy, Miranda, but I tread hopefully.

I now know that we are not only retreating from the society that has battered and drained us, but that we are ready to fight the challenges which loom large on the horizon. I slip away, walking down through the field, leaving my fellow-conspirators to their jovial meal. I unlock the folly, climb the stairs, close the blind, grab the tall stool and check the recess in the small attic. Yes, the box is there, and it is still packed full of bank notes. Am I a hypocrite or am I just lucky? No, I decide; there was no luck involved. I made a judgement call. With relief, I close the hatch, climb down, raise the blind and sit in the window seat. I survey the wondrous horizon, the sparkling waves, and the curlew fishing at the water's edge. At last, I am alone, and have time to think.

INTERROGATION

Morning

I am woken by the rude buzzing of a mobile phone, as the sun rises over the estuary. Realising that I must have dozed off to sleep, perched on the window seat in the turret of the folly, I scramble stiffly to my senses and grab the unfamiliar phone, wondering how Miranda and her gang managed to set up their own network while the populace was cowering under the debilitating shrill tones of a phone network in chaos. Right now, all I want is sleep in my comfortable bunk. I ignore the messages, hiding the phone under a cushion, hoping to dull its tones, and stagger to my bed. I crawl under the blankets, close my eyes, and sleep.

Hours later. drifting gently into consciousness, I pull the blankets around me and listen to the familiar sound of the distant seabirds accompanied by gusts of the powerful sea breeze. I will stay under the blankets as long as I can, in my undisturbed cocoon. The air inside the folly feels cold and damp on my cheeks; I know that I must light a fire and check what food I have in the cupboard, but I snuggle down, imagining the hot sweet tea which I will make, looking forward to the simple pleasures of a private bathroom, and clean clothes.

Thinking back to my trip to Oxford, the Christmas shoppers and carol singers, it does feel as if I have entered a bizarre dream. Yet again, society as we know it has become unrecognisable. Without the benefit of the internet, television, radio, I have no idea what is happening beyond my own immediate experience. I do know that when the first glitch hit, it knocked out systems across the world. We became a planet without the communications expected by advanced societies, and I have no reason to doubt that this is the case again. Although I have never been attracted to the celebrity culture of the television, I do really miss being able to tap into current news.

A faint reverberation disturbs my reverie, and I remember the phone. I am sorely tempted to hurl it over the cliff and into the waves, cutting any remaining links with Miranda and her cronies for good, but I know that I will be drawn back to check for messages once I am up, because I fear that there is some as yet unknown but vital role that I must play. I glance out over the blankets at the floor of the lookout, where my boots await my feet. The vegetable knife, which I didn't use, is lying on the rug. I must make an effort, and I sit up, swing my legs over the edge of the bed and stand. My limbs don't ache too badly, but I can see my breath, so I shove my feet into my boots, and head for the woodpile.

It doesn't take long to set and light a fire, and I crouch in front of the flames, blowing into the wood burner until the roar tells me I can close the front. Slowly the folly warms up. I tidy the debris from my hasty return, and boil the kettle. I retrieve the phone from under the cushion, settling in front of the stove to drink my tea while I look at the messages.

It is not a standard phone, and they gave me no charger, although that would be useless at present. It seems to be operating on solar power. I sign in using my fingerprint, touch the screen and several messages appear, all from Miranda, instantly creating a heaviness in my heart. I read, reluctantly, "need to know who met with Sec of State any info text me," and further down the stack of similar pleas, "need an 8-digit access code. Any ideas?" I thought that she said the phone was for occasional messages. The calmness which had pervaded my first hour back at the folly dissipates as I realize that I will not easily be rid of Miranda. I don't know whether I should trust her, but I do know that this is much bigger than I imagined. I wonder why she needs an eight-digit code, and why she thinks I can help with that.

I diligently scan each message which she has sent through, including a cryptic reference to mourning for a lost hero, decide not to respond, and stuff the phone back under the cushion. Once the water in the back boiler has heated, I wash, and scour the folly for food. There is very little. Thank goodness for the camp, and the sacks of vegetables from last summer up in the old coal store at the cottage. Just as I am deciding when I will walk up to the cottage, I see Maria and Poppy striding down the field towards the folly, seeking me out.

Maria greets me like a long-lost relative, and little Poppy leaps up and down with the enthusiasm of youth. 'She's been up since six, and I have been trying to keep her quiet. The others are still sleeping, but I thought we should eat together at lunchtime. There are several more mouths to feed now, and food is not plentiful. We must organise a party to walk out to search for food later. Sorry Robin, I am jabbering on; I have had no one to talk to all morning. How are you?'

I send Poppy up to sit in the lookout, and tell Maria that I feel surprisingly good, but hungry. Lunch together sounds great. I ask her how it has been living at the camp during this second glitch, and hear of their cosy Christmas, until they were unexpectedly interrupted by Miranda's gang.

'They wanted to know about Todd Humboldt, didn't they?'

'Yes. They still do, but why?'

'Last night Thomas said they were driven by their ideology. They want to end capitalism, end life as we know it, and impose a fresh start on the world. It sounds attractive, if it wasn't so impossible.'

'Maybe. I can't help thinking that we have a role to play in this, but I don't know what or how.'

'Robin, it will come to you, I am sure. You must be tired

and disorientated. Give that brain of yours some quiet time, and you will work it out, I have no doubt. But meanwhile, would you mind coming up to help me peel enough vegetables?'

I say that I will be up at the cottage in ten minutes, and watch the two of them walk back up the field. Then I access my stash of cash up in the roof. It is too small to be called an attic. There is a tiny hatch hidden in the ceiling over the lookout room, just wide enough for me to squeeze through. I have a small folding ladder, and can climb up, dislodge the wooden cover, and grope into the darkness where I have hidden the box of bank notes. Today I extract a thick pile of twenty-pound notes. I will give some to whoever goes on the search for food, and I need to reimburse Rhys at The Prince of Wales. I climb down, secure the hatch and am drawn to the window seat, where I sit and stare thoughtfully out over the estuary.

The water is ruffled into small waves today as there is a strong wind. I say out loud to myself, 'Who should I trust?' Confident in trusting my friends up at the cottage, I secure the money in my pockets, descend the stairs, exit the folly, somewhat reluctantly, and lock the door.

Lunch

We devour a basic but satisfying lunch of steaming baked potatoes doused in olive oil and sprinkled liberally with pepper, and a hot vegetable soup, all cooked successfully over the fire. Glyn arrives on his bike, in time to witness us eat the last few morsels, telling us that his wife had a successful trip to the supermarket earlier today after an enterprising mechanic disabled the electronics in her car, and succeeded in getting the engine to start. He says they are selling tins and packets. We have composed a long shopping list, hoping to feed the seven of us now at the camp for at least a week before needing to shop again. I provide the cash so that Thomas, Gid and Nathan can set off to attempt to collect groceries.

Glyn joins Maria, Eva and I by the fire in the small lounge in the cottage, blowing his hot coffee. He is telling us how life seems to be slowly returning to a semblance of normal, but without the benefits of power, mobile phones or internet. His face has aged through the latest trauma, and his ponytail is now more silver than black. He is worrying about getting the camp open again, and whether business will build back up without his aggressive advertising on social media. 'Also,' he says, warming his hands, 'people will no longer want to come here to escape technology, because they are forced to live in an IT shutdown anyway.'

I catch his eye and smile, reassuring him that the shutdown is only temporary, and as he succeeded in the miracle of building the camp back up after the sale and closure, I know that he will find a way to do it again, but I see from his face that he is weary. People are exhausted by the crises which seem to be characterising human existence. It is wearing them down.

'Of course, the answer could lie in the restoration of power, of the internet, and the lifting of whatever curse binds our mobiles,' Maria suggests. We agree that if Gid was here, he would scoff at this. He thinks it is impossible for society to fully recover, that we are on a slippery slope downwards into a pathetic ending of the human race, "not with a bang but a whimper." I stand with Maria. There must be a way.

It is Eva who cheers us up, with the last of the chocolate and more coffee, but she is puzzled, having joined our company so recently, 'Please can you explain to me what really happened here when the helicopters came. It's all a bit of a mystery. There is something that you are not sharing with me.' We tell her again about the night when the camp hosted the important and highly secretive visit, recalling the excitement, the nervousness, and the cacophony of the helicopters. 'And who *is* Miranda?' Eva ponders. A silence hangs in the previously genial air.

We don't know the answer to her question.

Maria decides that Eva deserves to be taken into our confidence, 'Eva, we should tell you something that you must not repeat. Although Robin, Glyn and Thomas did *not* see anything of our visitors that night, except shadowy outlines rushing from the helicopters to the dormitory, I did see the two men, in fact, I spoke with them.'

Eva sucks air through her teeth and raises her eyebrows, 'Who were they Maria? What were they really doing here?'

'I saw the two important visitors in person. The Secretary of State was talking with Todd Humboldt …'

'Really, Todd Humboldt, the trouble-maker. I remember the news reports last year. That is what Miranda and her gang want to know. Do you think that they consider he is the person who holds the secret of the glitch, who will know how to restore our systems?'

'Yes.'

~

There is a commotion in the hallway as the shoppers return, their faces serious. They drop the scant shopping by the kitchen table and squeeze into the small lounge, perching on the floor. They clearly bring news. Eva provides them with hot drinks, and it is Thomas who announces the news, 'We heard it from a guy who had come from London. Not sure if we can believe him, but he told us about two deaths; Todd Humboldt in Moscow, and on the very same day, a man in London. He said the man was called Karl Campbell.'

This has to be Karl, the ungracious philosophical leader of Miranda's gang, the man who drank our vodka, and who dragged Glyn and Thomas into the dormitory. I have no feelings for that man other than contempt.

Little Poppy breaks the silence, rustling a packet of crisps from the shopping and asking politely if they are for her. Maria sits Poppy at the kitchen table, leaving the door open, and tips the crisps into a bowl. I can see her face, troubled as she listens to the conversation, which is prompted by Gid, declaring where he stands, 'So, Todd has been killed, that rogue Karl has poked his nose in too far, and the press is all over it. No doubt Miranda is deep into this too.'

I confess to having heard from Miranda on the encrypted phone this morning, and relate the gist of her insistent messages. Gid is rattled as I admit to having left the phone in the folly. 'Robin, go and fetch the phone. We need it nearby in case there is news. I don't want to hear from them, but we are deeper into this than any of us wants, and we may have to act on our feet.' I rise wearily. I squeeze out of the crowded room and dive into the fresh air, relieved to be alone again. I breathe deeply and walk slowly through the grass, listening to the distant breakers on the rocks and the reassuring cries of the sea birds.

What does this mean?

Afternoon

I unlock the folly and look for the phone, which I find under a cushion up on the window seat in the lookout, but do not return immediately to my friends in the cottage. I settle at the window, building up the courage to look at the accursed screen of the phone to check for messages, and focusing on the curlew paddling in the shallows without a care in the world.

The Secretary of State talked with Todd here at Caernef, in the dormitory, but I am not convinced that Todd shared anything significant with him. It was a meeting to secure an agreement that he would *not* disable the internet. It was a diplomatic attempt to prevent any further glitches, but it failed. For an unknown reason, Todd exerted his secret knowledge a second time, in the approach to Christmas, setting society into chaos yet again.

Now I understand Miranda's previous message about mourning a hero. I recall the spark in her eyes when Karl delivered his speech to us in the dormitory. She clearly admired him and his grand aspirations. I slide the phone out and press my finger reluctantly on the reader, hoping there are no fresh messages, but there is one, which says, "Phone me".

It is the instruction that I least wanted to see. I can, of course, ignore it, but I feel honour bound to see this through. I take a deep breath and phone Miranda, pressing the phone anxiously to my ear, the odd ringing tone jangling, my heart beating unusually quickly. She doesn't answer. I give up, place the phone on the cushion and go down the stairs to stoke the embers and make a coffee, forgetting that I have no milk, so end up shovelling in sugar. Just as I am ascending the stairs, the phone rings. I jump, slopping coffee over the floor as I run to it, pressing the "accept" and putting it to my ear.

Miranda's unmistakable voice asks, 'Robin?'

'Hi.'

'Are you alone?'

'Yes.'

Miranda proceeds to tell me, in a hushed voice, how Karl had been careless, tried to gain access to the Prime Minister, and when the news came through about Todd Humboldt, Karl pushed even further, and paid the ultimate price. She says he was targeted by a gang of cyber-criminals, but I am not so sure. She seems to need to offload, and tells me more, describing the race to stop the glitch, and how Karl's followers are having to push boundaries to beat "the others".

'So, Robin, the man who visited Caernef was Todd Humboldt. Now we know,' she tells me, triumphantly.

I feign ignorance, and respond to her revelation, simply saying, 'We heard this morning.'

'Now, Robin, I need you to wrack your brains. I need a code, an eight-digit code. Apparently, Todd reset the entry code to his safe box after he returned from Caernef. He set up an incredibly intricate protection. An incorrect code blows the whole thing sky high. Robin we are so close. If we can get in, we can not only reinstate the internet, block the pulse in the phones, but we will be able to …' She stops.

'Be able to …?' I ask.

'Enact Karl's plan. Year Zero.'

She has lost me.

'Robin, are you still there?'

'Yes.'

'Good. Karl told me, before they got him, that the child knows the code. The child at Caernef. It was Karl's attempt at irony, not entrusting the code to an adult.'

'What?'

'The child, he said. I don't understand either. You must try find out for me. If you find out anything, alert me by a quick text, and we must talk. Don't put anything about the code in a message. Heaven knows who is monitoring us, … especially now. I must go.'

No "goodbye" and no "thank you". The line goes dead and I remove the phone from my ear. Miranda is clearly referring to Poppy. As Maria has told us, several times, Poppy played peek-a-boo with the two men that night, but I am not aware of the passing of any information to her, certainly no talk of codes. I know that I must return to my friends at the cottage. If Poppy is in any danger, I am duty-bound to alert Thomas and Maria, but I don't want to alarm them unduly.

I glance at the wooden box standing on my tiny desk overlooking the estuary and yearn for a smoke, but instead return to the kitchen, the phone in my pocket, drink a glass of water and take my painkillers, hoping that they will dull the aches which have invaded my head and my limbs; my body tense with the anxiety of Miranda's message, my mind troubled.

Anxious that my supply of pills is getting low, I wish that I understood better what was going on. We all need this glitch to end, for many reasons.

I lock the door to the folly and stare up at the lookout, longing to be able to spend time here without the worries of the survival of the human race on my mind. I want to be able to get up, read a book, go for a walk, and eat simple food. I want to breathe the cliff-top air and put reality aside, but I can visualise the expectant faces up at the cottage, waiting for any news, and I force myself to march through the grass up the hillside.

Night

There is no opportunity to speak with Thomas and Maria straight away, as during the hour that I have been away from the cottage, they have not only put the shopping away, but while washing up, Glyn has told them his news, that there is to be a party at the Prince of Wales tonight. It will be a grand event to cheer up the villagers, and to celebrate Rhys, the publican, having received a delivery, the first since the second glitch. I don't have the heart to turn their excitement into anxiety, and remain quiet for the present, but offer to remain back at the cottage with Maria, who doesn't think that The Prince of Wales is the right place for Poppy to spend the evening. I am not in the mood for celebrations. When they eventually quiz me about the messages from Miranda, I simply say that there is nothing new.

I want them to enjoy themselves for a change. We can worry about Miranda later.

We agree that we will start to plan for the future tomorrow, after the party. Glyn has ideas for reopening the camp, and I think Nathan already has itchy feet and wants to explore Wales. I reckon that the morning will be the right time to confide in my friends regarding Miranda's message, and her mention of Poppy.

I agree to sit with Maria later this evening when the others leave for The Prince of Wales, and we disperse. As I wander back to the folly, I hear pounding footsteps behind me. It is Gid, running, cigarette in hand and a beaming smile on his face.

'What's up Robin?' he asks, detecting the anxiety on my face. We walk together, stopping on the very platform of thrift where, only a few days ago, we clambered up to the folly, grimy from our journey, when the gang occupied the camp. I relate to him the gist of my communications with Miranda. At the mention of her name his face clouds over, he becomes serious, and urges caution.

'I understand you not wanting to worry the others, but you really must tell them tomorrow. There are forces involved in this fiasco which we know little about. I wouldn't be at all surprised if it was government security which saw to Karl. Maybe MI6.'

'Blimey. I hadn't thought of that.'

'No. You are too trusting Robin. Surely the events of the last few months have taught you something?' He is genuinely concerned for me, and puts his great tattooed arm affectionately around my shoulders. 'I must return your bread knife, it is up in the dormitory where Eva, Nathan and I are kipping down. Now, promise me that you will keep that phone on you at all times, and if anything comes through, tell me when we get back. Promise?' I promise, he slaps me on the back, and he heads off.

Despite the days lengthening, heavy black clouds roll in from the sea, and by seven o'clock it is nearly dark. I muffle up in a heavy coat, grab a torch, check the accursed phone is in my pocket, and head for the cottage. I can see Thomas join Eva, Gid and Nathan under the floodlights on the veranda to the dormitory and I am just in time to tell them to enjoy their evening. If anyone deserves to have a good time for a change, it is my friends. Glyn arrives in his wife's car, and they pile in. Spruced up, they look quite a different crowd to my bedraggled companions on the trip from Oxford. I wave enthusiastically and dodge into the cottage where Maria is reading to Poppy by the fire.

We are not in a hurry to get her to bed, and play games. Poppy is developing the confidence of her mother, and she shows me how she can now read some of her books for herself. Thomas has been teaching her to count in Arabic, and she recites the poetic words to me with great concentration while Maria makes her hot milk. I forget about the world outside, and am drawn into their cosy domestic pleasure.

Maria takes Poppy upstairs to bed, and so I go out to the woodshed to replenish the logs, as the fire is low, and the basket is empty. The lights from the cottage windows reveal swathes of mist. The air is damp, and the night dark. The log basket now full, I turn towards the door, but suddenly become aware of a shadow, and the crack of a twig. I remember when I approached the cottage from the wood, the first night that I met Thomas. This time there might be someone else out there in the darkness. I strain my ears, but only hear the hoot of an owl. Maybe I heard a fox. Reassured, I walk towards the back door of the cottage.

It happens so quickly. Someone hits me firmly on the back of my head, I drop the logs with a clatter and struggle to keep my footing. My arm is twisted up my back. A black figure shoves me through the cottage door, gloved hand firmly across my mouth. I see Maria's distraught face at the top of the stairs as two more figures in black hurry stealthily into the cottage. They slam the door shut, sit me on a kitchen chair, confounding my struggles. They are armed. A pistol at my back, I am helpless. Maria and Poppy are bundled down the stairs, Maria clutching Poppy protectively into her chest. This is all my fault.

Maria is held on a chair, like me, a pistol at her back. Poppy stands beside her, but I cannot see the little girl's face. The three figures are male, hidden under black balaclavas. I don't think we know them, but it is hard to tell. The third man removes his mask. He is older than I had thought, with short greying hair and a lined face. Although formidable, and deadly serious, he does not appear cruel, and as he catches my eye, he smiles kindly.

'We apologise for disturbing your evening. You do not need to know who we are, or why we are here, but we have been instructed to talk with the child. If you cooperate, no one will be harmed.'

'Then treat us with respect,' Maria shouts, furious, trying to rise from the chair.

The man speaks calmly, 'You help us talk with the child, and we will leave as quickly as we arrived. Please.' He gently turns Poppy's face round and she stares wide-eyed. I cannot speak, with a hand clamped firmly over my mouth. He crouches down and addresses Poppy,

'Tell me your name,' he tries. Poppy says nothing. The usually chatty child is completely silenced by her fear. Maria turns maternally to Poppy,

'It's alright Poppy. You can speak to him.'

'Your name is Poppy,' he tries again, picking up the picture book lying by the dying embers, 'Now Poppy, tell me about your book. Who is this?' Poppy remains dumb. She does not trust this invader of her home. Maria and the man coax a few words out of the scared child. Gradually she relaxes a little. The pistol presses uncomfortably into my back and I struggle to breathe. They ignore me.

'She can count to ten in Arabic,' Maria volunteers. She starts Poppy off, and the child's voice regains some of its confidence as she reels off the numbers. The man claps and smiles. They have chosen him for this job. He slowly gains a rapport with her, and builds up to the question which both Maria and I know is inevitable.

'Poppy, look at this picture.' He shows a photograph of Todd Humboldt's face. 'Can you remember seeing him, and this man?' He shows a photograph of the Secretary of State. 'They were here.' Poppy nods her head. 'What did he tell you?'

Poppy, having decided to perform, closes her eyes dramatically. She pretends to be thinking hard. She mouths the Syrian numbers again, and makes us all jump by exploding into one loud word, 'Boo!'

The man laughs. Maria explains, 'She is right. They played peek-a-boo. She remembers alright, but I was there and I didn't hear him say anything significant to her at all.'

'Something insignificant then?'

'No, he just asked her what her name was, and they played the little game. Then we left. There was nothing. I am sorry but nothing was said.'

'And to you, did they say anything to you, a codeword, a number, a clue?'

'No, nothing. I am telling you the truth. We really don't know. Now please, leave us in peace. We are not part of this, not at all.'

The interrogator replaces his mask. The two men holding us pocket their pistols, and they exit as quickly as they arrived, leaving the door wide open behind them.

INCINERATION

Midnight

I stand on the small doorstep of the cottage peering out into the darkness, watching the three men disappear, not upwards to the road, but stealthily across the meadow towards the folly. Filled with alarm, I strain my eyes, but they disappear from my view. Why wasn't I more vigilant? I cannot face Maria. I should have told her of Miranda's message. I am tangled up in something which I do not understand and do not like. I feel for the phone in my pocket, take it out and check for messages, but there is nothing. Why are they heading for the folly?

All that I can hear now is occasional familiar night noises of nocturnal creatures, the wind in the branches and distant waves breaking on the rocks. The damp air smells sweetly of vegetation and woodsmoke. I stay for several minutes, but the three men have melted into the darkness and there is no clue of their next actions. I take a deep breath and steel myself to return to Maria and Poppy.

Bolting the door as I enter the cottage, I find the lounge empty and the fire almost out. I hear Maria's soft voice upstairs, and gather some kindling. The front page of an old newspaper stares up at me from the kitchen table. I rip it off, screwing the photographs of nameless politicians into a ball and stuffing it under the kindling. Thomas has taught me how to light fires with maximum chance of success, and I blow gently, coaxing the flames which ignite from the barely glowing embers. The crumpled faces burst into flame, the sticks catch, and by the time Maria returns, I have reinstated the roaring fire.

My head is cowed, and I mutter a string of apologies, defeated by *them*, at this moment, broken. Maria sits beside me and takes my head gently into her lap, as if I am Poppy. She strokes my cheek, and speaks softly, 'Stop Robin, Let's save our anger to fight whatever comes at us next. Poppy genuinely doesn't know anything. They are clutching at straws. They need some sort of digital code to access the hack which causes glitches. And we don't have it. They must look elsewhere.'

Her kindness tips me over the edge, and tears flow down my cheeks, silently, making dark spots on her skirt. I think of my mother, who offered me comfort when I was very young. I think of my father, and feel nothing but derision. I will never really escape his grip. After all, I could not have created my new life at Caernef without him. I think of Poppy, who acted so responsibly for her young years. 'Is Poppy asleep?' I ask, dragging myself back to reality.

'Yes, Poppy is tough as they come. She is asleep.'

'Maria, have they gone. I mean really gone? They went off towards the folly.'

'They probably came in along the coast. Don't you worry.'

'In the dark? I am not convinced.'

'Robin, we must wait here, guard Poppy in case they return. The last thing we want is for them to come back. She wouldn't understand. We must wait until the others get home, and then we can check the folly with you.'

I know that this makes sense. We arm ourselves with knives from the kitchen, in case our visitors return, hoping not to have to use them, and we settle down by the fire to wait, determined not to doze off. We jump up at every small noise outside, but when eventually Thomas arrives home, we do not hear him until he unlocks the door, appearing with ruddy cheeks and wind-blown hair, but looking as anxious as we feel.

'Thank goodness you are alright. There was a strange

glow above the camp. We could see it in the sky when Glyn dropped us off by the parade ground. It was as if there was a fire.'

We quickly tell him about our unwelcome visitors, and reassure him that Poppy is fast asleep upstairs, as we peer out into the darkness in the direction of the folly. There is indeed a strange glow, similar to the lightening of the sky before the sun appears over the horizon in the morning. My heart beats faster as I fear the three men have, for some sick reason, torched the folly. And then we catch a whiff of burning in the wind.

'That is the smell of burning paper, or even plastic,' Maria observes, puzzled. I get my coat, determined to run down to the folly, but my way is barred by Thomas, who tells me to wait. I must not go down there alone. Maria and I stand trembling on the doorstep while Thomas runs up to the dormitory where Gid, Nathan and Eva are no doubt settling down after what sounds to have been a rousing party. We see Thomas beating on the door. He disappears inside and immediately reappears with Gid. They hasten back to us and Gid takes my hand. The two of us run anxiously down over the tussocks towards the folly.

The glow in the sky is diminishing, but the smell is strong. I am expecting to see the folly standing as a blackened ruin, but as we crest the field and descend, we can see the folly proudly silhouetted against the weakly moonlit sky. Gid's firm hand clings on to mine. There, on the platform of thrift in front of the folly is a smoking mess. Gid stops me moving forward, whispering, '*They* may still be here. Careful.' He checks in all directions, scanning the darkness, as clouds scud across the moon. 'Okay Robin, let's see what mischief they have been up to here.'

We walk forwards and can soon see pieces of ash fluttering in the updraft. I see the metal box which contained my savings discarded on the cliff-edge, and now see the charred and burnt bank notes which had been heaped up, in their bundles, like a malevolent bonfire of capitalism. I can imagine their faces when they lit the match and threw it on to the heap. They must have doused it in petrol or something highly flammable to cause such destruction.

Gid stares in disbelief, kicking the smouldering ash with his boot. I know exactly what has happened, but I feel no sadness, no regret. 'It's only paper after all. I didn't earn it. I didn't even deserve it. They have done me a favour.' Since the day that I received *the letter* finalising my inheritance, it has actually weighed heavily on me. I could never have predicted a bonfire, but I knew that I wanted a simpler life, not accountable to anyone, especially not to my deceased father. I want the satisfaction of having earned respect through my own actions.'

We enter the folly, left with the door flapping open in the wind, the hinges having been forced out of the wooden frame. Fortunately it can be wedged shut and locked from the inside. All my belongings have been rifled, spewed out on to the floor in a bizarre homage to my small and pathetic life. Books, papers, pots and pans, all thrown into disarray. I climb the stairs. The hatch above the lookout, into the small roof space, is open; my desk has been rifled, and the old Italian box where I have kept my painkillers and cigarettes is smashed on the wooden floor. Gid witnesses all my odd personal belongings strewn about, disrespected, and abandoned. He puts his arm around me, staring at the broken box, the blister packs of pills and the cigarette boxes, and we stand in silence.

Early Hours

Gid and I sit down on my bunk in the lookout. An unexpected calmness settles upon us. I genuinely don't care about the savings. My pride is bruised by seeing my pathetic belongings spattered around the floor, but I am comforted by Gid's presence. I don't mind him seeing me like this, now destitute, my life disrespected by our three visitors.

Even Gid seems to have momentarily lost his anger, and he breaks the silence, 'If only they would realise, we are on their side. We want to end this nightmare, provide the code, re-set the internet, remove the curse that affects our phones. We want to see an end to the materialism of mankind too. I'm with you Robin; money doesn't matter. What really matters is human dignity, behaving with integrity.' Reflecting that this young tattooed and pierced giant of a man makes a fitting philosopher, I squeeze his hand.

'Amen to that. What next then, Gid?'

'Common sense tells me to take you back to the safety of the dormitory for the night, and that we will tackle the folly in the morning, but I know you Robin, you will not rest until you are back in control here. How about we tidy up first, inside and out, and then sleep? I don't think the men will return tonight, but I will stay with you just in case. They haven't found what they were looking for because it is not here.'

'Yes. Thank you Gid. Let's get this place back to rights.' He stoops and picks up the two boxes of cigarettes, placing them on my desk. 'Gid, do me a favour and take those away in your pocket, smoke them and think of me in a former life.' He smiles, and slips them into the leg-pocket of his trousers, handing me the painkillers, which I put safely in my desk drawer. He scoops up the pieces of the broken box, turning over the false wooden book spines in his hands, and goes down the stairs in search of a bag. It doesn't take me long to tidy the lookout, to check my belongings and to replace the hatch.

Returning to the kitchen, I tell Gid that they have taken my camera. 'Ha,' he says, 'not for its worth, but because they think it may contain images with clues.'

'And all that they will find is photos of curlews, clifftops and wild flowers.' We walk back out on to the grass at the front of the folly, the chill night air biting and the now stale reek of smoke sticking in our noses. We decide there would have been no point in reporting the theft, even if we did have a camera, or a phone to record evidence, because in this strange time, wanton destruction seems commonplace, and the judicial system seems to be in disarray. I find a rake and a spade in my outdoor store, and we shovel the now cooling ashes into a small heap behind the folly, picking out the few banknotes which have not been completely burnt, and placing them in a bag. 'We can finish the job tomorrow and burn these too,' I comment, with a total lack of sentimentality.

We rake over the ground and once we are satisfied that order is restored, we go back into the folly, locking the door. As we tidy the two small downstairs rooms, we discuss the enigma of the lost code. 'Todd knew it. Surely he wrote it down, or shared it with someone? Isn't that what the security services will be focusing on?' I ask.

'They thought that he shared it here at Caernef,' Gid responds.

'Yes, but he didn't. We know that he didn't. Maria knows that he didn't.'

'They seem convinced.'

'They must have other lines of enquiry. They will know so much more than we do.'

'Maybe. But where does that bitch Miranda fit into all of this. She was thick with Karl. Now we know that Karl is dead, killed, but who by?'

I tell Gid that I think Miranda is a red herring, 'She is a failed politician who has become caught up in an underground movement. She targeted me at The Pike because she had found out about the secret meeting here. She seemed to know my guardian, Reginald, or to know of him. Gid, I would like to find out what has happened to Reginald through all of this.'

'Tell me about him, Robin.'

As we restore order in the kitchen, I tell Gid about my guardian, Reginald De Vere, starting with my childhood memories of his visits, and moving on to "De Vere Stratagems", and his role in various government missions over the years, which I knew very little about. 'He helped me out on a couple of occasions, when I needed job references. I wonder if he is still alive in this post-glitch chaos. I hope so. I have always respected him and valued his support.'

The kitchen is tidy and we move on to the small entrance room, where they seem to have searched behind everything, leaving a trail of debris. They have even looked under the logs and in the grate. Fir cones have spilled all over the flagstones. 'You wouldn't think that such a small place could be in such a mess,' I observe.

'Have they taken anything else do you think?'

'No, just the money and the camera. Everything else seems okay.'

'Good, now how about a coffee?'

'There's no milk.'

'Black will do fine.' We stand by the sputtering kettle, processing the events of the night, but come up with nothing new. Suddenly we both realise how tired we are. We swig our coffee. I tip half of mine away, worried it will keep me awake, but Gid doesn't seem to worry about anything. There is now no moonlight, and we stare out into the darkness.

'I'll stay with you tonight,' he declares resolutely, knowing that I will be unwilling to trudge back up the field at this hour. 'Do you think your bunk will take the two of us? Don't worry, we can keep our clothes on.'

I laugh, for the first time for days, at the thought of Gid, who must be well over six-foot tall, offering to squeeze into my bunk. We both laugh, and climb the stairs to try the bunk out for size. He eases his body under the blankets, leaving a small space for me, which I keenly occupy, smelling sweat and smoke as I bury my head in his chest and close my eyes. Gid holds me tightly, quickly starting to snore, and I drift into the rhythm of his breathing.

Morning

Surprisingly we both slept really deeply for the remaining few hours of the night. I wake first, and despite the warmth and security of Gid's sleeping grasp, am compelled to move as my leg muscles are aching uncontrollably from their cramped position. I hold my breath and slowly extricate myself, slipping out of the lookout and padding softly down the stairs without waking Gid.

I gaze out towards the grey water, and cannot avoid seeing the hastily raked blemish on the usually verdant clifftop. Reality hits me, my spirits drop, and my anger simmers. How dare *they* do this to me. I have never harmed them. I have only tried to play an honourable part in the game of life. All I have done is to help others, and stand up for what I believe is right. Losing my savings is not an issue, it is the disrespect which angers me. Quietly, I wash, straighten my clothes as best I can, and make a coffee. Even with sugar it tastes bitter, fuelling my fury. I picture the misleadingly kind face of the man who last night interrogated Poppy. Two-faced villain, I wish I had attacked him. I would have spat in his face, had I realised his intentions.

Gid stumbles blearily down the stairs, stretches and grins. 'Morning! I slept so well. Your bunk is surprisingly comfortable.' I make him coffee and we sit companionably. 'What's going through your mind?' he asks, detecting my pent-up anger.

'I am furious and ashamed all at once.' I struggle to put my thoughts into words.

'I can understand fury, but why ashamed?'

'Because I came here, a beneficent outsider. I had a dream, a vision of how things could be, but I have brought nothing but anguish to Caernef. It is my fault that Poppy was interrogated by an armed renegade. I am responsible for the fear which we now all feel here. The camp is closed, and people are frightened, all because of me.'

'Oh Robin, you should have been at The Prince of Wales last night. That would have banished your negative thoughts. It was a great party. Glyn, Thomas, Nathan, and Eva were all singing and laughing. The locals know that we are under fire here for some reason. They are supportive. Robin, *you* mustn't take responsibility for the fallout from the glitch. All you are guilty of is trying to set life back on its axis out here.'

Even Gid's bullish optimism cannot cheer me up this morning. I feel weary and empty. I fetch the accursed phone from under the cushion and hand it to Gid. 'Can you hang on to this for me today, otherwise I may hurl it over the cliff, which wouldn't be wise. I don't think I can stomach any more messages just now.' He takes the phone and it joins my cigarettes in his pocket.

It is a relief when Gid says that he should return to the others. He tries to persuade me to accompany him, but I want to be alone this morning. He promises to ask Nathan to pop down later to fix the door. As I watch him stride back up the field to the cottage, where there is probably a hot breakfast waiting for him, I regret that I didn't thank him for staying with me last night. I really am out of sorts, and decide that a bracing walk along the clifftop and down to the water's edge is the best medicine for me. Unburdened by phones, or by an inheritance, I march out along the path with only the key to the folly in my pocket.

I walk for hours and it is only the thought that Nathan might come down to repair the broken hinge of the door to the folly that persuades me to head for home. I march back up the cliff path and I realise how hungry I am, but know that my cupboards are bare.

As I approach the folly, I notice a large paper bag outside the door, surrounded by what looks like snowflakes. I bend down and inspect the doorstep. Tiny curls of wood shavings litter the step. Nathan has replaced the door hinge. I unlock, and take great pleasure in swinging the door open and shut. Peering in the bag I can see eggs, butter, milk and bread. For the first time today, I smile, taking my provisions into the little kitchen area, ready to scramble some Caernef eggs.

I devour my late breakfast, tidy up, and sit out on the doorstep with my milky coffee. Closing my eyes with pleasure, I do not notice Nathan approaching until he is nearly upon me.

'Morning Robin!' his cheerful voice alerts me. 'Actually, it is afternoon already,' he corrects himself. He is carrying a dustpan and brush. 'I came back to sweep up. I couldn't find a brush down here and didn't like to poke around. 'Are you alright?'

I am pleased to see him. His equanimity and youth fill me with hope, and I tell him that I am fine after a good march along the clifftop, a blast of sea air, and some scrambled egg. He says that the hens are laying well, and that there were enough fresh eggs for everyone up at the cottage this morning.

'Actually Robin, I wanted to have a word with you,' he says, nervously. 'Can we go inside?' I lead the way; we close the door and sit facing the empty grate. 'I have been thinking about this eight-digit code which everyone is talking about. The one to open Todd's safe box.'

'Any news, Nathan?'

'No. They are all trying to find out the code to unlock Todd Humboldt's massive hack. The one which has scuppered the whole world.'

'Blimey. So, it's out in the open then.'

'Yes. Anyway, we were talking over breakfast, and Maria told us all about those brutes who barged in last night … I'm sorry about what they did down here …'

'Did Gid tell everyone?'

'Yes. He said that you were amazing, that he had never seen someone keep so calm when their whole life had been trashed.'

I can feel myself blushing, and ask Nathan if Gid had mentioned the bonfire.

'He did, and that you didn't care! He said that you called it "only paper" and said they had "done you a favour". We live in bizarre times indeed.'

I show Nathan the charred remains of the few bank notes which had survived, saying that I will finish the job that they started once I have lit a proper fire in the wood burner. He touches the remains of the singed bank notes, saying that they are no good anyway, now they are made of plastic. They symbolise all that is bad about society.

Feeling our spirits flagging, I put on the kettle. He speaks over the sound of the steam, drawing me back to the eight-digit code. 'You see Robin, I was thinking. Miranda, and those louts last night, they kept on that Poppy knew a code. Well that is ridiculous. Maria is adamant that when Todd Humboldt came here, to meet the government guy, the only two things which he talked about with Poppy was asking her name, and playing peek-a-boo.' I agree, and he continues.

'A while back, I was into digital displays. We used to mess around with them, and I developed a habit of turning digits into words, just for fun. It is quite an art. I just wondered. I haven't told anyone else in case it sounds silly, but if you turn 'Poppy' into digits, running them backwards, the number would be 49909. Have you any paper and I will show you?'

I find a notebook and a pencil, and he sketches the digital cells, just like you used to see on LCD digital alarm clocks. He shows me, explaining, 'It is so simple. 'The "Y" isn't easy, but I know that people use the "4".'

'It's genius Nathan, but we both know it is unlikely. Also, there are only five digits and apparently the code has eight.'

'I've thought of that. Maybe the final three digits are 'Boo!' After all, that is what they were playing.'

'Boo? What do you mean? You've lost me.'

'Boo translates as 008, or 800. My guess is that the eight-digit code is "49909008", or 'Boo Poppy' backwards in digital script, but I may be barking up the wrong tree.'

Five-Minute Break

Nathan and I drink the tea. I praise his ingenious thinking, but secretly fear that the code he has come up with is too simplistic. We have no way of checking it anyway, and I am certainly not disposed to share it with Miranda on the encrypted phone. I tell him to give me time, as his secret discovery needs some thought, and we walk together up to the cottage, where we are welcomed by Poppy, who darts out of the door and drags me in by my coat, smiling and jabbering something about a letter.

It is reassuring to be in company again. Glyn has instigated rotas and chores, and the camp is buzzing with good intentions involving repairing, sweeping, feeding chickens and sowing of vegetables in Glyn's large greenhouse. I enter the cottage and Poppy stretches up to the table fetching the letter which she was talking about. It is, indeed, addressed to me.

Poppy returns to her game on the mat by the empty grate. Nathan heads off to find Glyn for instructions on his daily duty, and I study the envelope. I wonder how it was delivered. Maybe the postal service has restarted. It is stamped and the address is handwritten. No other clues are evident, and so I tear it open. Inside is a piece of writing paper. There is no message, no handwriting, only the unmistakable letterhead for "De Vere Stratagems". I turn the paper over and over, hoping to see something, but it seems to be an un-used sheet of paper. Either it is a trick, as I now know that Miranda's network of untrustworthy accomplices only wishes me harm, or it is genuinely from Reginald De Vere. If so, I guess it is a sign that he wants to see me. Not sure who to trust, or what to do next, I put the notepaper back into the envelope and hide it in my coat pocket, squatting down beside Poppy to take my mind off my worries. We play with her little farm animals, and I turn things over in my mind.

After a while, I begin to feel uncomfortable that I am not contributing to the extensive spring clean of the camp. Thomas calls Poppy to help him with the hens, and I find Glyn. He is digging over the empty vegetable beds ready for spring planting, and quickly employs me with a spade. Despite all the traumas befalling the earth, the floods, the fires, the pandemic, and now the glitch, the deep brown smell of the turning soil is the same as ever, reminding me of my childhood, reminding me of a time when things were simpler. I had tried to recapture that time here at Caernef, but it seems that, even in remote spots, we are cursed by the fallout from advanced human civilisation. As I stab the ground and turn the spadesful of earth, I am stabbing at the heart of our corrupt world.

'You imagining the vegetable bed is your ex-husband?' Glyn calls across the yards of beautifully turned soil between us, and I stab some more. He marches across to me. His boots are surrounded by skirts of mud, making him walk with huge high steps, but I find that I cannot laugh today. He bangs the mud off his feet with a spade and looks at my disgruntled face. 'What's up, Robin?' he asks kindly, adding, 'I heard about the folly. I can't believe the trash who have ended up out at Caernef. If I had been here, I would have given them a piece of my mind. They had no right …'

We sit on a low brick wall by the greenhouse. I often see Glyn sitting here, sometimes with Thomas, planning jobs for the day ahead. 'Glyn, I am sorry I have brought all this upon you, upon this magical place,' I begin. He squeezes my hand and tells me the glitch would have happened anyway. Trying so hard to reassure me, he ends up making me feel even worse because he is being so forgiving. He is more interested in his garden plans, and he reels off lists of vegetables which he is planning to grow this year, pointing out what will grow where, and when we will be able to harvest it. All that I can think about is whether, once our modest crops are grown, the world will be facing yet another crisis of some yet unknown kind, induced by the greedy human race overstepping the natural order.

Glyn only takes five-minute breaks, and looking at his watch, he stands, stretching in the sunlight, and resumes digging. I follow suit. The more I stab at the soil, the more convinced I am that I must try to see Reginald, but I am not sure how. I ask Glyn whether any more cars are back on the roads, and he says that things are slowly returning to something more like normal. Apparently, car mechanics are in great demand to reset vehicle engines, and trains are due to start on a reduced timetable this week.

An hour digging, and my spirits are superficially revived, even if my arms and legs are aching. A glorious aroma of cooking reaches us. Glyn checks his watch, mechanical of course, and announces lunchtime. In the distance, we see Thomas lifting Poppy high in the air to bang the gong outside the camp's large kitchen block, and we assemble in the dining room, where Thomas and Eva have set up lunch. They have somehow carried a huge pan of vegetable soup up to the dining room and are ladling the steaming mixture into bowls. There is homemade bread and real butter. Rhys the publican was right in saying that Caernef is a good place to be in a crisis.

ANNA KARENINA

Three Days Later

Thomas jogs down to the station twice a day and reports back. Today he seeks me out to update me. 'Robin, there is a notice down there. It explains what they are doing to get services back up and running. There's loads of details, "emergency disaster management," trains, signals ...'

I thank Thomas, resolving I will jog to the station straight away, so I can check this out for myself. The familiar route under trees and across the line to the dilapidated platform, is reassuring. There is indeed a large notice, which announces the intentions of Network Rail to re-establish connections between Wales and London. A series of dates and times of trains is provided. They talk of "resilience management" and "incident response" without revealing much detail. As Thomas said, there is a plan for signalling, using the backup 'UPS' or "uninterruptable power supplies" and to use 'bi-mode electrodiesels' on the line from Birmingham to Euston. It strikes me that they are having to de-digitise their carefully managed digitisation programme. The declaration is signed by the head of business continuity for Network Rail. It gives me some confidence in my plan to reach London.

As expected, the first few trains running back towards England are absolutely packed. After three days, demand has settled, and I decide that I will simply travel to the offices of "De Vere Stratagems" and seek out Reginald. There are still no means of direct communication, although gossip shared at The Prince of Wales provides us with valuable information about the world outside the camp.

We can see that, despite the most ingenious minds focusing on restoring the internet, and on removing the curse plaguing the phones of the world, no tangible progress is being made in restoring normal digital systems. People are saying that the internet may be broken forever, and enterprising experts are already planning some sort of rival arrangement which by-passes the cause of the glitch.

From discussions in the Prince of Wales, I believe that law and order have been largely restored, and I am therefore determined to travel alone this time, despite the protestations of Gid, and the others. I play down the trip, dress down, and share only with Nathan that I will follow up on his idea for solving the code. No point in raising expectations unnecessarily.

As schools are reopening after this latest emergency, Poppy waves me off, wearing her school uniform. Eva plans to volunteer at the local school, starting from today, and she is holding Poppy's hand, slightly nervous. I hug them both before I leave. I had hoped to slip off early, but despite heading for the first train of the day, everyone is up and wishing me well. The last time that I left the camp to catch a train, I ended up in Oxford during the second glitch, but today I don't feel any trepidation, just a numbness, and a deep rumbling anger.

I walk briskly along the lane, daysack on my back, and the hated mobile phone given to me by Miranda, recouped from Gid, back in my pocket. I have ignored all her messages and entreaties to meet, but will take counsel from Reginald, if I can find him.

My first challenge is obtaining a train ticket. There is no

news of the banks recovering, and our supply of actual cash at the camp has become very low, but I have scraped enough together for today's trip. There is a different train guard walking the aisle. He uses a mechanical ticket machine and looks nervous; I expect due to the quantity of cash he is carrying. We have been plunged back into a pre-digital age, and I am reminded of the well-worn phrase "be careful what you wish for." For years I longed for the advance of technology to slow, but not like this.

I gaze out of the scratched train window, unable to focus on reading the book which I have brought with me to pass the time. Even the exquisite views of the sea fail to raise my spirits today. I cling to my purpose of reaching "De Vere Stratagems", trying desperately to give my shattered life some purpose. All those values which I held so dear: equity, kindness and survival, float out of reach. I realise that I am deeply troubled, and do actually fear returning to London today. For an instant I regret travelling alone.

The journey seems interminable, but we finally draw in at Birmingham International, and I change trains with ease, mercifully now on a fast train to Euston. With no mobile phones to tap away on, passengers are chatty. I politely rebuff invitations to join conversations around me and simply listen. They talk of fear, of mistrust, of the incompetence of those in power, and of the daily hardships which they are forced to endure: food shortage, suspended bank accounts, uncertainty of employment. It is a depressing hour and a half, and I am relieved when we draw into platform eleven. There is no way that I am going down into the underground, and I exit Euston station to pick my way along the pavements, from memory, to Hyde Park.

Shops have opened, the damage from the post-glitch looting has been tidied, and the streets appear relatively normal, although no one is glued to their mobile phone. I see Marble Arch, and am reassured of my location. Without even pausing to consider any precautions, I walk round the park to the grand old building which houses the offices of many consultancies, including "De Vere Stratagems".

Having arrived, I get cold feet, and sit for a few minutes on a bench, considering my possible next move. I see two opposing options ahead of me; either I side with Reginald, working with him, and all that he stands for, the British establishment, to restore our systems, our phones and society as we know it, or I join forces with Miranda and her renegade gang and support them to trash capitalism and reset society to a new year zero. But I don't feel attracted to either - I just want things back to normal. I want to be able to recapture my personal freedom, and to retreat to the folly. Now I am only weary. I sigh, and glance up at the smart old terrace which houses "De Vere Stratagems", wondering whether I will find Reginald inside.

After the second glitch, and the terrifying aftermath, after several weeks of chaotic rebuilding, I am a shadow of my former self, and I have stopped trusting. However, I ring the bell and am greeted in person by Reginald's secretary, as if nothing untoward has happened at all. She is overjoyed to see me, and informs me that, although Reginald has popped out, he will be delighted that I am here. She leads me up the mahogany staircase where I can smell his coffee machine. A mechanical doorbell rings below, and she tells me to find my own way, as she treads back down the stairs.

I push gently at the heavy door to Reginald's office and peer into his inner sanctum, but stop short, my heart in my mouth, for there, sitting in his chair, reading a newspaper, sits Miranda.

Late Morning

'Good God, Robin, how marvellous! You haven't been answering my messages. How on earth did you get here?' The grand old desk is strewn with papers. Miranda has obviously been reading through them, 'Reginald has just popped out to meet someone. He is due back any minute. Come in and sit down.'

Is this a bluff? Has she broken into his office while he is out? Totally confused I find myself unable to speak or to enter the room. I stand, stunned. She sits smiling, looking very normal in jeans and a black polo-neck. She has lost the haggard look which characterised her on the road, and without scarves, disguises, militant companions, or a visible weapon; I wonder if I am in a dream, and she has been magically turned into more of a domestic heroine than a violent anti-hero.

'Robin, I do work here you know. I told you that I knew Marcella, and that Reginald and I were working for the British government. I even remembered "Anna Karenina" as proof,' she says, visibly puzzled by my obvious confusion.

'You sent violent interrogators to scare little Poppy and you … and you …' I struggle, 'you ordered the destruction of my inheritance.'

'What? Robin, come on in, sit down, have a drink, and let's get some things straight between us.'

I dislike feeling out of my depth; my clothes are shoddy and my head aches from the journey. I am at a disadvantage here, and she knows it, sitting me down and bringing me a glass of water while Reginald's coffee machine grinds into action.

'Now, what is this about Poppy being interrogated, and your inheritance being destroyed?'

I briefly relate the story of the night-time visitation to the camp, resenting every word that I say to this woman. Miranda is either a clever actor, or she genuinely knows nothing of it.

'All I can think of is that one of the splinter groups is responsible. They are much harder-line than we are, and they wouldn't hesitate to make a bonfire if they discovered a stash of bank notes in an attic. You can't trust them. It didn't take me long to realise that theirs was not the movement for me. I want to change the world, not to murder it.

Miranda fusses with the coffee machine, and I recall

watching her pick the lock in the chapel. I think of the expression on her face when she emerged from the house where we took the pickup, and I catch an image of the shrouded figure at the bar in The Pike. But I instinctively resent the apparently kind glances which she throws in my direction as she makes my coffee. She gathers some papers which she tucks under her arm, saying, 'Now, where has Reginald got to? He will be so pleased to see you.'

Leaving me with a steaming mug of coffee, Miranda descends the stairs. I can hear her talking with the secretary. Left alone in Reginald's office, I waste no time, silently placing my coffee on a Westminster Abbey coaster, I hasten across the room and fumble with the books on the shelf of his grand bookcase. I want to find "Anna Karenina" and to see what he keeps inside it. I successfully locate the book, slip the tome out, and unfold his finely written plans hidden in the pages. I just have time to read, "Year Zero" and "Operation Caernef". Hearing footsteps, I replace the papers, satisfied that there is a connection between Miranda's world of Year Zero and Reginald's strategies.

I slide the book back, and grab my coffee, sitting, innocently, awaiting the return of my host. So far Miranda's story makes sense.

Miranda reappears with Reginald. He looks exactly as he did last time I was here, in the same suit, upright and genial. He seems genuinely overjoyed to see me and shakes my hand many times, beaming, and saying to Miranda, 'You see, I know Robin; sending that blank letterhead worked a treat, much better than your satellite phone.' He turns to face me, and tells me that Meredith has told him all about our amazing journey from Oxford to Caernef.

'Meredith?'

'I told you, at the Pike,' Miranda says, condescendingly, 'I am Meredith Brenton. I have been going by the name of Miranda in my undercover role working for Reginald. This whole operation has been very risky.'

I have a vague memory of Miranda telling me this when

we first met at The Pike, but cannot reconcile myself with her real name, or with her not being my mortal enemy. I turn to Reginald, pleading for an explanation, and, while I drink my coffee, he talks me diligently through recent events. He begins with the stage-managed meeting at the camp, tells me about Todd getting cold feet and activating the second glitch, just before Christmas, catching them all by surprise, and moves on to the latest desperate world-wide attempt to unlock his massive hack, and the need for an eight-digit code to restore the world to normality.

'The code which Todd told Poppy,' Miranda cannot hold in her frustrations.

'Todd did not tell Poppy anything,' I snap.

Reginald retorts, politely, 'And so we are at a dead end, with all the countries of the world hanging on our every move, willing to pay inordinate amounts of money to get their systems up and running again. The rewards being offered are mind-blowing. The difficulty is that Todd set the passcode with intricate protection. Look, Robin, Tustian Hayward, the top civil servant assigned to this whole project is waiting for me to let him know the code. You and I could simply walk into his office in King Charles Street this afternoon, and if we succeed, we can claim the reward. He understands that we are so close to solving this.'

Miranda jumps in, 'Todd was clever. He encrypted his code. If you fail to get it right, it will blow sky high. He cannily prevented hackers from ever accessing the programme. Before Karl … he told me that there is layer upon layer of encryption, but that *the child* holds the key. Todd must have planned for all eventualities, including his own death, but it seems he left the human race one small window of opportunity to restore the systems which he used to hold us all to ransom. The code should by-pass the encryption. We are so close. God, Robin, this is not easy.'

Early Afternoon

Overcoming my surprise at finding Miranda ensconced in Reginald's office, I suddenly remember why I am here, and Nathan's code idea. I consider that it might be the time to put it on the table, but I still cannot bring myself to trust either of them. I need more reassurance. I turn towards my godfather and demand an explanation of Miranda's identity before we talk any further, 'Why should I trust *her*?' I ask him, with desperation, 'and how can we talk about this intensely serious matter while she is listening in? That is not how you and I have ...' I thump the desk in frustration, and am about to turn on my heel, when he motions to Miranda to leave.

'Meredith is as fiercely independent and focused as you are Robin. She has spent her lifetime campaigning for justice. Unlike you, she will take considerable risks to achieve the ultimate goal. I signed her on over a year ago and have had no reason to doubt her integrity. You have my word that "Miranda" can be trusted.'

I am only partially satisfied, and press him further, 'And you, Reginald? I have always thought you to be a pillar of the establishment. Why are you working with characters like Miranda, Karl, and Todd Humboldt? It still doesn't add up?'

He looks into my eyes with what I always believed to be a characteristic honesty, and I find myself wondering why I didn't probe him on the subject of his work much earlier in our lives. He clears his throat and continues, 'Robin, "De Vere Stratagems" is my life. I do not lead a politically motivated consultancy, I lead a living, thinking organisation. We weigh up evidence, and we provide options. We seek to influence those with the power to make significant changes to society. It can be that appearing as a pillar of the establishment is convenient in my line of work. I most certainly recognised the spark of the critical thinker in you at a very young age. My support for you over the years was by no means a result of friendship with your father. I championed you because I respected your intellect. Robin, I believe that you have a part to play in this current challenge which we all face.' He pauses, slightly flustered, as he has never spoken to me about his motives before.

'So you let that imposter, who hides her real name, tag on to my group of friends, forcibly take-over my home, tie us up, and threaten us. You let *her* friends shoot at Gid, even interrogate a young child. You allowed all this. It is despicable.' I can feel my blood boiling over. After months of tension, I am in no mood for parleying.

'I have always trusted you Reginald, always valued your counsel, but right now I am wavering, because of *her*.' I pick up my rucksack and make for the door. They both seem to know that I have come to tell them something about the desperately needed code, and he pleads with me to return to my chair and to calm down. I can hear Miranda lurking outside the door, no doubt ready to block my exit.

I am in no mood for calming down. 'It is all very well you offering me conciliatory words but you, Reginald, dragged me into this ridiculous situation, and *she* made it so much worse.'

Reginald gazes thoughtfully at me, and tries to gently coax me back onside. He talks to me about how he befriended my mother, a passive victim of my father's hubris. He tells me how, in playing the game of life, he has advanced himself, and is, only now, in a position to influence those "at the top". He reminds me about the years which I spent working with the disillusioned, those who had rejected society, those who slept in doorways, and those who had been overlooked.

I sigh, realising that he does know me better than anyone, but does he understand me? His mention of the years I spent working to restore the people's dignity when they had fallen on difficult times refocuses my mind. I begin to gain confidence and I reject his pomposity, this man who I had always trusted, collaborating with *her*.

'Robin, we need you to help us. Civilization has been

taken for a ride. Eight billion people are depending on us to find a solution. If we do not act, and act quickly, the real terrorists, those who shot Todd, and Karl, and those who torched your inheritance, will win, and heaven knows what will result.

'Tell me something I don't know Reginald.'

'You tell me something I don't know. Robin. I know how your brain works, making connections, seeking solutions. You know how scared people are now, millions of people are desperate. They have survived a pandemic, they were victims of the first glitch, and they have been frightened for a long time. They have been thrust into turmoil. Life as they knew it has ended…'

'I know this. I have seen it with my own eyes, but I have also seen the bastions of commercialism crumble. The glitch has presented us all with an opportunity to do things differently.'

Reginald raises his eyebrows and sighs. 'Robin, we are so close to a solution. This is not a time to push forward our personal ideologies.'

'I disagree.'

'You always were one to disagree.' Reginald's patience is wearing thin. The bizarre feeling that a small, insignificant and angry person like me, is sitting in an office having this conversation is overwhelming.

He is eager to get back on to matters relating to his work, 'Companies like mine are jostling to be the one to discover the code which unlocks Todd Humboldt's safe; companies all over the world, universities, great thinkers and problem-solvers. As you know, I have the ear of the British government, and we are placed advantageously. Contracts are in place. If I am able to come up with the code, they will try it. Meredith, I mean Miranda, is convinced that the child at Caernef holds the key. What do you think Robin?'

I remind my godfather, calmly this time, how Poppy was interrogated, and how the remains of my inheritance were torched. I betray no emotion. I say that, because he has pulled me, and my friends at the camp, into this, that our plans for the future have literally gone up in smoke. 'This all comes at a cost,' I assert coldly, finding my confidence, adding, 'where are the benefits of working with you?'

Miranda, who has been lurking outside the door listening throughout our tense exchange, returns silently, and Reginald moves to sit in the empty chair beside me. 'Apart from the obvious, that you and your friends would be able to live a normal life again, the reward is currently running into millions, with contributions from many countries. *If* we are successful, I would not take any personal payment of course, the benefit to "De Vere Stratagems" would be undeniable. There will, no doubt, be further large-scale crises to manage. I would split 50/50 with Caernef, assuming that you would match my stance, and not take a personal cut.'

This is an unexpected proposal, and I am tempted by another significant boost to the coffers at Caernef, but I still do not trust him completely. The look that passes between him and Miranda convinces me that he has already made a financial agreement with her. I have heard enough from them. I slam down the phone which I had been given back at the camp, leaving it on the desk, sling my rucksack over my shoulder, turn my back on them and march down the stairs, out of the door and into the fresher air of the park.

THE CURLEW

Afternoon

Fleet of foot, I dodge into the park and lose myself in the crowds before *they* can lure me back. I don't know why I head purposefully towards the river, pounding my feet on the pavements skirting Green Park, moving through the crowds, amazed that so many people are here sightseeing when the world is in such crisis. No one seems to carry a phone. It is both bizarre and uplifting to see the human race forced to talk again.

The glitch has done us a favour.

For a moment, I hope that we never manage to solve Todd's hack, and that we can re-establish our pre-digital behaviours. But I know that even if Todd has partially succeeded, the great thinkers who Reginald so admires will soon develop something new, probably even more insidious and commercially advantageous.

After twenty minutes of soul-searching, as I march towards Westminster through the afternoon sunshine, glancing behind every few yards in case Miranda is following me, I am all for returning to Caernef with my head bowed in failure. Why hadn't I just shared Nathan's guess with Reginald, watched the cogs of government turn and collected the reward money if it worked?

As I emerge on Birdcage Walk, I glimpse Big Ben in the distance, and I recall the name Tustian Hayward, Reginald's senior contact in the Foreign Office on King Charles Street. A helicopter circles overhead, and I tell myself that I am being paranoid as I consider whether Reginald and Miranda are tracking my progress. Am I foolhardy, or resolute? Drawn by the magnet of the unknown Tustian, I skirt the enormous Palladian buildings, taking care to remain as hidden as possible from above without acting suspiciously. I approach the forbidding iron gates of the grand government offices, walking straight up to the security guard.

'Good afternoon, I have an appointment with Tustian Hayward. I am here on behalf of Reginald De Vere,' I announce. Initially he bars my entrance, but a suited woman is exiting. She looks quizzically at my face, my casual clothes, my boots and my rucksack, and asks, 'Robin?' I nod, and she draws the security guard aside, talking to him quietly. He asks me to wait outside the iron gates, and then calls me over saying, 'Well, it seems you have friends in high places.'

'What do you mean?' I demand.

'She reports directly to the Minister, and if she says to let you in, that is what I must do.' He turns his nose up as he looks at me, and adds, 'Reginald De Vere vouches for you does he.'

The woman turns to me and snaps, 'Reginald phoned me and alerted us to *you*.' She struts across the pavement; I expect she is heading to De Vere Stratagems right now.

I stand alone, seething that Reginald seems to be one step ahead of me. While I wait, I crane my neck, trying to see what is inside the enormous doors, but can only watch smart office workers come and go. Have I been forgotten? I glance anxiously towards the road, relieved that there is no sign of the woman, Miranda, or indeed Reginald.

After what seems like an age, the security guard returns and beckons to me. He lets me through the doors into a vestibule where I am required to use the obligatory hand sanitiser before I stand and wait. He tells me that I must sign in and that someone will come down to collect me shortly. The queue moves slowly, and eventually I reach the desk, where I write my name and address in the visitor's book. The woman behind the desk asks, 'How *do* you say that?' as

I write "Caernef" and hands me a visitor's badge, which I hand round my neck. 'Sit over there. We will call you when they are ready,' she tells me in a dispassionate voice.

I perch on a deep leatherette chair, nervous now, wondering if I am wasting their time, wondering whether I will get to see someone who actually has the power to do anything at all with the information stored in my memory, and worried that Miranda will suddenly appear to goad me. The longer that I am kept waiting, the more doubtful I become. I am out of place in this high-ceilinged bastion of inefficiency, where primped-up bureaucrats prance up and down. I long for the headland at Caernef, for the curlews and the oyster catchers.

'Robin FitzWilliam,' I hear my name through the babble of voices, like being called in a doctor's surgery, rise, and am scooped up by an efficient young man who looks as if he should still be at school. He explains that he will take me up to the third floor, but first, there are security checks. I am searched very thoroughly, and have to leave my daysack in a cloakroom with a guard, who hands me a ticket. There is nothing of value in it, so I am not alarmed, and I finger the key to the folly remaining safely in my pocket.

We enter a wood-panelled passageway and I follow the young man, who strides upright and purposeful. We pass into modern corridors, and I catch glimpses of crowded offices, desks and blind computers, a life which I have left far behind me. After one final security check, and on the nod of the personal assistant guarding the door, we are taken into a small office inhabited by a senior official.

My chaperone leaves and I am invited to sit by the man, who simply introduces himself as "Tustian". He nods disdainfully at me, telling me that he is leading the government's post-glitch initiative.

'I was expecting you,' he explains, 'because Reginald phoned me half an hour ago. He said that you might come down to us. Now, I don't have much time, and I am focused on one matter alone, the reinstating of world-wide digital services.'

'And how do *you* think I can help?'

'This is not about you at all.'

'No …'

'Because you do not have the full picture.'

'No?'

'A great deal depends on this, far more than you can imagine. I don't want to waste time. I know that Todd Humboldt visited your place in Wales, and I am told that you may bring with you a clue as to the eight-digit code for his safe, which we seek. Is this true? You understand, I will need ministerial approval to proceed.'

If I am to deliver Nathan's hunch, I want to get it over and done with as quickly as possible. I dislike this man's brusque attitude, so reminiscent of my father, and I do not like the way that he looks down his nose at me. I have no intention of hanging around here, and I move towards the door, turning to face him, but threatening to leave.

'Yes. That is correct. I did not see Todd at Caernef, but he did play a game with my friend's little girl before he left. She is called "Poppy". The game was "peek-a-boo". If I can give you the correct code, do I claim the reward?' As I hear my words out loud, the whole idea seems ridiculously infantile.

Tustian raises his eyebrows, muttering disparagingly, 'Peek-a-boo,' and then snaps at me, 'Of course you would receive the reward.'

'I need that in writing first.' Determined not to be overwhelmed by the situation, I stand my ground. Tustian betrays no emotion. He calls in a secretary and dictates a short document, which is typed mechanically, in duplicate with carbon paper, while I sit clenching my fists. I contemplate marching out, leaving this bureaucrat and keeping the code to myself. I am not keen to share it with him. He hands me the sheet of paper, "… in the event of the correct 8-digit code being provided by Robin FitzWilliam, all reward monies to be awarded to her alone."

'Okay. But if we are successful …'

'Miss FitzWilliam, time is of the essence here … come on …'

'If we are successful, I demand total anonymity and for the reward payment to be invested in two trusts, one for homeless charities, and the other to promote outdoor education. I do not want to see a penny of it, and no reward should go to "De Vere Stratagems" as Reginald has not played a part in this.'

Tustian seems to stop himself swearing in dismay, and looking aghast, hastily instructs the secretary to retype the papers, adding, "Anonymity assured. Total reward to trust for homeless…" 'Now come on …'

'We must both sign.' He is irritated beyond measure, but is paid to keep his calm, and does as I ask, handing me the copies to sign. I place mine carefully in the back of my jeans, and take a deep breath.

Inside my head, I rehearse, 'Our theory is that the code picks up on poppy's name, and the word "boo", which could be the digits "49909" and "008".

But the word which comes out of my mouth is 'Peek-a-boo.'

Tustian shrugs, 'Is that all?'

'Yes.'

'Does it sound likely to you?' he barks at me.

'No less likely than any other suggestions,' I retort, surprised at the immense relief I feel at not having provided Nathan's probably correct code to this odious man.

He stands up, and without thanking me for my trouble, calls his personal assistant, who takes me into a small office nearby and offers me a cup of tea while I wait for him to return. I am all for exiting quickly, but cannot remember the way out through the bureaucratic labyrinth.

After a quarter of an hour, I open the door, but I wish that I had stayed safely inside the room, because I can hear an unmistakable voice booming down the corridor, the intonation of a confident pillar of the establishment:

Reginald. I cannot see him. As the murmur of conversation rises and falls, I retreat, sit down, and determine never to trust any of these bureaucrats or business-people again.

Still Afternoon

After another irritatingly long forty minutes, with nothing to do other than stare out of the window, anxiously awaiting Tustian's return, or the dreaded arrival of Miranda and Reginald, I am a nervous wreck. I fear that I will have made a fool of myself, giving the wrong code, even if Nathan's idea for the code was way off the mark. I worry that my posturing in front of Tustian will now appear ridiculous. I need to get out of this building.

I long to be back on the clifftop, out of this mad world which is so desperate to regain its digital props. I cannot imagine the charade going on behind the scenes here in Whitehall. Perhaps Tustian has gone into his afternoon meetings and forgotten about me. I hold my head in my hands.

The personal assistant peeps in, 'He says you must wait a little longer. He is with the minister. Can I get you more tea?' I say that I must leave, that I have a train to catch, and decline the tea.

Immediately she detects my intention to leave the building, she calls two uniformed security guards. They stand in the corridor outside the door. I sigh, asking for some water and she reappears with a one-use plastic cup filled to the brim. As I swig the water, I hear a commotion outside the small room where I am waiting. Exultant shouting, raised voices and hurrying feet. When I peer out into the corridor, beyond the guards, I see a herd of jubilant bureaucrats heading into Tustian's office, and Tustian himself, who rushes towards me, ushers me back into the small room, and hands me his business card saying, 'Contact me if you need to. For genuine anonymity, you must go now. I will ensure that our agreement is honoured.'

Confused by their apparent elation, I hurriedly tell Tustian in no uncertain terms that I do not want to see Reginald. He acknowledges this, but rushes out, abandoning me with the young man who led me up here.

I follow my guide without a word, back through the endless corridors. Glancing into large open-plan offices, I see computer screens blinking back into action, frantic tapping of keys, anxious faces. There will be parties tonight.

Handing the ticket to the cloakroom attendant, I collect my rucksack, and slip inconspicuously back out into King Charles Street where journalists are already jostling, ignoring me, seeking someone "important" for a soundbite.

In front of the building, I see Tustian, proudly talking to journalists. Standing close behind him is the shape of Reginald, and by the wall, on her phone, is Miranda. She looks up just as I hurry away. I don't think she spots me, but I see the smirk on her face.

I can't afford a cab, so hop on a packed bus, which is buzzing as the news travels from person to person, like a virus. They are getting out their mobile phones, and are showing each other the screens. There is no screeching. 'About fucking time.' 'Battery is nearly out.' 'Back to normal at last.' They cling to their devices while I clutch my rucksack to my chest and balance as the bus swerves round a corner.

We pass the theatres, hotels, clubs and museums, all thronging with chattering crowds. I close my eyes and breathe deeply, taking in the events of the last hour. I had been confident in failing to reveal Nathan's guess. I didn't want that pompous man Tustian to succeed. I didn't want the restoration of the digital systems which drag us down, but my red herring seems to have unlocked the box. Now I am nervous of being identified and mobbed. Gradually, as the bus swings and groans, and distance is established between me and the bizarre events of the last hour, a relieved anxiety takes over from my anguish. Perhaps there is a comfort in the restoration of normality, even if it will take time for systems to be recovered. We reach Euston, I jump calmly off the bus, walk into the railway station and navigate the buzzing crowds.

The automated departure board is being rebooted. The letters spin hopefully and land on familiar place names. I search for Birmingham International and spot with relief that a fast train leaves in five minutes from platform fifteen. I run, flashing my ticket as I dash on to the platform and leap into the train just in time. There are no vacant seats, but I secure a spot beside the toilet where I can perch in relative comfort on my rucksack. More passengers pack into the corridor, the doors close, and all that I can see is legs.

If it wasn't for the excited chatter all around me, and the visitor's badge which still hangs around my neck, I would not believe what has happened today. Unlike many of my fellow passengers I, of course, have no phone. I am desperately calculating whether this train, which should arrive in Birmingham in just over an hour, will enable me to catch the stopping train out into the backwaters of Wales. I think that I should make it, but am tense until I find out.

At Milton Keynes yet more passengers squash into the carriage, and I am compelled to stand up, otherwise I risk being kicked around the floor. It's merciful that we no longer have to "social distance", as I am packed up against my fellow-travellers so intimately that I can smell their perfume.

I watch an older woman switching on her phone, preparing to turn straight off, but when she is sure there is no shrill wailing, she taps hesitantly on the keys. I ask her whether she knows when this train arrives in Birmingham, and she looks it up for me, saying, 'How did we manage without these things? Thank goodness they have got it working again. I can hardly believe it. Now we can get back to normal.'

By the time we pull in at Coventry, I am reassured that I should be able to make my connection, having asked the guard, who is caught using the old-style ticket machine even though passengers are waving their credit cards at him.

We arrive at Birmingham International in good time, and I manage to obtain a drink of water from the medical point, so I can take my painkillers. While I wait on the platform, I continue to hear the exultant conversations around me. I seem to be the only traveller who is not clinging on to a revitalised phone. As the train draws into the platform, I push my way to the front and manage to secure a seat, sinking down with relief. Once we are on the move, I close my eyes, and know nothing more until we are well into Wales. The sky has darkened, it is raining, and I realise how hungry I am.

Day One of the Rest of My Life

It is dark by the time we arrive at Caernef halt. A solitary light is reflecting on the wet platform, and as I step from the train, I see two figures skulking in the shelter, out of the rain. I remember the first time I alighted here, full of hope, spotting the notice advertising the camp, thrown into the ditch, but right now I fear how I am going to cross the tracks without being seen by the people in the shelter? Is it Miranda and Reginald?

The train draws out, a brightly illuminated snake heading deeper into Wales, and disappears into the distance. Two figures approach me, calling my name, and I can see, with immense relief, that it is Gid with Nathan.

'Hi! We hoped you would take this train. It's so good to see you back. All okay?'

I am filled with confusion as I have been dreading facing Nathan ever since I refused the life-changing reward money.

'It's alright Robin, I told Gid about my guess. The news is everywhere. It's all sorted, the glitch has gone and we can get back to normal. Just tell me, did I get it right?' I look into his hopeful young eyes and say nothing.

'You didn't tell them about me, I hope?'

'No.' Rain cascades off the roof of the shelter, dripping

on to the platform, and I begin to see that Nathan, like me, doesn't want to become a soundbite, or a celebrity. 'Nathan, the reward money would have been massive …'

'I hope that you refused it, in line with our principles.'

'I did. I asked for it to go into trust funds for outdoor education and for the street sleepers. You both know how strongly I feel about this. It is abhorrent that in the twenty-first century people live out on the streets. I don't want to see the reward. I don't even want to hear about it. I just want to know that the struggling charities for people without housing will receive the boost they need, and that more children will be able to benefit from places like Caernef.'

'Perfect.'

'Gid, Nathan, only we three need know about this. I asked *them* for confidentiality.'

'Of course. We will say no more of it.'

Gid, his arm protectively round my shoulders, says, 'We must get back as the others have a present for you. Something small and personal.'

Now I am intrigued, and also relieved that Nathan approves of my course of action. I should have realised that he would. From his open face, I am sure of this. I trust his words, unlike those of my companions earlier in the day, even if his guess at the code was, ultimately, incorrect.

We walk through the rain, chatting about the camp, up the lane to the gateway, and over the rise where I can see lights glowing in the windows. Nathan and Gid lead me into the dormitory where Eva is waiting for us. She is overjoyed to see me safely home, and tells me all about the lifting of the glitch, that we are connected to the outside world again, and that there is to be a celebration later at The Prince of Wales.

Eva fusses over me as I am soaked from the rain, perceives how tired I am, and suggests that I head for the folly and catch up with them in the morning. They glance at each other. Something is going on. Gid rummages under the table and draws out a small package. He hands it to me, saying, 'This is for you. Can you take it down to the folly and open it there? Are you okay going back by yourself?' They know that I prefer my own company. I look up at their bright faces, and for the first time for many days, I smile.

'Thank you. I wonder what it is.' They grin conspiratorially. Nathan slaps me on the back saying today is a job well done. Eva hugs me, even though I am soaking wet, and as Gid kisses me on the cheek I catch a whiff of my old cigarettes on his breath.

Clutching the parcel, I leave them and walk down to the folly, pausing, even in the rain, to look out over the dark estuary and to listen for the nightjar. All I can hear is the waves on the rocks and the sound of the wind in the trees behind me.

As I unlock and enter the folly, the wood burner has been lit, there is an aromatic smell of cooking with a note on the table. I shake the drips off my hair, hang my coat behind the door, draw the blinds, and read the note, in Tomas's iconic scrawl, "Today is a good day. Supper in the oven x."

Wearily, I find some dry clothes, and carry the very welcome steaming bowl of stew carefully up to the lookout, return down the stairs to collect my parcel, remembering to lock the door to the folly from the inside.

As soon as I have devoured the supper, I unwrap the parcel. There, looking pristine, is my box, completely repaired and back to rights. I touch the wooden book-spines, marvelling at how they have repaired what, only a few days ago, looked like a pile of splintered wood. I guess that Glyn has been restoring it in his workshop. The tiny key is taped underneath, and I try it in the lock. It turns with its characteristic click, and my box opens. Inside there is no mobile phone, and no painkillers, but there are two cigarette boxes. Puzzled, I lift them out, and shake them. They rattle gently, and I tip out the contents, which have been gleaned from the hillside of Caernef. In one there is a bright blue jay's feather, empty snail shells, nuts and a couple of acorns.

In the other there are pressed flowers, sprigs of herbs, fronds of lichen, and a scrap of paper which says, in a childish script, "from Poppy xxx."

Placing the box by my pillow, I sleep.

I do not dream, but I am woken very early, as daylight streams into the lookout. I stretch, and stare out of the window, where the sun is emerging over the horizon, catching the waves and shimmering on the rocks below. I dress and rush downstairs, unlocking the door and bursting out on to the platform of sea thrift, where I stand, absorbing the peace. The waves splash lazily on the rocks. The tide is on its way out, and there, wading in the rock pools, is the curlew. As if to acknowledge my return to Caernef, it calls, piercing the air, and I sigh. Alone and unburdened, I finally realise that it is over. I am just thinking that my days can be peaceful once more, when the curlew is startled, flaps into the air, and I see Gid running down to the folly.

His face is serious. 'Robin, I don't know how to tell you, but it is back. The glitch is back. Our phones all started screaming at dawn ...'

ABOUT THE AUTHOR

Chris started her career cleaning toilets in a local outdoor centre for schools, while she studied for her degree with the Open University. Thirty-five years later she was Head of Education in Warwickshire.

Over the years, she has been involved in the work of three outdoor centres: Marchants Hill in Surrey, Hill End in Oxfordshire and Marle Hall in North Wales.

Now enjoying her retirement, Chris is an avid nature enthusiast and when she's not writing novels, she's catching up on re-reading all her favourite dystopian titles and modern classics.

#stoptheglitch is her second novel.

www.chrismaloneauthor.com
Twitter @CMoiraM

More **Burton Mayers Books** titles:

October's Son

John Michaelson's biographical horror takes readers beneath the facade of vampirism and exposes the dangerous subculture operating under the guise of real vampires. Packed with first-hand accounts and commentary, Michaelson's descent into the unknown will come as a chilling revelation to those hoping for an orthodox vampire novel.

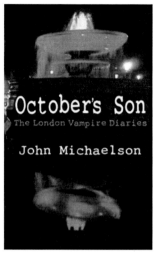

Published October 2015 – £9.99
ISBN: 978-0957338739

Another Life

Imagine if we could combine dreams and reality in a world where we live forever.

Oliver believes his life to be one of disappointment and failure. Haunted by the memory of a mysterious woman he encountered thirty years ago, and obsessed with finding her, he embarks on a journey embracing grief, hope, myths and legends to find her.

Published May 2020 - £8.99
ISBN: 978- 1916212626

Notes:

Printed by BoD in Norderstedt, Germany